Benji Shapiro's disappearance wasn't far from my thoughts. In fact, I couldn't stop thinking of that little kid. Especially late at night with the demons hovering about.

They had left me alone for a while but were now hanging out in dark nightmares. In one I was taken to a high rooftop. I saw myself, petrified, pleading, to let me live. Then I saw myself plummeting, the sidewalk rushing up to splatter me like a bug.

Rosie had heard me crying out, nudged me back to myself.

"You were having a bad dream," she gently told me.

"Mom," I whispered back. "This was something else."

Nightmares *were* "something else," a dark malevolence that left you screaming into the night.

And poor Benji had no one to wake him from his.

It had been three weeks since the boy was whisked off the street. Gone without a trace. Not a single neighborhood kid was about to forget that a real-life demon was out there, somewhere, lurking. And that he could come again, and for any one of us.

Paul Wolfenthal is a peculiar thirteen-year-old kid grappling with the absurdities of his young Bronx life, circa 1960. He visits the dead, hears voices in his head, despises Richard Nixon, is infatuated with his Marilyn Monroe look-alike math teacher, and is a choice victim for the neighborhood's sadistic bully. And then Paul really starts running into trouble.

Paul is, in fact, a kid in search of heroes, alive and otherwise, and finds them in John Kennedy and Harry Houdini, both of whom cross into his life. But these are strange and even dangerous times. Hovering in the shadows are "the demons" that haunt Paul's young childhood dreams, only to come alive and shatter his world. One steals away a neighborhood child. And then his president.

Set against the turbulent history of the times, *Bronxland* tugs on a kaleidoscope of emotions as an uproarious and heartrending coming-of-age tale. It is also the story of a place, a Bronx long gone yet still vivid in the collective memory of those who once called these streets their home. A place of the heart known to each of us, with our own story to tell of growing up, of trying to make sense of our life, with everything that comes along.

Welcome to *Bronxland*.

KUDOS for *Bronxland*

In *Bronxland* by Paul Thaler, Paul Wolfenthal is thirteen years old and growing up in the Bronx. Paul tells a hilarious tale of living in a close-knit neighborhood community, dealing with bullies, falling in lust with his beautiful teacher, and losing the love of his young life to his competition. Through his narration, we get a young teenager's perspective on people like John Kennedy and Harry Houdini, as well as a first-hand account of Kennedy's campaign in the Bronx and how his assassination affected his home town. We also get a look at how the Cold War with Russia affected young Americans who were told to "duck and cover" under their desks in the event of an atomic bomb—as if that would help. The story is well written and told in an autobiographical format—a heart-warming, heart-breaking tale of a young boy in a unique neighborhood, doing his best to cope with things out of his control. A really great read. ~ *Taylor Jones, The Review Team of Taylor Jones & Regan Murphy*

Bronxland by Paul Thaler is the story of Paul Wolfenthal, a thirteen-year-old boy living in the Bronx in the 1960s. Like any young boy, Paul needs heroes in his life and he finds them in his dad, his older brother Fred, and his teacher Mr. P, as well as in larger-than-life figures such as John Kennedy and Harry Houdini. But life isn't all about heroes, and Paul had to deal with daily life as well. He takes us through his trials with the neighborhood bully, his first attempts at young love, his disastrous mishaps—such as the naked picture of his teacher he got caught drawing in art class, and the birthday party for his best friend where Paul became the victim of his friend's sister and a game of spin the bottle—and his angst for another best friend who's accused of a crime he didn't commit. Then there were the horrible things Paul experienced, from the abduction of a neighborhood child and the boy's mother's mournful cries to the assassination of John Kennedy, whose death was a serious blow to the Bronx, John's hometown, giving us a close-up and personal look at some of our most turbulent times in history. The author takes us to a simpler time and place where families and communities stuck together, and people felt a sense of pride in their neighborhoods. Told in a unique and refreshing voice, *Bronxland* is a story you will enjoy reading over and over and one that you won't soon forget. ~ *Regan Murphy, The Review Team of Taylor Jones & Regan Murphy*

BRONXLAND

Paul Thaler

A Black Opal Books Publication

Black Opal Books

BECAUSE SOME STORIES JUST HAVE TO BE TOLD

GENRE: HISTORICAL FICTION/YOUNG ADULT

This is a work of fiction. Names, places, characters and incidents are either the product of the author's imagination or are used fictitiously, and any resemblance to any actual persons, living or dead, businesses, organizations, events or locales is entirely coincidental. All trademarks, service marks, registered trademarks, and registered service marks are the property of their respective owners and are used herein for identification purposes only. The publisher does not have any control over or assume any responsibility for author or third-party websites or their contents.

BRONXLAND
Copyright © 2017 by Paul Thaler
Cover Design by Jennifer Gibson
All cover art copyright © 2017
Author Photo by Jack Furtado
All Rights Reserved
Print ISBN: 978-1-626947-47-4

First Publication: OCTOBER 2017

Published by Black Opal Books **http://www.blackopalbooks.com**

DEDICATION

For Matthew, Robby, and Rebecca,
our beautiful Bronx kids...

and in memory of Mel Wolfson, a Brooklyn boy

PROLOGUE

A Time and Place

I'm not sure just where to start my story. Or whether you'll care about it anyway. After all, this story takes place a lifetime ago and, besides, who wants to read about some mixed-up kid growing up in the Bronx. Of all places. Maybe if I refer to my home by its original Native American name, *Rananchqua*, you'll think of it differently. Then again, maybe not. So, stop here if you must, but then you'll never know what happened to this boy in that time and place.

So much for trying to lure you in.

Well, let me begin at the beginning. I'd been a kid, a Bronx kid, back in the early '60s, and the world was my own. No one would mistake my growing up for Tom Sawyer's. No picket fences here. Just lots of gray cement and red bricks, not a tree or a wedge of grass in sight. And yet freedom was as natural as the five-story walk-ups that lined Tremont and Grand and Burnside avenues. It was a place where I could fly on my fire-engine-red Schwinn from day to night. And what could be better than pedaling over to the Stadium to visit the gods—the Mick, Yogi, Clete, Moose, Whitey? Nothing more to say.

We kids bumped into a few adults along the way but

were mostly free of those grown-up types. Not much parent coddling for sure. My folks worked hard to make a better life for my brother and me and either didn't have the energy to be on our backs or possessed the infinite wisdom to let us be. In any case our arrangement worked out just fine.

My neighborhood had its routine. Days were ruled by nonstop street games interrupted only by the dark of night or a mom's call for dinner. And there was no escaping the sounds of street life. The smack of a Spalding against a stoop. The grating steel roller-skate wheels that made it seem as if the pavement was in pain. The shouts of kids in constant motion, shattering any possible silence that dared to take hold. In my neighborhood, quiet just didn't stand a chance.

This is where I was born, spent my first sixteen years, great times, and some lousy ones. The Bronx wasn't perfect, but nobody said it was. No rose-colored glasses here. We had our demons: the neighborhood bigots, bullies, creeps, crazies, and outright psychos. They had a way of ruining your day. I managed to get by, though little Benji Rosenberg didn't have such luck, terrible luck in fact, I'm sorry to say.

It was also a time in which I woke up to discover the opposite sex. Not that I had any clue what to do next. There was this girl-of-my-dreams. That was Dee-Dee O'Hara, and then the other guy came along and that was that except for all the drama and torment. Anita "Bonita" also introduced me to matters of love—well, that's not exactly what she did —but that's way too embarrassing to get into here.

Was I a peculiar kid? Well, I liked to visit cemeteries and heard voices in my head. Did that make me strange? I'll let that go for now. Enough to say that I was a kid in search of heroes, dead, alive, and otherwise. I believed in Superman, and not just the comic book guy.

There were others. Alan Shepard reaching for the stars. "Rajah" Maris reaching for the right-field porch at Yankee Stadium that unforgettable summer. And, of course, JFK. I can't go back in time without thinking of him. He was special to me all right, but for a reason you might not expect. You see, John Kennedy had been a Bronx boy himself—that's right. He'd been one of us, even if his neighborhood was on the other side of the tracks. I still think of him now these many years after that awful November day.

For a kid growing up here, no other place seemed to exist even if the outside world had a way of sneaking up on you. At school we practiced hiding under our desks should we get hit with a nuke by the big bad Commies. We also could be dumb about other things, unable to see past our skin color. A bad thing, since I had a real pal in Joe Bailey, who was black, and a terrific guy before the meanness took over.

I stuck around my Bronx home long enough to see the cracks in the neighborhood grow deeper. America itself was starting to fall apart and moving headlong into a major nervous breakdown. I wasn't too happy about that either. By then I was no longer a kid, just one of so many young guys left to deal with the mess handed to us by some foolish grown-up types.

My family and relatives had their share of life's worries and finally joined the diaspora from the Bronx that set its sights on places like Rockland County and Queens and Long Island. I don't think my folks ever looked back, and perhaps there was no reason to. For them, Bronx life was about survival, taking care, responsibilities, getting by. They never led a kid's life there or felt the invisible space in which we existed.

But I feel compelled to come back now. Maybe it's nostalgia, or just the feeling that we all share that time in the flight and stumbles of childhood. It is where we all begin our life stories. And that's worth remembering. It's been said that you can't go home again, but even if we can't return to our past, we can visit, digging through the fog of time to rediscover those simple, complicated days.

Each of us has a story to tell of growing up, of trying to make sense of our life with everything that comes along. This is mine.

PART I

1960

CHAPTER 1

Tommy Branigan

Tommy Branigan was born on the wrong side of crazy. Not that he'd mind being thought of in such a way.

Hunched, bony, and pockmarked, with dirty blond hair slicked back into pigeon wings, Tommy prided himself on being an all-American greaser. I got the feeling that he'd spent way too much time watching old repeats of *Rebel Without a Cause*, fantasizing about the guy who races his hot rod off a cliff in his duel with James Dean. It was just too bad Tommy never made his way out of the '50s, or, for that matter, didn't take up hot-rodding. I don't mean to imply that I carried a death wish for Tommy. But would making the world safe for normal human beings really be considered such a bad thing?

Tommy was hard to miss in the neighborhood. It wasn't just that he carried the sneer and swagger of a hood—or as much a hood that a fifteen-year-old could be. The guy was just whacked-out dangerous, radiating a punch-you-in-the-face attitude if you dared to cross him. Which, for me, never once entered my mind. I was just fine keeping my distance and my face intact.

There were only two problems concerning my relationship with Tommy. First, he lived on Davidson Avenue, around the corner from my Tremont Avenue apartment building. Chance meetings in the neighborhood were inevitable. Worse, Tommy Branigan was about to become my new classmate in Miss Crouse's seventh-grade class at Macombs Junior High School 82. I was an okay student, a decent enough kid. Tommy wasn't on both counts. So you can understand why we were instantly enemies. Let me rephrase this: Tommy hated me. My only feeling about Tommy was an icy chill of fear. It would have made perfect sense to find a tall tree to hide out in when bumping into him on the block. Too bad not a single tree dared to grow on this side of the Bronx.

Tommy had already managed to get held back a grade— and given that he was more than two years older than the rest of us, we suspected that another part of his life must have been spent in juvie hall. This was Tommy's second go-round in seventh grade—a stigma unimaginable to me. I came out of a working-class family where school was second only to synagogue. The idea that you could be "left back" carried a shame that was, simply, unspeakable. It's safe to say that my friends and I shared a common scripture. That following the Sixth Commandment, Thou Shalt Not Kill, stood the Seventh Commandment—Thou Shalt Never, Ever, Get Left Back. It was understood that disobeying this Seventh Commandment automatically negated the Sixth, freeing your parents to wring your neck—from their view, a case of justifiable homicide.

So, no wonder that in looking at Tommy Branigan we did not just see a bad guy pissed off at the world. Tommy had committed the most egregious sin in our eyes. Being left back made him a leper in our midst. And he knew that we knew, which did not make him any happier.

I suppose it didn't help matters that Tommy's dad was said to have been an enforcer for the Irish mob. That was until the cops, fed up with dead bodies piling up on Bronx streets, put Brewster Branigan away for a good long time.

At least that was the gossip that floated around the neighborhood and, I should add, considerably spiced Tommy's own tough guy reputation—not that it needed an added boost. I didn't totally believe the stories about his father. No gangster named Brewster could be a killer. President of Yale, maybe. Psychopathic killer, not likely. In any case, I wasn't about to test my theory by bringing it up with his son.

❧❧❧

I wasn't sure what was worse as I stared at myself in the bathroom mirror—meeting up with Tommy later that morning or dealing with Rosie, my mom, prepping me for my very first day at JHS 82. Hovering on my shoulder, she fingered globs of Brylcream into my hair, transforming the top of my head into a glistening, hardened pompadour.

"Ma, 'nough already," I growled.

"We're almost done," she chimed.

"You're getting the stuff in my ear!"

Rosie gave me that look, the one that took pity on her imbecile second-born son who couldn't quite fathom the importance of being well groomed. She kept this evaluation to herself as she carefully studied her work. I was making the big leap into junior high that day, and Rosie wasn't about to throw her son into the lion's den without his pompadour in place.

"What a good-looking boy!"

It was about this time that I felt like crawling back to bed. To think, four months earlier I had been bar mitzvahed and officially proclaimed "a man" by the rabbi. And here Mom thinking I was five, smothering my head with goop—naturally I would have asked God where He was in all of this, but I didn't think even He had a chance understanding my mother.

Rosie finally detached herself from my head. My hair

flipped into a small bun gave anyone interested a clear view of my face. I was certain that even a tornado striking the Bronx couldn't possibly knock a single hair out of place. And Mom surely must have been comforted knowing that her son was properly coiffed should a natural disaster strike.

As for me, I was less than happy about the clean-cut image. Crew cuts were cool, even scraggly was okay. Pompadours, well, I might as well have hung a sign around my neck that read, "Jew Boy—Red Meat for Bullies." And my neighborhood had more than its share of such psychos. Of course none was worse than Tommy. I could only hope that if he ever threw me on top of my head in his own bit of fun, my Brylcream-plastered hair would protect my brain from serious damage.

"Make a good impression," Mom went on cheerfully, clearly not in tune with my inner angst.

Rosie gave me the once-over, nodding approvingly, as I bolted from the bathroom. I scuttled over to the kitchen to pick up my tin lunch box decorated with a soaring Superman—my hero whose godlike tales were told in treasured comic books stuffed in my bedroom drawer. I somehow doubted whether the Man would settle for the tuna fish on white bread, accompanied by a usual chocolate Entenmann's doughnut, my lunch in a few hours, but what could you do.

"Bye, Ma," I said as I reached for the doorknob.

"Bye, sweetheart, have a wonderful first day," she chirped, beaming as if her son was going off to Harvard.

With my Superman lunch box in one hand, a marbled composition notebook and plastic bag carrying three number two lead pencils in another—and my pompadour solidly in place—I bounded out of apartment 3A onto Tremont Avenue and headed on the five-block journey over to JHS 82. I could only hope that I wouldn't run into Tommy on the way, greeting me in his usual friendly, articulate way. Something like:

"Hey shithead, eat shit."

At those times, I never thought it was a good idea to tell Tommy that he was being redundant.

CHAPTER 2

The 710 Chain Gang

I was determined to be cool that first day at Macombs JHS 82, not just some twerp hanging around the hallways in a pompadour—I really needed to talk to Rosie about that. A few months earlier, I'd been king of the mountain as a sixth-grader at PS 26. Okay, so king of a pathetic mountain. But I kind of liked the way those kindergartners looked up to me as if I was some sort of big shot. Now I was the one looking up, eyeing the older guys well on their way to growing mustaches, along with the girls parading around still in their summery halter-tops and ignoring the idiot that kept staring at their chests. (I couldn't help myself—breasts were just a very new experience for me.)

"Hey, *bro*, checkin' out the babes?"

Sammy Spigelman.

The guy had a way of sneaking up on me, and, in general, was a royal pain in the butt. Not to mention, my best friend.

"Nice set on that one," Sammy announced, smirking, as he bopped up alongside me. He was pointing directly at a long-haired girl wearing a tight T-shirt, who angrily shot back a "fuck-you" glare. "A bit too jiggly for my taste, bro, don't you think?"

"Sammy, can't you *cool* it!" I moaned, mortified and hoping for a heart attack, anything quick and final. "And what's with the 'bro'?"

"You know, 'bro,' it's the talk. Jets, Riff, *West Side Story*."

"That's 'Daddy-o'—not 'bro,' you jerk."

"Okay, 'Daddy-o.'"

"Sammy, let's just get to class!"

Too late, but I should have known that.

Sammy was already on the move, snapping his fingers to an imaginary beat, bobbing his head in time, and giving me his squinty gangster gaze. Then he started belting out the Jet's gang song, no doubt dreaming about taking on the Sharks.

"Sammy," I pleaded. "I promise to get you your own switchblade for your birthday if you just cut it out."

The guy was well on his way to Mars, or some other planet, and didn't seem to mind that we were standing in the middle of our crowded school hallway. Or that every kid around us was staring at this lunatic on the loose from the asylum—along with his friend, who automatically was guilty by association.

"*Sammy*—"

Sammy snapped his fingers to cut me off. "Cool it, Action!" he barked.

I closed my eyes, and let out a deep breath.

છ૭૭

Sammy was born Samuel, but he disowned that name long ago. He was Sammy or Sam and prided himself as something of a hooligan, the kind that rooted for Al Capone, his hero, over Eliot Ness on *The Untouchables*. He had a way to go as Scarface considering he was still waiting for a growth spurt, had yet to shed his baby face, and simply didn't scare anyone. Besides, Jewish kids just weren't that convincing when it came to the tough guy act. Let's just say that Sammy didn't stand much of a chance making his bones with the local gangster crew, the Fordham Baldies.

Still, not a bad guy.

The good news, we were in the same seventh-grade class together. That also happened to be the bad news. JHS 82 must have gotten wind of Sammy's reputation and considered me his partner in crime. As such, I found myself buried in a pit called Class 710. The end of the line. Not that Sammy minded.

"So, we've made the big time," he proclaimed, proudly waving a school letter that he had received in the mail. "Bro, you and I can take over!"

"Yeah, great," I groused. "Maybe we should just skip the whole school thing and go straight into armed robbery."

I wasn't sure if Sammy knew I was kidding. I had the identical school letter in my pocket that I swiped from the mailbox before Mom and Dad discovered their son's new status as the family moron. I kept the news to myself—printed in black and white next to my name was my class assignment: 710.

Apparently JHS 82 had evaluated my potential to succeed and decided I had none. I mean, absolutely none. Okay, so my final sixth-grade report card wasn't great but neither had I killed anyone. You would've thought that worked in my favor.

We all knew where we fit in from the start at 82. The top class, 701, even got its own initials—the "SP." I wasn't sure what these letters stood for—I came up with "Supersmart People," but I don't think that was it. Those braniacs were pushed to finish junior high in two years instead of three and were destined to be future Einsteins.

Next came 702, your ordinary smart kids, and so on. As the numbers got higher, kids got dumber or so the school branded them. By the time you got down to class 707 or 708, students were assumed to be preparing for careers as car thieves, or worse. These kids were, in fact, rough around the edges, but it probably didn't help them being identified as members of the criminal class, so to speak, in seventh grade.

"Jeez, Seven-Ten!" Sammy said excitedly. "I didn't know classes went that high. You think the school made a new one for us?"

"Yeah, nice to feel special," I said sourly. "Maybe we'll even get our own separate jail cell."

"Hey, look on the bright side."

"Yeah, and what's that?"

"Well," Sammy paused, weighing the question. "I have no idea."

"Sammy, this is impossible," I grumbled. "Jewish kids aren't the chain gang type."

"Hey, you an anti-Semite or somethin'? We got our bad boys. What about Meyer Lansky or Bugsy Siegel? Those guys would fit right in with us."

Sammy was not helping me out. Class 710 was nothing but a huge mistake. It had to be. I was about to face lockup with thirty-five other misfits, isolated from "normal" kids allowed to move from one subject class to another—I guess the school didn't want whatever we juvies had to spread. I'd tough it out if I had to, but the reality was clear. I had arrived at JHS 82 only to end up in Sing Sing.

And then, as if on cue, the school bell rang beckoning us to our cellblock. I checked out a hallway bulletin board telling me where I could surrender. I trudged up to the fourth floor in search of Room 424 with Sammy on my tail.

"Bro, time to get it on!" Sammy boomed, excited and already on the move down the hallway, bouncing from one leg to the other, back to being Riff, the tough-guy, finger-snapping leader of the Jets. He was whistling yet another tune from his favorite street-gang movie and looking ready to rumble.

I could only pray that Sammy wasn't about to reenact the murder of Bernardo.

CHAPTER 3

Seventh Grade with Swastikas

I gave our classroom the once around. Room 424 wasn't much different from any other in the school. Nailed to the floor were thirty-six sets of worn wooden desks and chairs, six rows across and back, a perfect square, neatly regimented, much like our education.

The place had the usual. Maps, portraits of famous people, pictures of the solar system. Also a large paper alphabet strung across the front wall. The last time I'd seen that thing was in kindergarten. I was pretty sure we all had our A-Zs down, even if Tommy Branigan had a hard time getting past the letter "F." I was relieved to see he was now catching a few "Zzzs" in his corner seat after a tough night prowling the streets. Tommy just needed his shut-eye.

The rest of us were fidgety with first-day nervous energy waiting for our teacher to finally settle in and settle us down. Sammy plopped down next to me still on overdrive, his hands drumming the wooden desk in rhythm to his feet tapping out a beat. The guy simply couldn't keep still.

I got comfortable at my desk, checking out the names of previous students immortalized in black ink on the square wooden top. Two students named Bobby and Suzy apparently were once in love since their names were ringed with a heart. Another guy had carved a large penis onto the desk-top. I guess each student expressed his inner feelings in his own way.

"Hey, Sammy, take a look at this," I whispered.

Sammy nodded approvingly.

"That's one incredible dick," he said, seriously examin-ing the artwork. "Pretty realistic, don't you think?" He then leaned over to work his index finger around the contours of the carving. "Why do you think he left out the balls?"

Sammy had a point, I thought. I mean, why carve such an important thing and leave out the balls?

"You'd think the guy would get it right," he said, reading my mind.

It was then I felt a set of eyes drilling into me. Tommy glowering from across the room as if I was his sworn ene-my. Maybe he was angry having been woken up, or felt left out of our penis critique, or thought that his education was stunted being in 710. But I didn't think that was it. Tommy was just not a happy guy.

Sammy kept up with his analysis ("Jeez, the size of this thing. The guy had some imagination.") when our teacher shushed the class and quieted us down. Miss Crouse wore the bright smile of a brand-new teacher who had no idea what she was in for. Thirty-six pairs of stony eyes gave her the up and down as she carefully wrote her name in extra-large block letters on the blackboard. I was starting to think that I really was back in kindergarten with Miss Crouse about to announce our naptime.

Instead, our teacher stepped back beaming as if she had drawn a Picasso on the board. I could see Sal Castalano giv-ing her the whaddaya-kiddin'-me? look. But our teacher was not about to be denied. She picked up a long wooden pointer and tapped it on the blackboard.

"So, children, your teacher this year—that's me—" Pause, big smile. "—is—M-I-S-S, C-R-O-U-S-E like in 'HOUSE' or 'MOUSE.'" Pause, big smile.

The rhyming thing was not exactly an icebreaker. But

even our silent treatment did not stop Miss Crouse from letting us know how happy she was to have us all in her class.
The only thing missing that morning was our cookies and
chocolate milk. Maybe afterward a game of Hide-and-Seek.

Sammy leaned over, confused. "Hey, Paul. Is this lady
for real," he muttered, "or a wack job?"

I wasn't sure myself but wanted to give Miss Crouse the
benefit of the doubt. Even with her patty-cake ways there
was something about Miss Crouse that I liked. Maybe it was
the fact that she was young and pretty. Or sounded like
Snow White. Or wrote like a six year old. Or treated us like
six year olds. Actually, it was the young and pretty part.
That was definitely it. I sat back and listened as she went on
about "the wonders" of seventh grade.

I could see that Sammy had made up his mind. "Definitely, wacko," he mumbled to himself.

Miss Crouse went on bubbling about all "the bright faces" in class when I decided to zone her out and check out
the new kids. I was having a hard time finding those bright
faces, but at least the class seemed like a decent bunch. The
two exceptions were Tommy and Alan Plotz. Tommy, of
course, was to be avoided at all costs. Plotz was simply un-
avoidable.

I caught a glimpse of Plotz in the back row staring off into space. He'd been in my fourth-grade class and had grown
since then. And that wasn't a good thing. His body had become larger and rounder, reminding me of a 240-pound
snowman dressed in a plaid shirt and black pants about to
split in half at the seams. He barely squeezed into his desk
with his bulbous ass spilling over his chair and into the
aisle.

I knew Plotz—only teachers called him by his first
name—all too well from elementary school and had no
doubt that he brought his special gift to JHS 82. The guy
stank from body odor. Not the ordinary bad body odor that I
was used to after running around all day. Not the bad body
odor that made my mom's nose crinkle before ordering me

to jump into the shower. No, this was something else: a hellacious vomit-like smell that I was positive had been banned under the Geneva Convention.

It had been this rotten stink that compelled Mrs. Petrow, our fourth-grade teacher, to quarantine Plotz in the far corner of our classroom. The move didn't do much good especially during warm weather months when an inhuman stench seemed to rise up from every corner of the room. I was convinced that Plotz was responsible for putting poor Mrs. Petrow in the hospital later that year.

I might have felt sorry for Plotz and the barrage of name-calling that kids threw at him behind his back. But the guy just wasn't a kid to warm up to. It was one thing to be obese and stink to high heaven—though I assumed he had indoor plumbing at home and was capable of taking a shower every now and then. But having an obnoxious, snorting personality was pushing it. So I really didn't think a lasting friendship was in the cards for us.

I was jolted from my daydreaming when the wall speaker sparked the classroom. We all knew what was coming. Since kindergarten, each morning started with the "Pledge of Allegiance" and "Star Spangled Banner," the public school version of *shul* with everyone—from students to the janitor—submitting to a higher power, the good old USA.

Miss Crouse was already motioning us to get out of our seats. Hand over heart and under God, she led us on, her head upraised in search of the Big Guy Himself. The rest of us recited the pledge in monotone before singing off-tune our beloved anthem to a crackly recording.

"Excellent, class!" she said, misty-eyed over our rendition. "How wonderful!"

"Paul, I gotta get outta here!" Sammy blurted too loudly. "She's freaking me out with the Cinderella thing. I don't think she's even human."

Before I could calm Sammy down, Miss Crouse stretched out her arms as if they were wings—I half expected her to start flapping and take off from the ground.

Instead, she had an "important" announcement. Something in her eyes, now sparkling, told me that this was the moment she'd been waiting for since the day she was born.

"Boys and girls!" Dramatic pause (she liked doing that). Then Miss Crouse eagerly told us her plan. "You are seventh graders now and mature enough to pick your own classroom seat. When I give the signal, I want you to stand and then find a seat to your liking. It will be yours for the entire year, so choose wisely."

Hey, what *was* this? Maybe I'd been wrong about Miss Crouse. Whatever it was, she had my attention.

ତୟତୟ

I had lived my public school life clumped in the back row, a fate tied to my last name. When it came to assigning seats each year, every teacher I ever knew used the same scientific approach—it was known as the "alphabetical order." As our family names were called, we wound into our seats in serpentine fashion, moving from front to back of the classroom. Names closer to the end of the alphabet got the bum seats. Mine ended in W, as in Wolfenthal—so I was always stuck in the "bleachers." Great for Yankee games, lousy for a near-sighted kid without his glasses. Not that I would be caught wearing them anyway.

How could I forget Mrs. Woods, my second-grade teacher, who warned me time and again about mimicking Asians. It didn't cross her mind that I squinted because I was too blind to see the blackboard from my seat. I wasn't about to let on. Eyeglasses were a fate to avoid at any cost, second only to wearing urine-soaked underwear to school. I kept my black, horn-rimmed glasses secretly buried in my backpack. They were nearly identical to those worn by rocker Buddy Holly. Even he looked weirdly cross-eyed with them on. So, better to squint and get by in the back row rather than run into the taunts heaped upon other unfortunate myopics. They were better known at school as "Four Eyes."

ↁↁↁ

"Now, class, are you ready? On my signal," Miss Crouse announced excitedly, getting more ramped up with her idea. This class, *her* class, was about to start a revolution the likes of which had never been seen at Macombs JHS 82.

She could not have been more right on that one.

I suppose that Miss Crouse had expected some orderly transition, with nice boys and girls politely making their way through the classroom to find their seats. A beautiful thought. But our teacher had clearly lost her marbles, not that we didn't suspect that already. She really should have known better. Too bad she didn't. And so, Miss Crouse lowered her hand—and then there was no turning back.

The classroom exploded into a mass of monster children, each of us on high adrenaline ready to destroy anything in our path for a choice spot. And at that moment, no power on Earth could have stopped us.

"*Slowly, slowly!*" Miss Crouse, her voice shaking, was coming to grips with this horror version of musical chairs. Class 710 was officially out of control.

Thirty-six wild-eyed kids were now barreling down aisles and climbing over desks in search of the perfect seat. I was proudly part of the pack. I instantly eyed second seat, fifth row, and made my dash across the room, lunging into the chair, edging out Donny Broz, who wound up face down on my lap before rolling back into the aisle. Not a bad start to seventh grade, I thought contentedly. The seat was not too close to the teacher—front seats were only for brown noses—but close enough to check out the blackboard free of my glasses. Perfect in fact.

I sat back enjoying the view, having a few laughs. Kids were charging through jammed aisles, diving headlong into contested seats. Others were using their rear ends as battering rams to shove any challenger away. Seventh grade was getting better every second.

It was then I saw Sammy sprawled out in a nearby aisle, glaring angrily at Molly O'Malley. In the battle of butts, no one was going to bet against Molly's.

"Hey *bro*, what's happening?" I shouted out to Sammy.

"Yeah, funny, funny," as he got to his feet.

"You should know better than to go up against Molly."

"I was there first!" he barked.

"You know, survival of the fittest."

"Molly's not fit. She's a fat horse."

"Take it up with Darwin."

And, then, just as quickly, Sammy was off and running, catching sight of a vacant seat in the first row.

"Class! Class Seven-Ten!"

Miss Crouse was way past her happy moment, now furiously patting the air with two hands, begging for us to calm down. Calm was just not a possibility at the moment.

I sat smugly settled in my primo spot and couldn't help but crack up at the sight of my classmates in the throes of battle. It was then that I noticed Dee-Dee O'Hara on the other side of the room.

If truth be told, I had a serious crush on Dee-Dee since third grade. She had grown up to be this pretty Irish Catholic girl, with flaming red hair and hazel-green eyes, and dimples when she smiled. While my parents might object to any future wedding plans, I was completely hooked. She was always friendly, and I felt that she liked me, but her shyness, and mine too, got in the way.

But now—and I could not believe my eyes—third seat, second row, directly in back of Dee-Dee, was empty. And calling out to me.

At that very moment, Dee-Dee turned my way, and our eyes met. Then that shy, dimpled smile of hers. I could feel my heart step up a few beats. I mean, what did Dee-Dee expect me to do? Abandon my prized seat just for the chance to sit right next to her—to be that close together—for the entire school year?

Yes. Exactly.

A warning flashed in my head, but I ignored it. Instead, I took off from my seat and raced across the room. Frenzy had taken over, my eyes fixated on third seat, second row. In fact, no other seat existed in the classroom.

Only this one.

Right behind that pretty girl with the hazel-green eyes.

And nothing was about to get in my way.

Like a pinball caught between bumpers, I barged through the crush of my classmates. Elbows out, feet churning. It was just about then that I started to get a bad feeling. Really bad. Only as bodies cleared did I discover my fate. Definitely not the one I was looking for.

Third seat, second row was taken.

Sitting in back of Dee-Dee O'Hara was Tommy Branigan.

Of course.

If Dee-Dee was disappointed, she mostly kept it to herself. She was no longer eyeing me but hunched over her desktop. No smiles or anything. Maybe she was thinking that she had lost her golden chance with Paul Wolfenthal. Feeling sorry for herself, poor girl.

That must have been it.

Or maybe I was hallucinating.

The truth was, I felt as if I'd been hit square in the face. Miserable luck to lose my chance with Dee-Dee—and to Tommy no less. But at that moment I was waking up to another feeling taking over—it felt something like a panic attack. In fact it *was* panic, the kind you get in a nightmare when you're about to be flattened by a trailer truck. Only now I was very much in the real world and waiting to be crushed.

I was the last man standing—and frantic.

I could see Larry Stone sitting comfortably in my original, perfect seat, hands behind his head, nice and relaxed.

Good for Larry—that louse. In fact, every seat seemed to have been taken. My head was spinning like one of those crazed cartoon characters about to be blown to smithereens. Desperate, I scanned the rows of desks and chairs, praying it wasn't too late.

I never stood a chance.

"Hey, Paul, *bro*, over there!" Sammy called out, thumbing to the back row. And then he started to giggle, that weird "heh-heh-heh" snicker of his—never a good sign.

I dragged myself to the back of the classroom and found the last vacant desk. It had been empty for a reason. Alan Plotz, larger than life, so to speak, was seated right next to it.

I just managed to squeeze past his overblown rear-end that blocked the narrow aisle between the two desks. Plopping into my seat, I felt trapped in some nightmarish *Twilight Zone* episode in which my every wish was cursed. But as reality quickly sank in I could clearly see that I was of this time and place. And that Plotz was going to be my very close neighbor. For the next ten months.

I instinctively sniffed the air—a hint of rotten eggs already hung in the air, but the day was still young.

"Hey, Paul, whaddaya say?" Plotz whispered as if he was catching up to a long-lost pal. "This class sucks."

I really wasn't planning on a conversation with the guy. "Plotz, we haven't been here an hour," I said wearily.

"I know when something sucks, and this class sucks the big one."

Another Shakespeare in the making.

Plotz snorted, having failed to get my class-sucks vote. But I was in no mood—this was going to be a very long year, and I made a mental note to buy a gas mask.

I turned back to Miss Crouse, still shell-shocked, but she thanked us anyway for our cooperation. She had to be kidding. Still, I wanted to like her. Miss Crouse had this open face, reddish-brown hair that tumbled to her shoulders, and a wide smile. But as a new teacher she was way too eager to please. A mistake, big time. As I looked around the class-room, I could see each of us mentally sizing her up. Then I glanced over to Tommy. I had no doubt whatsoever that he was eyeing her jugular.

Our teacher had yet to realize it, but she had a major dis-cipline problem on her hands. On one side were the brown noses willing to beg, borrow, or steal for her attention. On the other end stood Tommy, who once shared with me his personal philosophy about school. It went something like: "Don't *ever* think about waking me up in class unless you *really* want me awake and fucking with you." In fact, I be-lieve those were his exact words.

It was then from my back-row seat that I noticed Tommy had rolled up his right shirtsleeve. No big deal, until I took a closer look. Scars ran up and down his arms. They were short and longer scars that zigzagged from his wrist, along his forearm and up to his muscular bicep. One set of scars was deeper and longer than the others, lopsided Zs that were joined in the middle. A swastika. *My God.* I couldn't take my eyes off the marking. Why *that*?

It was later that day, as we worked on a math sheet, that Tommy got to his own assignment. I glanced over to his desk as he secretly pulled out a small metallic object that he palmed in his right hand. The razor blade gave off a soft glint between his two fingers. And then, quietly, he cut him-self. I stared in shock.

Tommy had sliced his forearm, a three-inch cut that, in-credibly, barely bled. I could see him squeeze the surround-ing skin causing a small amount of blood to bubble up around the wound. I guess when it scabbed Tommy would have yet another scar to add to his collection.

Perhaps he was working on a portrait of Hitler himself.

I wondered if I was just seeing things. But there was no denying that Tommy was all too real.

I wasn't the only one to notice Tommy's act of self-mutilation. Sammy was shaking his head after school. "Can you believe it, Paul? He cut himself—with a razor! Why would he do that?"

We both knew the answer to that question. Tommy Branigan was certifiably nuts.

"You shouldn't go blabbing about this to anyone," I warned Sammy as we turned to leave the schoolyard for home. "Seriously."

Sammy nodded grimly.

There was no telling what other use Tommy had in mind for his razor blade.

CHAPTER 4

Sins and Cemeteries

Hey, Paul, how 'bout we go and swipe a few Three Musketeers," Sammy goaded me on as we headed home after our first day at JHS 82.

Sammy wasn't being funny at all, and I thought a hard stare would shut him up. Who was I kidding?

"Just thought you wanted your chocolate fix and needed to cop a bar," he added off-handedly. "I mean you're a pro at this sort of thing."

"Sammy, screw you," I shot back. "Just forget it."

"Hey, think of it this way," Sammy went on. "You don't have to lay low anymore. That guy will never find you around this neighborhood."

I didn't need Sammy to remind me that I'd been on the lam since elementary school, and that a certain candy store owner was on the lookout for me. Yeah, I'd been a thief back in sixth grade. Not that I was proud being a criminal but those Three Musketeers chocolate candy bars had a way of messing with my mind.

The candy store near PS 26 had been easy target. All I needed to do was wait for the owner to turn his back, then snatch a few bars from the outside counter rack. One time, the last time, I was caught red-handed. Life moves quickly when you see the end coming. I could still see the red-faced owner, murder in his eyes, storming out of the shop, homing in for the kill. Then there was the thief—me—taking off like a bat out of hell down Tremont Avenue, on his way to breaking the four-minute mile, the pinched Three Musketeers now squeezed to death.

I really regretted spending sixth grade feeling like some low-life delinquent, hustling by that store each day, head down, afraid that the candy man was still out for me. If Jews had a confession box, I would've confessed my sin and prayed for forgiveness—and hope that word of my redemption reached the candy man. For now, I was just glad to be out of that neighborhood and the guy's reach.

"He'd have killed you if he caught you," Sammy grinned, seeming fired up at the idea. "That woulda added a little spice to your rep, don't you think?"

"Nice to know you're a pal," I said wearily.

"Hey, just next time get me in on the heist. Think the James boys."

"Yeah, Jesse, you're in," I sighed.

"Nah, I'm Frank. A nastier guy."

Then, without missing a beat, Sammy was on to his analysis of 82.

"Man, I'm getting sick of school. When is it over?"

"Kind of complicated math," I replied fake-seriously. "Today was day one. So that makes 179 school days to go."

"Hey, why the big number? A downer, bro."

"Just wanted to give it to you straight."

"Yeah, thanks a lot. I thought we were best friends. You might want to return my bar mitzvah gift."

"Really, a nice card. You know there's a slot in the card where you're supposed to put a check."

"Yeah, funny." Sammy looked at me seriously, unsure, "You're kidding, right? Did my mom stiff you?"

I deadpanned for a second then mussed his hair, and we both cracked up.

As for me, I couldn't complain about JHS 82. Okay, so it

hadn't been the greatest start to junior high. Yeah, there were the missing-screw types like Tommy and Plotz. And maybe not the brightest bunch in 710. At least no real homicidal types—though I was giving Tommy a huge benefit of the doubt on that score.

Maybe it was Miss Crouse who made the difference. She was a universe apart from the likes of Miss Horowitz, my third-grade teacher, who rightly earned the nickname Miss Horror Witch, both for her scary looks and mean attitude. It was really nice having someone like Miss Crouse, young and pretty. I might have mentioned that before.

Sammy was back to cracking wise as we strolled on. "Hey, Paul, what's the difference between your girlfriend and a walrus?" he joked.

I shook my head, preparing myself.

"One has a moustache and smells like a fish, and the other is a walrus."

"Nice try." I shrugged, though this one was better than most of Sammy's cracks.

"Hey, let's get the guys for a stickball game." Sammy was ready for the free afternoon ahead.

"Nope, sorry. Got things to do."

"C'mon. Too nice a day."

"Yeah, maybe later on, but I'm out on the bike," I said, catching the shake in my voice.

Sammy paused, shook his head. "Bro, not Woodlawn again!"

"Nah, something I need to do for my mom."

Sammy gave me a smirk, the one that called me a liar. And he was right about that one.

We approached my building at 50 West Tremont with hardly another word, the energy of our walk fading fast.

"Later," he mumbled, moving on to his own apartment building on Grand Avenue.

"Yeah, later," I replied, feeling guilty.

It was lousy lying to Sammy, but I didn't want to get into it with him again. I tried once to explain, but he just gave me another face—the one that shouted: "Are you a crazy, stupid, idiotic, idiot?"

Way too much redundancy to deal with.

So what if I liked to visit cemeteries. I didn't think anyone else would understand, but I felt like I belonged in such places. Not underground, mind you, no death wish or anything crazy. I just felt welcomed there. Did that make me weird? Okay, it made me weird. The point was, it was cool being around dead folks with their incredible stories even if actual conversations were tough given the situation. And I was sure that they didn't mind the company.

I also had been lucky to discover that a bike ride away was Woodlawn Cemetery. The place was heaven, so to speak. Kind of a graveyard version of Madame Tussaud's, only better without the creepy wax look-alikes. The cemetery was the real deal, and no admission fee to boot. I generally liked coming on an actor or athlete or adventurer, but once in a while I'd settle around the grave of an intellectual type, a scientist, a writer, a political guy. I thought of myself as being well rounded that way. If I was really lucky I'd come across some mobster—these guys always had a lively tale. Too bad that the really tough ones like Al Capone were buried outside the range of my bicycle. I promised myself though that one day I'd get over to Mount Carmel Cemetery in Hillside, Illinois, to visit old Scarface.

I guess all this made me some sort of dead celebrity stalker. But I could live with that.

I left Woodlawn on hold to first check in with Mom. A stoopball game was already going on with the guys only stopping to let me hustle up the steps and into my building. I was tempted and thought of joining them. Stoopball, after all, was *the* coolest street game. Throwing a rubber Spalding at a certain speed and angle against a stoop created a force of energy that was unmatched. Depending on the physics, the ball could either dribble away or rocket into old lady Goldberg's ground floor window, thereby shattering it. It was tough on us, too, since she always refused to return our ball afterward.

I resisted the game and made my way through a steel gate and up three flights of stairs to apartment 3A. There was Rosie, all warm smiles and hugs. I was happy to see her home. Most days she worked long hours at a small food market that she and Dad ran in the South Bronx. Then the expected two questions as I walked through the door.

"So, how was school?" And before I could answer, "So, what do you want to eat?"

It wasn't actually a question to see if I was hungry but shorthand to let me know that food was coming my way whether I was hungry or not. In fact, Rosie already had the answer to her own question, which she apprised me of in the form of another question.

"So, a malted and doughnut?" she asked, turning to the fridge, still not waiting for my response. Not that I objected.

The malted was chocolate, of course, the doughnut was Entenmann's, frosted chocolate, the large size. I didn't resist. There could never be enough sugar to ingest in our family dietary plan. That included a snack or two in between our regular big meals. Mom wasn't a very good cook, but that didn't stop her from acting on her most basic maternal instinct—feeding her children. And so, I contentedly washed down chunks of Entenmann's with a large glass of thick malt before heading to the door. It was best to keep quiet about my travel plan. Enough to say that Rosie wasn't a fan of graveyards.

"Don't come back too late, honey," she called out. "We're having meatballs and spaghetti for dinner."

"Sure, Mom. See you later."

I headed to the building's storage room to pick up my trusty Schwinn. Then I took off for Woodlawn Cemetery.

CHAPTER 5

Isidor and Ida

I made my way down Tremont to the Grand Concourse. In truth, the roadway had no right being in the Bronx—after all, how can you play stickball across six lanes of speeding traffic? I discovered the road had been modeled after some place called the Champs-Elysees in Paris. I couldn't think of another time when Paris and the Bronx were mentioned in the same breath. Certainly not on the Grand Concourse where Yiddish was about the only European language heard and no other wine grape existed that wasn't contained in the holy Manischewitz.

To me, and everyone else of my persuasion, the four-mile stretch was simply "The Concourse." If you had money, you lived in one of the fancy Art Deco apartment buildings with doormen and elevators. If you didn't, you lived in one of the five-story walk-ups on Tremont Avenue or any other street on my side of the tracks—literally, the Jerome Avenue IRT.

I took my usual bike route past the Loew's Paradise, checking out the marquee with the latest double billing. I loved the Paradise. The theater was beginning to show its age, but nothing compared with its marble columns and busts of Columbus and Shakespeare and Mozart. It still was a palace where a kid could get lost watching a movie under-neath a domed ceiling filled with twinkling stars. It was the closest I'd ever been to such a night sky.

It was just my bad luck though that the reality of Bronx streets could find its way into the Paradise. I was still leery from a close call a week earlier. I'd been by myself for the must-see double flick of *Corridors of Blood* and *Horror Hotel*, when a rough-looking bald guy sat down next to me. Given that almost every one of the 4,000 seats in the theater was empty, I didn't get a good feeling.

It was only a few moments into the film when the bald guy asked out of the side of his mouth, "So, did I miss much?"

I hesitated then made a mistake. I answered. "Uh, no, just started," I whispered back nervously.

He wasn't through talking, all hush-like, as if I was some close buddy or something. I could hear him sucking in air. And then he stretched his leg to the side, and rubbed his knee against mine. Now I could hear my own heart thump-ing.

I stared straight ahead at the screen, but I had stopped watching.

"So, you want to do it?" he rasped.

I stopped breathing. I didn't know what "it" was, but I knew for sure that I didn't want to "do it."

He let the question hang in the air. And then. "Do you want me to do it to you?"

I was nailed to my seat. A scream froze inside my throat.

I could feel the guy's eyeballs on me, his wheezing heav-ier, raspier.

On the screen someone was being dismembered.

A minute passed, another, but the bald guy waited. Wait-ing for what? Finally, he slid out of his seat and out the the-ater. I was freed from my unmovable state, though it took some time to settle my heart down. I stayed another hour watching Boris Karloff do his scary thing, but he had noth-ing on the bald guy.

A week later I remembered nothing of the movie.

☙☯☙

I shook off the memory and sped the two-and-a-half-miles to where Jerome and Bainbridge avenues crisscrossed. The junction was the last stop on the IRT, not to mention the very last stop for those folks lying underground across the street.

I pedaled into Woodlawn Cemetery.

I had the good sense to bring along my map this time. Woodlawn was huge, and I imagined getting lost forever among the stones only for my bones to be discovered years later. Now that would be a fine how-do-you-do. I could only hope that my family would be given a discount on my plot.

Biking through the cemetery was not very respectful. My Schwinn wasn't even painted black but racing red, but I had no choice if I was going to get to where I was going. I made my way along the crooked lines of stones and mausoleums, checking my map along the way. Not exactly "Hollywood Homes of the Stars," but I thought I might have a career here as a tour guide for the "Graves of the Rich and Famous." Quite a few among the 250,000 departed here. A money-maker for sure.

I took a route past a few familiar spots. To the left was Lot 185 with a gravestone belonging to William Barclay Masterson, better known as Bat Masterson. His epitaph was engraved in the stone: "Loved By Everyone," which really cracked me up since he wasn't exactly the lovable type, having gunned down a bunch of guys who got in his way. I was hooked on the TV western with actor Gene Barry as Bat, and found myself stupidly singing the theme song as I drove past.

I had visited Bat's grave before but was bummed to learn that his gunslinger days were overinflated. Yeah, he had some shootouts with his buddy, Wyatt Earp, and had a rep as a hard-assed lawman in Dodge City. But the guy hung up his six irons only to become a sports writer and some sort of boxing promoter, dying of a heart attack *at his desk*. Jeez, what was *that* about!

At least Gaetano Reina was the real deal, a Mafia boss from the Bronx who lived and died by the gun—actually, a shotgun blast to the head as he left his mistress on Sheridan Avenue. Great story. The godfather was now resting peacefully in his four-column mausoleum topped by a large cross. I slowed down to pay my respects to the tough guy.

I picked up speed moving past Herman Melville's stone with its scroll carving (though I never thought much of his whale story). Then Elizabeth Cady Stanton's memorial that reminded me of an oversized chess rook, and mausoleums containing the departed Augustus Juilliard (my brother had gone to his music school) and James Bailey, the Ringling Brothers Circus guy.

I purposely went out of my way to ride past Diana Barrymore in her family vault. She was an actress and the daughter of the famous film actor, and her death had been all over the papers back in January. She had killed herself overdosing on alcohol and sleeping pills. At thirty-eight. Sad, sad, life.

I finally came to some small stone buildings surrounding a strange-looking tomb. My destination that day. The tomb reminded me of an Egyptian funeral barge in one of those epic Bible movies. This one, though, was the final resting place of Isidor Straus. Inscribed on his tomb: "Lost at Sea, April 15, 1912." Not really a well-known guy, but his story grabbed me. I'd been hooked on the *Titanic* ever since seeing *Night of Darkness*. The movie hit me even harder after I found out that a dozen or so of the 1,500 dead were buried at Woodlawn. One of those lost lives was Isidor's.

I knew his story by heart. Isidor was sixty-seven, rich, married to Ida for forty years, and owned Macy's department store. I was more of an Alexander's department store kid myself, but that didn't matter now. Stories of bravery and nobility got to me, and the Strauses had both.

The movie version ran in my head. Isidor refusing to leave the dying ship while women and children were still on board. His beloved Ida also shunning a lifeboat seat, insisting on sticking by Isidor's side. "We have lived together for many years," she told her husband. "Where you go, I go." Then handing her fur coat to her maid boarding a lifeboat, telling her she needed to keep warm in the freezing North Atlantic. And, finally, the couple, huddling in a pair of deck chairs, holding hands in those last minutes when a huge wave strikes, washing them into the sea.

Isidor's body was recovered. Ida was never found.

I don't know why I was so caught up in their story. Actually I did know. Maybe I saw in the Strauses something of my own folks. My dad, Max, also an immigrant Jew from Eastern Europe, came to America to carve out a new life. He traveled by steamship with little more than his violin in hand. The family legend had it that a shipman heard Dad's rhapsodies coming from steerage class and asked him to join the ship's band on the first-class deck.

That violin would be Dad's good-luck charm. This was especially true when he first met Rosie at a hotel in the Catskill Mountains in upstate New York. She had caught sight of this dashing band-leader, with sky-blue eyes, his passionate gypsy melodies soaring from the stage, and that was that. By the time my brother, Fred, and I came along, Max and Rosie had built a life together. Not always an easy one, but they survived and had each other. And I had no doubt at all that Rosie, like Ida, could ever think of her life without her man.

I spent some more time hanging around with Isidor, thinking about his life, and my own, before coming on a biblical memorial inscription near his tomb. It was meant for his lost Ida.

"Many waters cannot quench love—neither can the floods drown it."

I ran my hand along the inscribed words, and turned

misty-eyed. Just a beautiful thought to sum up their long lives together.

Really a corny story.

But only if it never happened.

≈≈≈

I biked home from Woodlawn worn out and in desperate need of a drink—my "regular"—at Mel's candy store on the corner of Tremont and Davidson avenues.

"Hey Mel, set 'em up," I told Mel as I bounded onto a tall stool.

Mel was missing some teeth with a black patch over his left eye, and looked like an extra in some bad pirate movie. But there was no mistaking the fact that he made the best egg cream in the Bronx, maybe even the world. The drink didn't have an egg or cream, but Mel was a master with U-Bet chocolate syrup, seltzer, and a touch of milk.

"So, what're ya up to?" Mel asked in that gravelly voice of his. "I assume nothin' good."

"Just robbing a few banks, nothing too serious," I jibed back.

Mel was cantankerous but a good guy who liked to tell his stories.

"Did I tell ya the time I made one-hundred-ten free throws in a row?" he rasped.

"Yeah, about forty, fifty times," I sighed. "I think that's a record for telling the same story over and over, Mel."

"Don't be a wise ass," he shot back testily. "You're in the presence of a schoolyard basketball legend. I was known as Dead Eye."

I was about to crack wise about Dead Eye's real dead eye, but I was afraid of the rat poison he would mix into his egg cream concoction.

"You might think of helping Wilt the Stilt with his foul shots," I said, ready to move on from the back and forth.

Mel kind of growled, slapped down the egg cream in a tall glass on the counter, and turned to the sink to wash a dish.

I was left to sip my drink, eyeing a familiar cardboard box on the counter stacked with plastic covered gold packs. I tinkered through the pile finally deciding on my lucky one. I put my nickel on the counter and tore the pack open—six baseball cards and a large slab of bubble gum. The baseball gods stared back at me. Warren Spahn. "Moose" Skowron. Harmon "Killer" Killebrew. Gil McDougald. Juan Marichal's rookie card. And a bonus card. I just about leapt for joy.

"Hey Mel," I shouted out. "Roger Maris!"

Mel turned to check out the card I had hoisted in the air. "Yeah, the guy has a shot at forty home runs this season," he said. "That's Mickey Mantle territory."

"Yeah, that would be something."

"That's something all right. But so are one-hundred-ten foul shots in a row. Remember that or get ready for a kick in the ass."

"Will do, Mel," I smiled, but dead tired and ready to call it a day.

I slurped what was left of my egg cream, pocketed the cards, and waved s'long to Mel. It was getting dark, and I needed to get going.

Biking up Tremont for home, I swear I could smell Mom's meatballs and spaghetti from down the block.

CHAPTER 6

John's House

S nap!
"*Tommy!*" a furious Dee-Dee O'Hara cried out. "*That isn't funny!*"

Tommy was having his fun again. I guess he was tired of cutting his arm or picking his nose, his usual way of passing time in class. Poor Dee-Dee had the bad luck to be sitting in front of the guy.

Grabbing the back of her blouse, Tommy had latched his fingers under her bra strap and pulled back the elastic strip as far as it would stretch. Then he let the strap go.

"Slingshot!" he shouted gleefully, as the strap smacked against Dee-Dee's back.

A few boys snickered. Tommy, with his alligator grin, chortled. Dee-Dee was mortified and close to tears. Miss Crouse was not amused.

"Tommy—*to the back!*" Miss Crouse wearily told him. Tommy had nearly worn down our teacher only a month into the school year.

Miss Crouse was turning out to be an okay teacher, still holding on to her sweet Disney character. But the cracks in her experience left her struggling. She tried to walk the line between being "nice" and "not-so-nice" but really couldn't pull off the mean teacher act. For the most part we weren't bad kids, but then there was Tommy. And Miss Crouse didn't have an answer or an attitude for him.

Tommy slowly rose from his seat, sauntered to the back of the class, and sat down on a movable wooden chair next to me. It was kind of a dunce chair, but with Tommy's frequent visits the spot was known as the "Psycho's Corner." We decided it was best to keep the name to ourselves.

So there I was with Plotz on one side and Tommy, my new neighbor, on the other. I silently prayed that this wasn't the day Tommy decided to carve a new tattoo on his arm. Luckily, the guy wasn't in an artistic mood as he hunkered down in the seat, closed his eyes, and nodded off. I made a mental note not to wake him up.

The class also settled down—though sniffling Dee-Dee was still having a hard time—as Miss Crouse turned to our social studies lesson. It was all about the upcoming national election, a few weeks away. These two guys running for president were going at it, and I wanted to hear what our teacher had to say. If only Plotz would shut up.

"Hell, not even close. Nixon has a hard-on for those Commies," Plotz snarled out the corner of his mouth, then taking his fist to his crotch and pretending to masturbate. Planting the image in my head of Richard Nixon with a boner was none too appealing. But I guess Plotz needed a visual aid to round out his argument.

Anyway, there was no point getting into it with Plotz, not that he was about to stop mouthing off.

"Nixon got my vote," he proudly went on. "Besides, this other guy looks like a fag. Probably is a fag."

I couldn't help myself. "Plotz! He's married to Jackie Kennedy! Cut the stupid talk."

"The fags always put up a front. She's probably a lesbo anyway."

Alan Plotz was some package deal. He appeared to be a member of the human race, but I was sure I was wrong on that one. I didn't know what was worse—his idiotic ramblings or his smell. I tried to tune him out, but there was no getting around his body stink. (Even Mom gagged when I came home infected with Plotz's aroma before pointing me to the shower.)

Plotz's blab had finally given way to Miss Crouse who was holding up two photographs for the class to see. One was of John Kennedy, the other, Richard Nixon, both smiling and looking confident. Miss Crouse tried not to show any favoritism, but no way could I see her choosing the squirrely Nixon.

"Remember, we get to decide the next most powerful leader of the free world," she said in her bubbly way. I didn't want to be a killjoy by mentioning that we couldn't vote and had absolutely no say in who would be our next president.

Besides, Plotz was back at it again.

"The fag would be better off running as a Jew," he smirked.

"What the *hell* are you talking about now, Plotz?" I shot back giving in to his moronic ramble.

"The guy's a Cat-o-lick," he went on. "You might as well elect the pope."

Plotz's round face brimmed with self-satisfaction, convinced that he'd nailed JFK. As much as I couldn't stand that smug face, Plotz was right about one thing. When it came to religion, all that "love thy neighbor" stuff went out the window. Dad told me that lots of people hated Kennedy because he was a Roman Catholic bent on turning the country into a "Church of America." Plotz could definitely be counted among the stupids.

I was hooked into the political goings-on and had a definite favorite. The only live president I'd ever known was the guy in office, who was old, bald, and liked to play golf (an alien sport that no self-respecting Bronx kid could ever imagine playing). John Kennedy was something else—cool, a movie star type, even with the strange nasal voice. I didn't hold that against him, or anything else. Without even trying he had my vote if they ever let me vote. And there was a very good reason.

You see, John F. Kennedy had been a Bronx boy. Yep. Really. No lie.

I had discovered this important truth leafing through a book at the library one afternoon. At first I couldn't believe my eyes. But there he was in a photograph. John, ten years old, a Bronx schoolboy, sitting stiffly for his class picture. It turned out he lived a bike ride away from my neighborhood. Too bad his family later moved to nearby Bronxville—not to confused with the *real* Bronx—and finally to Massachusetts, a move that obviously ruined his Bronx accent, but what could you do? Whatever else, the kid had been one of us. And once a Bronx boy, well, you know.

Okay, so John lived on the other side of the Bronx, the rich and fancy section they called Riverdale. But who cared—it was still the Bronx. No two ways about it. I'd never found a reason to head over to that area with its grassy fields and tall trees and fresh air. Who wanted to live like that anyhow? I was told that the place also had amazing views of the Hudson River. I'd seen pictures of old Henry sailing down the waterway, but that was as close as I'd ever gotten to the river.

It was true that John was not exactly a public school type of kid, but went to one of those stuck-up privates called Riverdale Country School. The all-boys school didn't even have a number to it. This was no PS 26 or JHS 82. But John and I had something else in common. Let's just say, we both weren't in the top of our class. His report card: a B in Penmanship, C-minus in English, D in French. Overall, a C average. He won some "Best Composition Award" at his graduation, so maybe his folks didn't give him too hard a time. My grades weren't so hot either in sixth grade, but PS 26 did give me a paper certificate for good attendance. Hey, not so bad. At least I showed up.

☙❧❧

I thought back to John's class picture—there he was, sitting in the middle first row, wearing a dark suit and tie, and looking as if he had a stick up his butt. In fact, not one of his schoolmates seemed as if they were having an especially good time. It was their tough luck that they never had the chance to attend 82. No suits and ties there. Well, except for the white shirt-blue tie for Wednesday assembly.

I found another important piece of information that afternoon in the library. John's old Bronx address. I knew where I heading next. Not Woodlawn this time. I was more interested in where this kid *started* his life. I wrote John's address in black marker on the back of my hand, and the next day went in search of his boyhood home.

I studied my map before jumping onto the Schwinn—the trip was new territory for me. I pedaled down to the Concourse and across to the Kingsbridge area. I followed the elevated train tracks, and found my way up a steep road until I came to the edge of the Bronx. This was Riverdale. Streets with fancy high-rise apartment buildings and pretty private houses and green parks.

And here was the Hudson River, drifting on as far as I could see. Lining the opposite shore was an incredible forest of gold-and-red leafed trees. So this is what autumn leaves looked like, I thought. On my block about the only sign of fall was seeing my pals move from their tees to sweatshirts. Nothing like this.

I might have hung out longer here but needed to get going. The days were already shorter and the sun was low in the sky. I eyed my map again before heading down a stretch of country road with the name Palisade Avenue.

This was the Bronx I never imagined. Along the narrow road, I sped past woods that rose high enough to block out the last rays of the sun. A train, out of sight, chugged-chugged along some distant track. Nothing at all like the screeching Jerome Avenue IRT sparking along the EL. I had yet to come across a single car, just a lone woman strolling, walking her dog. The only other sound was my bike gliding along the pavement, a calmness that never would have been tolerated in my neighborhood.

The road stretched through the wooded area for about a mile before I came to what I first thought was a country park. But a large sign told me where I was: the Riverdale Country School. So this was John's school. I checked out the grass ball fields and low-rise buildings that I guessed had classrooms, a gym, and everything else. No one would confuse this place with JHS 82. No students were around, but I was certain that these kids weren't the class 710 type. No reeking Alan Plotz or Herbie Kaplan, whose talent was shouting out "horseshit" each time he blasted out a sneeze.

I wound past the school and up a twisty road before coming to a stop next to a gated estate. I could see families milling about the grounds, all enjoying the afternoon.

"Are you coming in?" asked a smiling guard at the entrance. "Free admission today."

I stood at the entrance, peeking in. The place was like something out of another time with its old stone buildings, green lawn, flower beds, and a scenic view of the Hudson River in the distance.

"Welcome to Wave Hill," the smiley guard went on, sweeping his arms as if introducing me to the King's palace. "Teddy Roosevelt and Mark Twain once stayed here. Twain even built a tree house here, where he invited his guests."

"A tree house?" I was even more confused.

The guard nodded excitedly, his eyeballs popping wide.

I was convinced that Rod Serling was about to show up at any second, but even this crazy world, *this Bronx*, had to be beyond *his* wildest imagination—and getting weirder. Not to seem impolite I gave the guard a half-wave and a short smile. (No way was I going to win a smiling contest with him.)

"Thanks, maybe some other time," I lied.

He didn't seem too disappointed, still grinning as he waved back.

Then I quickly hopped back on my bike, still wondering what planet I had arrived on, and went on my way.

I didn't have to go far, as I slowly pedaled up the road. I double-checked the address imprinted on the back of my hand. I had come to a run-down, abandoned house at the corner—5040 Independence Avenue.

John's house.

I didn't bother booting down the kickstand, letting my bike fall to the ground. No fence bordered the property, so I just walked onto the front lawn. No signs of life. An old car was parked in the driveway. I thought another family might live there now, but I couldn't be sure. I went over to a large window and peeked in. Nothing much to see. The insides had been gutted with wood planks scattered about, but no workers were in sight.

The house wasn't at all what I expected. A huge three-story rectangle made of cement blocks. Somehow I imagined a grand manor from some history book. There were a few nice touches, I suppose. A stone porch, large windows, and lots of grass and trees. Not a bad backyard for the Kennedy boys—John and his brothers Bobby, Teddy, and Joe—all here. I wouldn't have minded getting into a touch football game with those guys.

I counted windows, some twenty rooms, which I guess that family needed with the seven kids and everyone else. John's mom was also a Rose—though I found out that she wasn't exactly the warm, cuddly type with a chocolate malted waiting for him after school. I sat down on a stone step, trying to imagine what once was.

I wondered. Who were *John's* heroes?

What did he dream about?

Would we have been friends?

Okay, so this place, and John's life, was nothing like mine on Tremont Avenue. No matter. John and I had breathed Bronx air. We were pals in that sense. Well, maybe this was a bit of wishful thinking. But I felt connected being here anyway, hanging out in a space where John had led his own kid's life.

I stayed a while longer, letting my mind wander. Easy enough, since the only sounds about were from a few chirping birds. But the sun had already sunk into the trees across the river leaving a red ribbon in the dark sky, and my Schwinn didn't have lights. I took a last look at the big house and silently gave my best wishes to the Kennedy ghosts. Then I hopped back on my bike, and hustled my way home, this time not bothering to stop at Wave Hill and the smiley man.

e/3e/3

Miss Crouse ended the lesson by announcing our homework assignment.

"Children—" (She just had to stop calling us this.) "Vice President Richard Nixon and Senator John Kennedy are going to debate on television this Monday evening, and I want you to watch."

"Crap!" Plotz cried out. "Does this mean I won't be able to watch *The Flintstones*?"

This time Miss Crouse ignored him and bubbled on about Nixon and Kennedy and how excited we should be. "It is the first time *ever* that we can see a presidential debate on television!" she exclaimed.

Miss Crouse did a nice job stirring me up, and I couldn't wait to watch.

Then the dismissal bell rang.

Tommy Branigan, rousing from his afternoon catnap, had the last word as we got up to leave, muttering to anyone who cared to listen, "Fuck 'em both."

CHAPTER 7

Anita Bonita

The weather finally cooled down what was left of the summer heat. The change gave us kids even more energy, and the courtyard was alive with a fierce game of stoopball and noisy roller skaters. Me and my boys huddled in the corner with serious stakes at hand. Our prized baseball cards.

It was then that Anita Goldman glided out of my building, a first-class distraction. The girl was a neighbor of mine but older and not at all a family friend. She had a "reputation" around the neighborhood, one that earned her the nickname "Anita Bonita." I don't think the name was intended as a compliment, though I think Anita actually liked it. In fact, she got an early start to her career, and, sad to say, it involved my family.

When Anita was seven she had enticed my six-year-old brother, Fred, into a game of "doctor." She proceeded to shove down her panties to show Fred "hers" with the promise that Fred showed her "his." Apparently both kids had their curiosity satisfied. But it was soon afterward that Anita's mother came storming into our apartment accusing my brother of practically raping her darling daughter. Mom wasn't about to back down—after all, no one dared to accuse her Freddy of such things (though Rosie let my brother have it when Anita's mother left). As for Anita, I had the distinct feeling that over the years she continued to play "doctor" with other boys around the block. Maybe she was just taking an early interest in her medical studies.

I made it a point to stay away from Anita, who now was no longer a kid but a pretty, flirty teenager about five years older than me. It wasn't only the old trouble with Fred that made me keep my distance—Anita just gave me the shivers. Every once in a while I'd catch her checking me out as she walked by, slyly smiling. A smile with a scary attitude. I didn't want to think about what she was thinking, but of course that's exactly what I thought. Was she thinking *that*, and with me? Or maybe I was just an underage pervert letting my imagination get the better of me.

Anita swayed closely by me now as she made her way out of the courtyard, and I caught a whiff of her perfume. But she didn't throw me even a glance walking by. Thank god. So why couldn't I stop from eyeballing *her*? She had on one of those peasant blouses that left her midriff bare and puffed up her breasts. I worked my way down, my eyes glued to her curvy butt tightly molded into a pair of hip huggers.

And just then Anita half turned her head, catching me in the act. She smiled, that sly smile, again, that smile with an attitude, and then she winked. *What was that—a wink?* Was that the wink that said, *"I'll show you mine, if you show me yours?"* Of course either part of that deal terrified me. I was in sudden panic attack mode with Anita watching me watch her ass. She then cast her spell.

Suddenly, I freaked. *What the hell was happening inside my pants?*

Actually I had a very good idea what was going on and instantly covered my crotch to hide a hard-on that had crammed up the front of my jeans. This wasn't the first time. Recently, I found myself waking up each morning with a throbbing boner. Kind of confusing. I mean, how did this thing magically happen? Also annoying since it kept me stalling in bed before breakfast until I was back to normal. But having a boner here on the streets? In broad daylight? *And in front of Anita Bonita?*

Well, Anita obviously had something against the Wolfenthal men—and should have felt ashamed doing what she does. This spell thing.

But from what I could see, Anita Bonita seemed perfectly satisfied, no regrets at all, as she left the courtyard, chalking up another score.

"Hey, Paul, let's play!"

What was that?

I turned.

Sammy.

"Hey, you okay?" he asked. "You need a run to the toilet?"

That wasn't quite it but thought it best not to explain why I was crunching my arms around my crotch.

"Nah, good to go," I replied weakly.

It took me a minute or two to settle things down, so to speak. I inspected my pants and finally got back to my gang.

❧❧❧

Our baseball collections grew or shrank based on our surgical skill with baseball cards. The game was called Match, and my rep as a steely-eyed player was well known.

This time I was up against Sammy, no second stringer when it came to Match. I immediately went on the attack, gripping a card between my thumb and middle finger, and then flipping it into the air. The card turned twice in midair flashing a player's picture on one side—"heads"—his baseball stats on the other—"tails."

I flipped six more cards, with each telling the same story as the first. Sammy and I hovered over the pavement and saw the faces of all seven players looking back at us. All heads. A slam.

And now Sammy had to match in order to win.

"Bro, you're leaving me no room here," Sammy grumbled. "Not even a single tail."

"Pressures on." I dug the knife in deep.

"I'm not done," Sammy snapped.

"Yeah, you are."

I could see Sammy's eyes narrow, his gunslinger squint. He shook his hands to get loose, and then took aim. He instantly got into synch—his first six cards came up heads. The guy was good! One more heads would finish me off.

So I needed to dig deeper, pulling out my reverse psychology move. "Hey, Sammy, you got me, I'm dead. No pressure at all."

"Shut up, Paul!" Sammy shot back. "Don't try the psych job on me."

"Just giving you a boost."

"Yeah, right."

Match was a game of "feel," and the worst thing a player could do is tighten up. I could now see Sammy thinking, tightening. And with the last card resting between his fingers, he paused—a second or two too long!—before flicking his wrist. The baseball card seemed to turn in the air in slow motion. Sammy let out a groan even before his card hit the pavement.

"Shit! Shit! Shit!"

Sammy was being repetitive, and such bad language. But I thought it best not to give him another dig while we hunched over the card. Tony Kubek's baseball statistics. Nice career. But tails. No match. Each one of Sammy's seven cards belonged to me. Later I'd stack them with hundreds of others stored in my closet.

"Damnit, Paul," Sammy griped. "You got my rookie Mickey Mantle card. C'mon, give me a break and take a trade for it!"

"Sorry, m'man," I said in my fake-sympathy voice. "No mercy allowed in Match."

Okay, so I wasn't being a pal, but I couldn't help myself.

Suddenly, one of the stoopball kids let out a holler. Throwing down his Spalding, the kid raced over to a portable radio that was blaring through the courtyard. "Guys, we're in trouble!" he shouted.

We all sprang into motion, spilling over to the stoop. Mel Allen, the Yankee broadcaster, was spelling out the latest danger to our guys. The Yankees were about to win the American League pennant—but the hated Boston Red Sox were not going down easy in the ninth. Down one run, the Sox had men on first and third and two outs. And their best hitter was coming to the plate.

Allen's voice was familiar to every Bronx kid. He was our "Voice of God." And now he was about to tell us the fate of our beloved team…

"Stengel has come out to the mound. He's pulling Ralph Terry.

"He signals to the bullpen. It will be the lefty, Luis Arroyo.

"He will have to face Pete Runnels, who leads the league in hitting this year.

"Runnels settles in the box, and here comes Arroyo's first pitch. Runnels swings…

"A pop-up to third. Boyer's under it.

"The Yankees win…

"The Yankees have won the pennant!"

Allen raved on, but we imagined the scene for ourselves. The Yankees were jubilant as they stormed the mound, falling over each other in celebration.

So did the boys at 50 West Tremont Avenue.

෨෩෨෩

The day after the Yankees won the pennant, John Kennedy went on television to take on Richard Nixon.

CHAPTER 8

"Such a Good-Looking Man"

Dad adjusted the rabbit-ear antenna as we settled around the small RCA black-and-white TV in our living room. "I think you got it now, honey," Mom called from the couch.

The screen moved from a blur of squiggly lines to a picture of a group of men on some stage, somewhere. Dad checked out the screen, nodded his approval, and sat down next to Mom. I was perfectly comfortable sprawled out on our living room rug.

None of us knew what to expect, and I had the feeling neither did these guys in suits on the screen. One white-haired reporter named Smith sat at a tiny desk that must have come straight from my old PS 26 kindergarten classroom. I guess his job was to act as referee for the main event. Some other reporters on the set swiveled around in their chairs to introduce themselves to us. But I had enough with their talk—it was time to get on with this showdown.

Finally, the main event. On stage came John Kennedy and Richard Nixon—and, so, the great debate, the talk everywhere, was on. I imagined that every television set in America was tuned into this great battle for the presidency.

Honestly, it didn't look like much.

My guy, John, didn't get off to a good start, confused whether to sit or stand when asked his first question. Not that it made a difference to any of us.

"He's such a good-looking man," gushed Mom. "And so young!"

"Mom, I'm listening!" I groused.

"He's certainly a better man than 'Tricky Dick,'" Dad chimed in, the family conversation revving up even before much of anything was happening.

"What's a 'Tricky Dick'?" I asked, giving in to the family talk.

"He's the other fellow, Nixon."

"What's with the weird nickname?"

"He has what you call in Yiddish, *genevishe oigen*."

"That helps a lot, Dad."

"It means he has shifty eyes."

Shifty eyes? There was something to Dad's observation. You could tell a lot about a person from his eyes, and Nixon had a problem with his. I could see that when the guy made a serious point, his eyes got kind of squinty as if was pitching us a used car sale. He also had these thick, dark eyebrows that formed a "V" on his forehead. A psycho look and not really a great selling point for a guy with his hand out for votes.

John was something else. He seemed to jump off the screen into our living room, looking tan and sharp in his dark suit. Should he lose as president he probably could get a leading role in a movie playing one.

Nixon was back on to the screen talking about "the men in the Kremlin," but I could see something wasn't right as he rattled on. The guy came across as if he was trying to climb out of his skin. He was not the family favorite by any stretch, and we had no intention of cutting him a break. Even so, there was no getting around the fact that he looked awful.

"I'm getting itchy just watching him," I said. "He looks sick."

Mom nodded. "He needs make-up—badly."

Or at least a Miami Beach vacation, I thought.

I wasn't exactly a fashion expert, but Nixon in his dull-gray suit had the look of someone who had casually dropped by the TV studio for a cup of coffee on his way to a doctor's office for a checkup.

"What's with his clothes?" I asked Dad. "Doesn't Uncle Harry sell that outfit downtown?" I was only half-kidding. In fact, my father's brother, Harry, owned a clothing store in Chinatown, and I could have sworn that Nixon's suit came off his close-out rack.

The debate went from bad to worse for the man. Nixon seemed to be melting into a puddle of bodily fluid right before my eyes. I was especially glued to a glob of sweat that glistened on his chin and stuck there.

"Can't someone tell him to wipe his face?" I said to no one in particular.

Finally, Nixon took out a handkerchief, dabbing the sweat from his upper lip and forehead. It wasn't long though before his face was wet again.

The man was already getting under my skin ten minutes into the debate. It was one thing being a Republican—the family nemesis—but looking like a guy who walked out of a sauna wearing a ratty suit was just too much.

The political blab grinded on, and soon even Nixon's sweat bubble didn't hold my interest. Both men were gabbing about something called farm subsidies, but I didn't care at all about the cost for pigs or much of the political talk for that matter. I wasn't listening anyway. I was watching.

And I couldn't take my eyes off of John. When the man meant to emphasize a point, he pumped his fist, thumb up, as if he was hammering a nail. He was calm and cool, and I believed every word he had to tell us even if I didn't understand much of anything he was saying. Okay, I was a little dim, but JFK wasn't about to steer us wrong.

Then there was sweaty Nixon making his pitch again, his black eyes darting back and forth as if he was caught lying on the witness stand. He probably was thinking that this TV thing was a real bad idea, and hoping to make a quick exit.

Could this guy possibly be our next president?

Dad seemed to read my mind. "What a Republican *shmendrik*," he muttered.

I didn't know much Yiddish but I knew Dad wasn't giving Nixon a compliment.

Mom finally decided that she'd had enough and took off to bed. Dad and I watched until the end. For all the hoopla, I found the debate pretty boring. It wasn't the politics anyway, but the two men that made a difference to me.

Dad had it right, pointing to John on the screen, "Now that's a *mensch*."

I understood the Yiddish this time and went to bed that night, thinking about John Kennedy, and happily fell into a peaceful sleep.

CHAPTER 9

The Voice

I guess I wasn't a totally normal kid growing up. To state the obvious. Let's just say I had a vivid imagination and liked sharp objects. You would be surprised how these two go together. Like the time I was five and cut off most of my hair while lying in bed. The haircut left streaks of bald patches on my head, giving me an authentic concentration-camp look. I was neat about the whole thing, though, making sure my departed hair was neatly piled on top of a toy drum.

Rosie screamed, horrified, the next morning when she came into my room and saw her retarded son. At the time I didn't understand why she was so upset. I thought the bald streaks were kind of cool. In truth, I had no clue why I did what I did. I was five, and just a moronic kid, so that explained that.

My fixation with sharp objects obviously ran deep, even in my sleep filled with nightmares. And weirdness. I had even taken up sleepwalking. Not in that zombie sort of way, with arms outstretched like in some horror movie. Only creepier. One such night I had slipped out of bed and made my way into the kitchen where Mom and Dad were talking. My presence put a stop to that. They called out to me, but here was their adorable boy, now a scary voodoo creature, in some sort of trance. My folks were used to me being strange, but it's safe to say that this current spookiness was over the top. Especially after I went over to the cutlery drawer and pulled out a humongous steak knife. That absolutely got their attention.

Deciding not to shake me from my hypnotic state—who knows what could have happened next?—they trailed me back to my bedroom. The large blade in my small hand was pointing the way. I then climbed into bed, tucking the knife under my pillow, and fell right to sleep. Dad inched over and carefully took away the blade, but held off telling me about the episode until years later. Perhaps he was afraid I would be traumatized by the story. Either that, or he needed more time to seriously consider whether to commit his five-year-old son to a loony bin.

In looking back, though, I realize I hadn't been crazy at all. Perfectly sane, in fact. There were creepy monsters out there, hovering in the night outside the window. What was a little kid to do? I needed to protect myself from the demons.

༄༅༄

I guess what happened later on was no surprise. I was seven now and drifting off to sleep in my bedroom—the night when the Voice first came to me. It was a raspy Voice, with a message to deliver. I suspected that it had been hiding in my head for some time and decided it was a good time to step out. I might have guessed. The dead of night is when the Voices make themselves known, creeping into a kid's shadowy places. And, so, here was one such stranger, alone with me in bed, speaking to me. And freaking me out!

I couldn't move, shout for help, or even burst into tears, just petrified and frozen in terror. It was as if my body had turned to stone with my mind in a panic and my heart beating rat-ta-tat-tat-tat. I remembered some biblical story about a girl who was turned into a pillar of salt for disobeying God. But I was only seven and way too young to feel the wrath of anyone or anything. But here was the Voice. This bogeyman. And I had no idea what it had in store for me.

I swear I felt the stabbing edges of a pitchfork in the back of my throat, choking me—that sharp object fixation again—making it hard to breathe and impossible to scream. I would have if I was able, but all I could do is listen. Then, incredibly, I discovered that the Voice wasn't a monster at all—in fact, it had come to my room that night only to settle me down. This kid full of fears.

I could hear the Voice distinctly.

'There is no need to be afraid. You are safe.'

I thought that this might be a ridiculous piece of advice considering the source. Hearing voices in your head wasn't exactly a confidence builder. But I was drawn to it. I wanted to believe that everything was okay, that there was nothing to be afraid of out there in the world.

'You are safe.'

Again, words coming through the dark, the Voice, a friend, calming me down. And this time I breathed more easily. My nightmares gone, I drifted easily into sleep.

It was a shame, though, that the Voice turned out to be a lousy prophet. Later on, I would find out that the world, in fact, was a very dangerous place with real demons, alive and living among us. They wore different disguises, looking like anyone else. And they could be terrifying since they basically lived to create meanness, cause harm.

Then one such monster came along and shattered my neighborhood. He was not some imaginary horror. He was as real and evil as could be. I was no longer seven then—I was older, yet still a kid at thirteen. And I wholly remembered back to that night, the Voice with its reassuring words still echoing in my memory. *'There is no need to be afraid,'* it promised. *'You are safe.'*

And how sadly cruel those words were that day when little Benji Shapiro disappeared.

CHAPTER 10

Missing

It was a very bad night, the worst. A woman was crying out from the courtyard below my bedroom window. A frantic voice. Calling out a name, pleading to some invisible being. "Please, give me back my son. My little boy."

I was scared to my bones. Nothing could sound more terrifying.

I finally built up the nerve to look out my window. A woman stood there in half shadow underneath a courtyard lamp. I could see her scanning my building, searching for a response, any sign. I felt her desperation even three floors up in my bedroom.

The woman seemed so young to be a mom, but it was hard to tell for sure. Her face was a mask of pain weighted down by the crush of her fears. Again and again she cried out her son's name, each syllable a stretch of sound. With each repetition, her plea became more despairing, as if her son's name itself was flailing in the wind.

BEN-JI!
BEN-JI!
BEN-JI!
BEN-JI!

From my bedroom window I could see three cops standing next to the woman. Soon, my neighbors also made their way into the courtyard. Not that they could do anything but feel sorry for her.

Rosie, distressed, suddenly hurried into my room.

"Don't go anywhere," she told me. "I need to go downstairs."

"Mom, what is going on?" I asked, but I was afraid that I already knew.

"Something horrible."

"Mom—"

"Later," she stated. "Do not leave this apartment. I'll be back soon—that poor woman."

Mom left the apartment when the young mother started up again. Calling out to her little boy. Pleading. I wanted to shout out my window, tell her that everything would be okay. But I didn't believe that for a moment, and neither would she.

I now saw Mom in the courtyard coming up to the woman. She didn't know this family, but it didn't make any difference. The two women were joined in the cruelest of ways. Benji's mother's nightmare was also her own, only that her child was safe.

Rosie was speaking softly to her, an arm around her shoulder. It was hard to see what good that would do. The young woman was panicked, her body twitching with nerves. Then one of the cops began handing out a large photograph. Even from my window I could make out the picture, the face of a boy. This boy. It was the best that the cops could do. Which wasn't much of anything.

Finally, the woman, along with the police, left the courtyard to make their way to the next building. There was a minute or two of quiet until I heard her cries again a half-block away. A name being called out into the night.

Benji.

The courtyard stir below went on after she left. Scared talk buzzing up to my window. Mom was finally back in the apartment, and came into my room. She gave me a look as I lay in bed. More than sadness in her eyes, something deeper. And I understood what I'd always known and felt from Rosie. Her absolute love. I was her son, her flesh and blood, her Paulie-Boy, and nothing in the world was more precious. It was a feeling that bonded her to Benji's mom now, sharing in her despair for her lost boy. A pain so bottomless. Unbearable for any mother to carry.

Rosie bent down and took me in her arms and gave me a tight hug, her cheek touching mine. And that sad look again.

"What's going on, Mom?"

I already felt the answer in my heart, but needed to hear it from Rosie. Some little boy from the neighborhood was missing. Taken.

"His name is Benjamin Shapiro. He's six years old and lives on University Avenue," Mom said, trying to calmly recite the facts as she was told. "He was supposed to take the school bus back home this afternoon. But he never got on the bus."

"What do you mean he never got on the bus? Where could he have gone?"

"That's what everyone is trying to figure out. Benji's mom has been searching the neighborhood for hours looking for him." And then an afterthought. "Maybe he just wandered off after school."

"Mom, is that possible?"

I was waiting to hear a hint of hope in her voice. Perhaps he was lost, or with a friend, or maybe…

Rosie sighed, sadly, and then turned away before I could see tears trickling down her face. But I had and wanted her to stop. I soon found myself misting up also, though I wasn't sure whether it was because Benji was missing or that my mom was hurting.

৩৵৩৵৩

The next day Benji's picture was plastered on every

street post. The image of a smiling, tow-headed kid stared back at me. Benji could have been any one of the first-graders that I'd once bumped into roaming the hallways of PS 26. There was nothing much to distinguish him from any other neighborhood kid except for a fact highlighted on his photograph in large, bold letters: *MISSING*.

The same photo appeared in *The Daily News* that morning next to an old family picture. This one was of his mother, glowing, holding Benji in her arms. A loving picture from another time when the world was right. The news story gave the basic facts with little else to report. Laura Shapiro, twenty-seven, had raised Benji by herself after a drunken driver had killed her husband three years earlier. Now her boy, Benjamin Aaron Shapiro, was missing. Last seen waiting for a school bus in front of PS 26. Three-feet-eight-inches tall, fifty-five pounds. Brown hair, blue eyes. Missing a front tooth. Wearing blue jeans, a tan T-shirt, and Keds sneakers.

I could see Laura's features more clearly in the photograph with Benji. She was young, Hollywood pretty, reminding me of the actress Natalie Wood. I couldn't take my eyes off the picture. There was no suffering in her smiling eyes then, only love for her little boy. But what now? What must she be feeling? What will become of her?

I remembered the time I had been Benji's age. In bed drifting off to sleep, I imagined a nightmare like this, when my world was turned upside down, when I no longer felt safe in the arms of my family. I had seen this coming. So I'd conjured up the Voice to tell me things I needed to hear, and it told me not to be afraid.

For a while I did feel safe, but I never should have held out that hope. It was just a lie I told myself—the truth was that evil lived outside my bedroom, on the streets. And that no kid was ever safe. I should have warned Benji Shapiro to be careful.

But I didn't, and now Benji was gone.

CHAPTER 11

Waiting for Houdini

What Bronx kid didn't look forward to Halloween with its goblins, ghosts, and other spooks? I would have felt the same if it wasn't for the real creepy stuff around the neighborhood. It wasn't just these days getting darker and gloomier. I was feeling much the same myself.

Benji Shapiro's disappearance wasn't far from my thoughts. In fact, I couldn't stop thinking of that little kid. Especially late at night with the demons hovering about. They had left me alone for a while but were now hanging out in dark nightmares when I fell off to sleep. In one, I was taken to a high roof-top. I couldn't make out who it was that dragged me there—just a blurry presence—but I saw myself, petrified, pleading, to let me live. Then I saw myself plummeting, the sidewalk rushing up to splatter me like a bug.

Rosie had heard me crying out, nudged me back to myself and the real world. My pajamas were soaked in sweat, my throat sore from hollering.

"You were having a bad dream," she gently told me.

"Mom," I whispered back. "This was something else."

Nightmares *were* "something else," a dark malevolence that left you screaming into the night.

And poor Benji had no one to wake him from his.

It had been three weeks since the boy was whisked off the street. Gone without a trace. The story already had drifted off the pages of *The Daily News*. Even Benji's posters showed the wear of bad weather, though his picture was firmly planted in my head. Not a single kid around the neighborhood was about to forget that a real-life demon was out there, somewhere, lurking. And he could come again, and for any one of us.

Not a great frame of mind for Halloween.

It didn't help that my pals weren't around that night. Parents were on watch, and no kid of theirs was heading anywhere off the block. I had another one of my feelings, this one telling me to lay low and just forget the whole trick-or-treat thing. But disrespecting Halloween seemed sacrilegious. Besides, I wasn't about to be scared off by some kidnapper. At least that's what I told myself anyway.

And, so, I decided to push these dark feelings aside and try to get into the spirit of the night. Yeah, as usual, I should've paid attention to those warnings. Letting me know that those spirits floating around weren't on my side. They were out to get me.

I really should've listened.

❧❦❧

Trick-or-treating usually gave my friends and me an excuse to cause some small trouble. The usual stupid mischief, maybe a chalk drawing on the door of someone holding back on the sweet stuff. We could never eat all of it anyway, but who cared? The idea was to fill your bag with as much junk as you could grab and then sort out the good crap from the bad. My large plastic superhero bag stood ready to carry

the night's booty. But first I needed to get my act together
for the evening.

I was of an age where I'd outgrown the buckskin outfit
with its fake leather fringes and coonskin cap. The getup
was once the coolest for an eight-year-old kid doing his best
Fess Parker imitation—who *was* Davy Crockett!. But I was
older now and there was zero chance catching me with that
cheap polyester buckskin and rat hat. It had taken me days
to stop itching after one Halloween night traipsing around in
that costume

A different idea this time. I'd put together the costume a
few days earlier—it hadn't been easy attaching a bloody
plastic axe to my bloody T-shirt. Being an axe-murder victim seemed cool at the time. But the getup seemed all too
real to me now with Benji gone. Someone might not even
get the joke, thinking I was just another Bronx kid who'd
been mugged.

"Just lovely," Mom said, smiling and sarcastic as she
came into my room. "Aren't you waiting for Sammy and
the rest of your friends?"

"His mom won't let him come over," I replied. "All the
guys are sticking around their block."

I could see Rosie stiffen. "Well, don't wander around too
far by yourself," she said, her face tightening, realizing that
I'd be on my own in the neighborhood. "Don't stay out too
late. It's already getting dark."

Fred, oblivious to it all, sauntered in to add his two cents.
"Try not to scare the old ladies," he teased.

✧✦✧

Halloween was going okay, but nothing more. Weirdly
quiet, with only a few of us kids making the rounds. That
jumpy feeling was starting to hit me again, something brewing in the air. I tried to let it pass, but it wouldn't let go. So I
sat on my stoop, taking a break. My thoughts drifted back to

the previous Halloween, one that I wasn't about to forget. I mean, you just don't go visiting Harry Houdini every day.

I idolized the great Houdini, this Jewish kid from New York, even if it was the East Side of Manhattan. I had read everything I could about him. What could you say about a guy who couldn't be held down by handcuffs or leg irons, or even a straitjacket. I had a poster on my bedroom wall of him suspended upside-down in a locked glass-and-steel container filled with water. A caption noted that Houdini had held his breath for more than three minutes before being "rescued." Amazing, crazy guy.

I never did tell my parents about my long subway ride to visit his grave. Another one of my cemetery trips in search of a hero. Houdini was one of them, and I was excited to find out that he'd been buried in an old graveyard in Queens. It didn't feel right lying to Mom, telling her that I was hanging out with friends after school. But I felt if Houdini in chains could escape a locked steel crate sunk into New York waters, I should be able to break out of the Bronx for the afternoon. Well, that's what I told myself anyway.

Of course, had I been truthful with Mom, the conversation would have gone something like:

Me: Mom, I'm going to a graveyard in Queens to see Houdini.

Mom: Very nice, and have a pleasant trip. Oh, by the way, please make sure you get a nice plot next to him because you'll need it once your father finds out.

Strange how that survival instinct kicks in. I thought it best just to keep the trip to myself.

Following a maze of subway lines I made my way down to the tip of Queens. There I found myself in a land—make that an entire continent—of dead people. Machpela Jewish Cemetery was sandwiched among a slew of bigger cemeteries that stretched farther than I could see. It was as if every human being who had ever died had come to be buried here. Even for a graveyard lover like myself, this was a bit much.

Machpela had seen better days. Old headstones spilled over the grounds reminding me of a huge box of blocks that had been randomly dumped. Houdini's resting place was the exception—a large U-shaped granite monument designed for a king. Jewish graves were usually simple. Not this one.

Steps led up to the monument where a statute of a woman rested against two engraved names, "Houdini" and "Weiss," the family name. Houdini's bust stood on top of his tomb, giving me the creeps. I felt like the guy was giving me the eye, checking me out from the great beyond. I wouldn't put anything past the man.

I thought I'd come to pay Houdini a quiet visit, but the guy attracted his own company. Amazingly, a party was breaking out around his gravesite. I soon found out that, each Halloween, worshipers armed with broomsticks, wands and card games came to Machpela to honor the man. A séance was under way as I came up to his grave. A strange celebration since I knew that Houdini loved to expose those phony spirit mediums.

"They're waiting for a sign."

I nearly jumped out of my skin.

An ancient guy with a scraggly beard and a thousand wrinkles had silently crept up to my shoulder.

"Sorry, young fella," he croaked. 'I'm no spook so you can put yer eyeballs back in yer face."

I whipped around, getting a better look at him. I thought he must have been the oldest man still walking the Earth. He reminded me of Charlton Heston as old Moses in *The Ten Commandments* except he was missing most of his teeth. The side of his face twitched making it seem as if he was getting an electric shock every two seconds.

"What was that?" I replied nervously.

He pointed to the crowd around the tomb. "They're waiting for Harry to make his way back from the grave," he rasped. "He once said that if anyone could come back, he'd be the one. Hasn't happened yet. But those folks there aren't givin' up hope."

I eased up to the gravesite and rested my hand on the stone, imagining Houdini underground and rising from the dead. The old man read my mind.

"That's not the first time he's been buried. I remember the time in California. Buried alive some six feet deep. He wasn't even in a casket! Goddamn stunt almost killed him. He even cried out, real desperate, finally clawing his way up to the surface. Never really made it out by himself. His men rushed to rescue him, unconscious in the dirt. Even the great Houdini couldn't take on the weight of the earth."

The old man thumbed to a nearby memorial stone covered with small rocks. "That belongs to Bess, his wife. Ain't buried there, though. Some other place in New York."

"Why isn't she here with him?"

"Yeah, thirty-two years married. Machpela's a Jewish cemetery. Bess was Roman Catholic, her family wanted her among her own kind."

"That stinks," I said. "Seems like they should be together."

"Damn right. Devoted to the guy. Even when he was gone, old Bess held séances for years waiting for a secret signal from her man to prove he'd come back from the afterlife. Wouldja believe that?"

"She really believed he could return from *the dead*?"

"Yeah, the guy didn't make it, but I'm sure he gave it a good try."

"And Bess?"

"It was Halloween of '36 when Bess told the world that she'd finally lost hope. And just like that she ended it all. 'It is finished. Good night, Harry!' That's what she said, young man. Seems like only yesterday."

There was something about this old guy, and I was caught in his spell. For all I knew he could have been Houdini himself back from the grave after all this time. Houdini with gummies and a tic.

"How do you know so much about him?" I asked.

"Seen him enough times. Couldn't get enough. I was a little like you. Inquisitive type."

"You *saw* Houdini?"

"Oh, yeah, saw the guy get out of a straitjacket under water. Then there was the time they hung him from a skyscraper tied up in ropes. If I didn't see it with my own eyes, I'd never believe anyone could escape that stunt. Insane man. Broke my heart when he passed on. Some guy punched him in the gut on a dare. Wasn't prepared, busted his appendix. Died Halloween, 1926. Fifty-two years old. Damn, damn shame."

I pointed to the group holding hands next to Houdini's tomb, chanting his name, waiting for a sign.

"What do you think about their chances?"

"I don't know, it's been thirty-four years," the old man sighed. "But I wouldn't mind hearing from him again."

☙❦☙

I mentally took note of the candy pile in my bag that included a batch of my beloved Three Musketeers. No other apartments in my building were left to conquer as I ambled out of the courtyard and onto Tremont Avenue. It was already late and pitch dark, and I should have called it quits. But I wasn't ready to go home yet, and, besides, I didn't think it would hurt to pile some more of the sweet stuff into my bag.

I was wrong on that one.

"Hey, shithead. Nice costume."

Tommy.

It was bad enough bumping into the guy during daylight. It wasn't great at nighttime either. And on Halloween. Tommy wasn't in costume, not that he needed to dress up to be scary. The night shadows made his pockmarks look deeper, the bones in his face sharper. "I gotta real one of those at home," he said menacingly, pointing to the plastic axe sticking out of my T-shirt. "Would love to show you sometime."

Right, Tommy. I could smell the alcohol heavy on his breath as he edged closer. He was fifteen and already a bad drunk.

"Where's your girlfriend, Sammy? I hear he sucks dick."

I couldn't look up to face him. Just needed to get away. I tried to pull past but he stepped in the way.

"Hey, wherya goin?" Tommy garbled as he reached into my bag, swiping a fist full of candy. "Hey, lotsa good crap there. Thanks, shithead."

I ignored the theft and hustled my way around him. It was just then that I felt the sting of something hard hitting the back of my head.

Tommy then hurled another piece of rock candy that flew by barely missing me this time. Another shot, this one glancing off my arm. Then another, this one got me square in the face as I turned. I could feel a welt already rising on my forehead.

"Changed my mind," he snarled. "This shit will give you cavities." He flung the rest of the candy at me, showering me with the barrage, and let out a hoarse laugh. There was nothing light about the sound. Air filled with hate.

The black atmosphere lingered as Tommy staggered

away having had his evening fun. He looked as if he was more interested now in throwing up.

"See you around, shithead," Tommy muttered as he retched and lurched down the block.

I hoped that he was wrong about that. But who was I kidding. There was no getting rid of Tommy.

I couldn't make sense of people like Tommy Branigan whose sole purpose in life was to hurt others. I was one of his kick-arounds and didn't like the part one bit. But I was helpless. My thoughts went back to poor Benji, who found himself taken by another crazy into some dark place. And also helpless. Where was he now? I hated to think about that. Or about a basic truth of life.

Bad people lived among us.

And I was sure Tommy Branigan was a member of that club.

CHAPTER 12

The Old Lady in 4G

I was still feeling the sting from Tommy's assault—and it wasn't only my face that was hurting. My axe-in-the-chest costume perfectly suited my lousy mental state. This Halloween from hell. I could swear that even the jack-o-lanterns with their twisted smirks were mocking me from windowsills. I mean, who came up with this holiday anyway, pushing kids into stupid costumes to wander gloomy streets in search of crummy candy, pretending they are having the time of their lives?

Crap. Crap. *Crap!*

So why then did I decide to take one more run at Halloween instead of just heading back home? Was it because I was stubborn and stupid? That I refused to give in to the demons that terrorized kids, that messed with their minds, that stole them from their families?

So, *why?*

I had no idea.

❧❧❧

Forty West Tremont Avenue was old and falling apart much like its tenants. I didn't know a single kid who lived in the place or was dumb enough to treat-or-treat here. Well, I must have been confused, the concussion from one of Tommy's candy projectiles. And so I went inside the building to roam its dreary hallways. Idiot that I was.

The hunt was rough going. A few residents laid out small candy dishes outside their door with hard candies covered in sticky wax paper, the kind that was impossible to unwrap. This was the junk some recluse kept in his closet for years before deciding to dump it on some poor schmoe for Halloween. Yeah, that was me again.

Most tenants had no intention of unlocking their door for some kid with a bloody axe stuck to his T-shirt. One creepy guy angrily yanked opened his door to tell me to go to hell. I thought he was taking the Halloween theme way too seriously.

I headed up the building's dark stairwell to the fourth floor for one final shot. Like every other floor, the hallway was absolutely still. I'd have been better off visiting some cemetery other than this one at 40 West Tremont. At least crickets were around to keep me company there.

I did a quick survey and randomly picked a door: 4G.

I buzzed the apartment and waited a few seconds. No answer. One more buzz, and more silence. It was when I turned to leave that an old woman cracked opened the chained door. I could barely see her face through the door slit.

Just an eyeball staring at me.

She shut the door and that was that until I heard her wrestling with the chain. And then the door opened. She stood there without a word. Nothing distinguished her from the scores of tiny, old gray ladies living in the neighborhood. Ancient-looking, worn down by life and its troubles. Her beady black eyes glared at me, giving her small, delicate face a ferocious appearance, as if she'd been angry her entire life. She gave me the once-over, not at all impressed at the sight of the axe-murder victim in front of her.

"Trick or treat," I managed to mumble.

The old lady just continued to glower, not a single word, before finally stepping to the side of the open door. Then she pointed her bony index finger and beckoned me into her apartment. Stooped and scowling, she was doing a great impression of the Wicked Witch of the West, and I half expected some flying monkeys to appear.

I don't know why, but I followed her in. Maybe it was because I didn't want to seem impolite. Maybe I thought she had a stash of Three Musketeers that she'd secreted away and was ready to hand over. Maybe it was because I was an absolute moron. Yeah, that was definitely it. At least that was settled.

And, so, I shuffled into 4G. The room was pitch-black except for some candles illuminating a few photographs sitting on a table. I wondered if she was running short on electricity. Or conjuring up a ghost of some sort. As it turned out, not a bad guess.

"Look!" she ordered, pointing her crooked finger to a large portrait hanging on the wall of a young man in a military uniform. "That's my son."

I nodded, a tight smile, the only response I could come up with. I was only hoping she didn't intend to take out her entire family album for a show-and-tell.

"He's dead," she went on. "They killed him. Those dirty rotten bastards. Those Nazi bastards."

I was nodding again, but not smiling this time. This was far from one of those happy family remembrances. Then I noticed that all of the pictures on the living room table were of her son. In one, he looks all of ten years old, at the seaside frolicking through a wave. In another beach photo, his mother is hugging him tightly, keeping him warm in her arms. That woman was unrecognizable from this old lady stooped in front of me.

I stared at the wall portrait. The only light in the room came from some flickering candles that made her son's face come alive—and I could swear he was glaring at me!

If I didn't know better, I would've thought that this was

some sort of Halloween prank. But I did know better, and this was no joke. The neighborhood was filled with victims from the war. Old apartments with old ladies with pictures of dead sons. Others had numbers tattooed onto their fore-arms, some of them the walking dead. I had heard their sto-ries. My dad had told me about his own scare leaving Po-land right before Hitler came storming in nearly bringing an end to the world.

The lady in 4G wasn't as lucky, wasn't lucky at all. She was off the deep end, and I really needed to get out of there. The problem—my feet were plastered to the cracked vinyl floor. I could hardly move, or breathe for that matter.

"Come over here!"

She was pointing her finger again, directing me into the kitchen. I managed to lift up my feet and shuffle over. The place smelled like roach powder, and I thought I was about to hurl Mom's meat loaf. On a beaten up Formica table sat a large wooden box.

"Take that!" she ordered, pointing to the box.

I didn't think the box was a big payday for Halloween—instead, it was filled with a half-dozen empty seltzer bottles. The bottles with rounded glass and metal levers were famil-iar to any Bronxite. Seltzer was a must for egg creams, and Mom kept a regular supply. At this moment, though, I was pretty sure that the old lady wasn't thinking about whipping me up a drink.

"Go to the store and get me back my bottle deposit. *Now!*"

"Um, isn't there, um, a delivery guy who picks these up?" I asked nervously.

"Not anymore," she rasped.

"Uh-huh" was the only response coming out of my mouth.

I really didn't know what the hell was going on, but I eyed the old lady and knew I had no choice. She was witch-like scary, and I wasn't about to tempt fate. For all I knew, the guy in the portrait hadn't been her son at all but someone who had refused to return her seltzer bottles only to meet a violent end from a spell cast on him.

And, so, I put down my superhero bag, picked up the heavy box, stumbled out of her apartment, and slogged down Tremont to the bottle store. I got the attention of a few people on the street, who looked at me cross-eyed as I passed by. I mean, was it really that hard to make sense of this kid with a bloody axe in his chest, lugging a box of seltzer bottles in the middle of Halloween night? Obviously, they didn't see the deep human connection between axe-murder victims and Moshe's seltzer bottles.

By now I had lost it. Really.

Not that my luck was about to change. Even a half-block down from the bottle store, I could see that it was too late to cash in. I stood for a minute in front of the darkened store, willing the shopkeeper to show up. No luck. So I now had two choices. I could dump the bottles and head home— yeah, sorry, crazy lady. Or return the bottles back to her and hope that she would let me live. Not really a choice at all. Everything in my bones told me to get rid of the damn bottles. That would've been the smart thing to do. But who said anything about me being smart.

I trudged back up Tremont Avenue lugging the wooden box, but I couldn't catch a break. The street was in deep, dark shadows, and it was rough being on the move with the heavy box blocking my way. So that explains why I crashed into the old guy walking with his grandkid. I'd no idea where the two had come from—they seemed to have materialized out of thin air when we collided. For a moment, the box of bottles was in danger of crashing to the sidewalk, gone for good. Broken bottles that would have solved my dilemma. Too bad I held on.

The old man wasn't in a forgiving mood, giving me the evil eye. "You are a very stupid boy," he hissed.

I wasn't about to argue. The guy was Halloween-scary with stringy white hair, a pointed white beard, and black, angry eyes that seemed to glow in the night.

I glanced over at his grandkid, unsmiling, wearing a baseball cap, tipped to hide most of his face. He didn't seem too happy with his granddad, and for good reason. The old guy just wasn't the gentle, loving grand-pa-pa type you play gin rummy with or come over to visit for a hot dog and knish.

"Sorry, mister," was about all I could muster.

The old man gave me another evil eye before grabbing hold of his kid and marching away.

I kept thinking that I had arrived in some alternate world where Halloween had come alive with its own creepy cast of characters. Tommy, the old lady, and Evil Eye. I wouldn't have dared to go see *this* horror film at the Loew's Paradise. Way too scary.

I finally made it back to 40 West Tremont and climbed the stairs to 4G. The old lady somehow heard my footsteps and was already at the open door. I gave her the bad news straight. Just one word.

"Sorry," I mumbled, holding out the box of bottles. I was making a habit of apologizing that night.

She gave me a squinty look, but I was relieved that she wasn't waving her arms in the air, casting a spell. Actually, she kind of snorted and left me standing there, turning to some other room in the apartment.

I quietly stepped inside, shoving the box of bottles into the corner, and retrieved my superhero bag. I was about to make my escape and halfway back out the door.

"Wait!" Her crackly shout from the next room stopped me from taking another step.

What now?

The old lady shambled back, more stooped and tired than before. Then she slid a small bunch of coins from her hand into my bag. All the while she kept her eyes on me, not a mean look, but something else was on her mind. Something she wanted to tell me, this kid with the axe on his shirt. The old woman was tough to figure out, but I wouldn't have minded the talk. Really. She was less scary now, and sad-der. But she didn't say a word, keeping the thought to herself. So, I nodded thanks for the coins, and left it at that.

I couldn't help but take one more look at the portrait behind her. Another mother's son. Taken. Gone. Then I opened the door and walked out, catching the sound of a chain latching behind me. And as I made my way from 4G, I could hear the old lady's pained voice penetrating the silent hallway. "Those Nazi bastards," she was crying out. "They killed my Mickey. They killed my beautiful boy."

CHAPTER 13

John, Rosie, and Me

Saturday afternoon. A brisk day in early November. Earlier, the guys had given me a call to shoot some hoops at the schoolyard. Instead here I was with Mom on a bus to Fordham Road and on my way to buy a suit for Robby Rosenfeld's bar mitzvah. No one had bothered to ask me before we began our trip: "Paul, would you rather play basketball with your friends today, or go shopping with your mother?"

That would have been the polite thing to do. And certainly I would have weighed each choice carefully. And who knows what decision I would have reached. I mean basketball was my favorite sport, loved the game, but what kid could pass up the chance to go shopping—on a Saturday—with his mother—to Alexander's department store no less.

When I get angry, I get sarcastic, and that afternoon I was really pissed. Giving up my Saturday afternoon to shop at Alexander's was extreme child abuse as far as I was concerned. I hated clothes shopping in general, and especially at Alexander's with its store matrons, who told me how cute I was, measuring me with their eyes, and then loudly declaring to anyone within shouting distance, "So, you look like a husky!"

Okay, so I could have lost a few pounds. But did the entire world need to know about it? At Alexander's they did. In fact, the store had invented a new clothing size for Jewish boys from the Bronx. It was called a "husky." I guess Alexander's was trying to be diplomatic when they found a word to tell Mrs. Wolfenthal that her somewhat chunky son waiting to get fitted for a suit was not really fat at all. He was only "husky." How nice. They should have just gone ahead and named the oversized garment "fat boy." Small, medium, large, and fat boy. At least that would have been honest.

I hated the store. But I didn't count.

❦

Fordham Road was the Mecca for shopping and Alexander's rose from its center. Most shoppers thought of the place as sort of a house of worship at the corner of the Grand Concourse and Fordham Road, answering their prayers for bargain-priced stuff. Saturday was a particularly popular service with lots of mothers and kids in tow.

Something was obviously very different about this trip though. A swirl of street activity surrounded Rosie and me as we approached the store. Men, women, and even small kids, all looking keyed up, were beginning to pack around the Concourse.

I doubted whether these folks were part of the Saturday shopping crowd out to buy a suit for Robby Rosenfeld's bar mitzvah. Some other happening was about to go on, though it took me a minute to figure it out.

I could see that an outdoor platform had been set up next to a yellow-brick building with a bald eagle over its entrance. The stage was decorated with American flags and red-white-and-blue streamers.

Some kind of political big deal was in the works to get this crowd to show up. I wondered if the mayor himself was coming. Elections were now three days away, and politics was definitely in the air. I was starting to get revved up myself walking through the crush of people.

"Mom, can't we hang here to see what's going on?" I asked.

"Honey, we can't," Rosie said. "Sel, Ettie and the kids are coming over later and I'm making a brisket. We need to buy you your suit and get home."

I didn't think a visit by my aunts and cousins was enough of a reason to miss the big event. And certainly Mom's brisket was no incentive—I loved Rosie, but, honestly, cooking was simply not her strong suit.

"C'mon, Mom," I pleaded, but by then she was taking me by the hand into the hellhole that was Alexander's.

❧❧❧

I hated Alexander's ever since I was a little kid. Rosie would drag me along on her shopping forays, my patience gone before even taking a step into the place. And then the hunt in search of the "bargain." At least this was Rosie's plan. As a six-year-old, I had my own idea, with the cavernous store turning into a fantasy place for my adventures. The maze of clothing racks was suddenly transformed as I went in search of bad guys or aliens through the rows of dresses and stacks of brassieres and underwear.

My world was usually shaken when I realized that Mom was lost. Of course Rosie knew exactly where she was. I was the one with the problem. The reality shock immediately doused my fun, followed by a surge of panic and a stream of tears.

Coming to the rescue was, of course, the store matron, taking me by the hand over to the nearest service desk. Over the store loudspeaker, she made each and every patron aware of my dire predicament, along with my mother's apparent neglect in choosing shopping over her child's welfare. She barked into the intercom leaving no doubt of Rosie's guilt. "We have a lost boy at the service desk. Will the mother of Paul Wolfenthal *please* pick up her child directly—he is very upset!"

My mom, relieved, angry, and humiliated, soon came bounding down the aisle to the service desk and promptly scolded me for the hundredth time about wandering off in the store.

We then took the escalator down to the main floor, about the only fun activity that afternoon. Still exasperated, she gripped my hand a little too hard as we exited the store onto Fordham Road. And, so, another pleasant afternoon spent at Alexander's had come to an end.

Nothing much had changed seven years later. I wasn't getting lost in the department store anymore. But I was still back with Mom, this time heading to the second-floor boys' clothing in search of the perfect bar mitzvah suit. We approached a saleslady who eyed me up and down, and pronounced, way too loudly. "Husky, right?"

Humiliation knew no boundaries at Alexander's.

❧❧❧

We left Alexander's with my dark blue suit covered in a black plastic bag. Mission accomplished, and I guess I should have been relieved knowing that I wasn't going naked to Robby Rosenfeld's bar mitzvah. But heading out the store exit, we suddenly found ourselves wedged into a gigantic crowd, and trapped. The streets outside Alexander's, had become a forest of humanity. It was if the entire Bronx had shown up, filling every inch of sidewalk on *both sides* of the Concourse.

"Mom, *what is this?"* I said excitedly, caught up in the street energy.

I could see that all eyes in the crowd were focused on the speakers' platform. That included mom's.

Rosie seemed spellbound—someone had gripped her attention from the stage. "Let's find out," she replied, suddenly determined.

Rosie tugged at my arm as we pushed our way through the crowd, finally squeezing into a spot close to the platform.

"Look!" I called out to Mom, pointing up to the stage.

I had recognized the gray-haired man standing at the microphone. He was our governor, Abraham Ribicoff.

"And there's the mayor too!" I shouted, eyeing Robert Wagner standing among the group of politicians.

Amazing. I had never been this close to anyone nearly as famous as these guys.

Rosie stood next to me without a word, strangely quiet, also staring at the men on the platform.

I could see that the governor was having a hard time being heard over the crowd noise. More than twenty-thousand people, I found out later. A number more suited for a Yankee game than a political rally outside of Alexander's.

"This is incredible, Mom!" I called out to Rosie.

She nodded, but I had the feeling she hadn't heard a word. Her eyes were still locked on the stage.

Then the crowd began some loud chant, something I couldn't pick up at first. The governor seemed to understand the message though, stepping away from the microphone. He then turned to the political guys standing in back of him. To one guy in particular.

I glanced across the platform and then saw him. And I understood just who had caught Rosie's eye. And everyone else's.

Shouts from the packed crowd now resounded as one and boomed along the Concourse—everyone calling out to the man on stage who had just stepped forward.

"J—F—K!

"J—F—K!

"J—F—K!

"J—F—K!

"J—F—K!"

John F. Kennedy was in the Bronx. And he was standing fifteen feet in front of Rosie and me.

The explosion of noise followed John, now making his way to the microphone. I couldn't take my eyes off of him. I had only seen the guy in shades of gray on my small black-and-white television. In person, he was so full of color, full of life. He looked tan and relaxed, his smile radiating across the Concourse.

Everyone in the crowd was bundled up in our warm coats and hats that brisk day. All except John, who shrugged off the weather in his light overcoat. No surprise there. Every kid could tell you the story of PT 109. John saving the life of one of his crewman after his boat was rammed by a Jap destroyer. Swimming miles to safety in enemy waters, towing a wounded shipmate by a belt buckle *clamped in his teeth*. I mean, what was a little cold weather for *this* guy.

I glanced back at Rosie, still in a hypnotic state, as we pressed closer to the platform.

And then John started to speak, accented words that I had grown familiar with over the campaign. The crowd settled down to listen.

"I come to the Bronx as an old Bronx boy. I used to live in the Bronx."

(I knew that! I knew that!)

Cheers.

"I agree it was the Riverdale end of the Bronx, but it was the Bronx. No other candidate for the presidency can make that statement."

Laughter.

"I do not know the last time that a candidate from the Bronx ran for the presidency, but I am here to ask your help. It is the highest responsibility that a citizen of a free country can have, to pick the president, and it is the president's responsibility to set before the American people the unfinished business of our society, to rally them to a great cause."

Cheers, only louder, then wild applause.

John had barely mentioned his opponent, Richard Nixon. Instead, he spoke about "the future of America" and "the time of revolution and change."

I hung onto his every word. It was if he was talking directly to me, and it would not have surprised me if every person there felt the same.

"The presidency, as Franklin Roosevelt said, is above all a place for moral leadership, and I believe in 1960 the people of the great Republic, as in 1932, are going to choose to go forward, and right in the lead will be the Bronx County of New York."

John finished with waves of love coming his way from the huge crowd. He finally turned from the microphone to rejoin the mayor, governor, and the other pols, all seeming very pleased. And, slowly, the crowd started to break up, holding onto the moment before getting back to their lives. I wasn't going anywhere, planted in my spot, awestruck at the sight of the man still standing in front of me.

"Mom, he's talking to those other guys. Can't we go over there and say hello?"

Before Rosie could say a word, I bolted past some policemen and over to the edge of the platform. The politicians continued to chat as they climbed down a few steps to make their way to a waiting Lincoln convertible.

"*Mr. Kennedy*," I called out, unsteadily. "*Mr. Kennedy.*"

John F. Kennedy turned his head, eyes on me. Then he came over.

"How are you, son?" he said, smiling that bright toothy smile of his.

Up close he looked much younger than he did on television. I remembered his school picture, the kid he once was. That Bronx boy. And now he was here. With me.

I could barely utter a word, shaking badly. When I finally spoke, I think it was something like, "You know, I'm from the Bronx, too."

"Is that right? And how do you like it here?" And that smile again.

"Yeah, uh, great," I sputtered, my head nodding as if it was caught on a broken spring.

I don't know if I was pleased or not when Mom came by, my bar mitzvah suit slung over her arm, and introduced herself. I mean, she had interrupted our man-to-man talk. But then something amazing happened. Rosie and John started to chat, easily. Shooting the breeze. They seemed relaxed, as if they had been lifelong neighbors.

The talk was about kids—I heard my name. Another name, Caroline. It was family talk. I was half expecting Rosie to invite John—I was sure they were on a first name basis by now—over to our apartment for a little chopped liver and some white fish. Maybe Jackie could play Mah Jongg with the girls on Wednesday night.

I was in some fantastic dream world here on the Concourse with Mom schmoozing with John Kennedy. *Could this possibly be?*

Mom and John's talk finally broke up with John reaching out to take Rosie's hand. They stood there like that for a few seconds before letting go. I could see Rosie's eyes glowing, face shining. I had never seen that little girl look in her before.

Then John turned and reached out his hand to me, and I

shook it. His hand was surprisingly soft, a comforting touch.

I found my voice and wished him good luck with the election. He smiled and nodded. "I'm counting on your vote, Paul," he said, eyes twinkling. I nodded back, and decided not to remind him that I couldn't vote. I was pretty sure he knew that already.

John gave me an "attaboy" tap on my shoulder, a sign, maybe, that we were pals. At least that's how I took it. And then he was off, making his way back to the Lincoln.

I could not move until I saw his car disappear down the Concourse. Rosie also was not ready to let go of the moment. There we were, a mother-son statue, frozen in our tracks, gazing at a car, and a man, now out of sight.

We slowly came back to ourselves and began to stroll along the avenue, both of us lost in thought. I knew that we would never go to Alexander's again without looking across the way and thinking of this November day.

I was in no mood to rush home, a decision made easy as we passed my favorite ice cream parlor.

"Mom, how about Jahn's?" I asked, pointing to the store window filled with faces deep into huge bowls of the creamy stuff.

"Yes, great idea!" Rosie bubbled, her smile ear to ear. "But no Kitchen Sink."

We both laughed. The infamous Sink, filled with a mountain of every ice cream imaginable, was uneatable. Anyone finishing the monster dish was promised another free one by Jahn's. Legend had it though that many a teen almost died trying, but no one had ever gone the distance with the Kitchen Sink.

"Maybe we can toast our next president with the Banana Split," I happily replied.

"Perfect," Mom giggled, and I also laughed, the glow of the afternoon still in us.

⌘⌘⌘

Three days later, I settled in with Dad, Mom, and Fred around our TV set as election results came in. Chet Huntley and David Brinkley, the newscasters, sat facing each other at a small semicircular table. Studio walls were covered with all sorts of grids and scoreboards and large spools of tape with signs that read "Electronic Data Processing."

Nothing moved very quickly as reporters gave whatever little news they had. A rotating board of numbers gave viewers the latest tally of votes. About the only break from the boring coverage was family footage of the Kennedys with their three-year-old daughter, Caroline—so, there she was—and a more recent film clip of a cheery John and Jackie entering the Boston Public Library to vote.

The early returns had John ahead but Nixon was closing in. It must have been nearly three in the morning when I finally conked out. I woke up early and groggy but rushed to the set. John had squeaked by Tricky Dick. Sitting by myself in front of the TV, I silently rooted on my new president.

The screen took me to a place called Hyannis Port in Massachusetts. There was John in the front passenger seat of a Lincoln, behind him a parade of cars carrying his family. Along the way admirers were throwing confetti. When the procession came to a stop at a nearby Armory, John climbed out of his car, threw a short wave to the crowd and entered the building.

Standing next to Jackie on the Armory stage, John looked different from that time on the Concourse. He seemed wearier.

I could see the puffiness under his eyes. He had to be glad that the campaign was over. His victory speech was the usual, thanking Richard Nixon and President Eisenhower for their telegrams supporting him.

He then asked us for our "supreme national effort" as we headed into the '60s.

He had mine, absolutely.

But before leaving the platform, he had one final announcement. "Now my wife and I prepare for a new administration—and a new baby."

I was all smiles. How amazing—the Kennedy First Family. What a wonderful ring it had to my ears. I'd always associated old men in gray suits with the White House. Not anymore. John, Jackie, and their young kids crawling and playing around that neighborhood.

That sounded just right to me.

PART II

1961

CHAPTER 14

Gas Attack

Patriotism was in full swing in Miss Crouse's class that morning in late January. After attendance was taken, we were on to our daily ritual, pledging to the flag before mangling our national anthem. I guess we weren't through with America yet. Pointing to a TV set that had been wheeled into the classroom, Miss Crouse told us that a "historic event" was in store for us later that afternoon.

"Children, Mr. John F. Kennedy will be taking his oath of office today to become our thirty-fifth President—and we will get to watch his inauguration. How exciting is that!"

I can't say that the class was jumping for joy at the news.

"Can't we watch something else?" asked Margie Gubitosi. "*Leave it to Beaver* is on."

A few students buzzed support for Margie's idea, but I didn't think the Beaver was going to make it with Miss Crouse.

"Shouldn't we vote on which program to turn on?" Sammy joined in. I guess Sammy had learned something about democracy, but Miss Crouse was not about to fall for it.

Miss Crouse shook her head slowly, and left it at that.

Sensing a revolt, our teacher turned to our homework. She would deal with JFK's inauguration later.

◌◌◌

I also wanted to get on with the morning. I had counted down the days since Miss Crouse "special" homework assignment. She had told us to memorize a famous poem that "speaks to us" about "the meaning of life" (our teacher was at it again), and then stand and recite it in front of the class.

I was up for the challenge, and ready to show off. I even felt sorry for those timid types that couldn't take the pressure. So I went after the big one. "The Midnight Ride of Paul Revere," by this guy, Henry Wadsworth Longfellow. No other kid would've dared take this one on. The poem ran 142 lines, 986 words to be exact—just tough enough for me. Of course, I had driven my parents crazy—they were set to shoot Paul Revere if their son didn't shut-up with his nonstop rehearsals around the house.

Yeah, a ton of memorization, but so what? Paul Wolfenthal's time had come, and he was ready to give life to his newest hero!

I wasted no time as Miss Crouse asked for volunteers. A few hands went up along with mine. Dee-Dee O'Hara was picked first. She stood up and nailed some poem called "The Road Not Taken." Something about reaching a fork in a road and deciding which way to go. Not my problem. I was looking straight ahead.

Applause for Dee-Dee had yet to die down when I shot up my hand. Miss Crouse grinned, nodded her approval, and called me to the front of the class.

I scooted up next to her desk and scanned the faces of my classmates.

Every eyeball was on me.

"Kick ass!" Sammy shouted to spur me on.

The class busted out laughing.

"Sammy!" Miss Crouse chided, not thrilled with his style of encouragement.

"Really sorry, Miss Crouse," said Sammy, who was not sorry at all.

No matter. I wasn't about to be denied. Aiming for a dramatic effect, in a hushed voice I began the epic poem.

> "'Listen my children and you shall hear
> Of the midnight ride of Paul Revere,
> On the eighteenth of April, in Seventy-five,
> Hardly a man is now alive
> Who remembers that famous day and year.'"

I felt that I was on a Broadway stage—I might as well have been. Man, was I good, actually great, very likely the best "Paul Revere" orator ever. I looked out over the classroom and could see that every kid was already hooked. Even Plotz in the back row seemed semi-alert.

Miss Crouse had taken out a copy of the poem to prompt me if I blanked on a word or two. But nothing was about to get in the way of my heroic story.

> "'He said to his friend, 'If the British march
> By land or sea from the town to-night,
> Hang a lantern aloft in the belfry arch
> Of the North Church tower as a signal light,
> One if by land, and two if by sea,
> And I on the opposite shore will be.'"

I was rolling. The story of Paul Revere came alive. My hero's ride from Boston to Lexington to warn countrymen about the looming British Army was stirring. Impossible not to get caught up in his adventure. And just a perfect morning for such a great American tale. Later on more history would take place, but I was riding high now with Paul Revere. Yes, Revere, Kennedy, Wolfenthal. Not a bad combination at all.

"'Ready to ride and spread the alarm
Through every Middlesex village and farm,
For the country folk to be up and to arm—'"

The best part was coming, and I had no doubt that Paul would be proud of his namesake telling his tale. Nothing was about to stop either of us.

Except that there was this pungent odor coming from the middle of the second row and wafting through the room.

I stopped myself in mid-sentence, instinctively sniffing the air. My classmates were also beginning to react to the smell that had quickly spread.

The problem became instantly clear.

"Hey, who cut the cheese?" yelled Stanley Madison, and the word was out.

Just then Tommy let go a second fart, an enormous, vibrating, gaseous explosion that blanketed the classroom with the nauseating stench of rotten eggs.

"Tommy, stop clearing your throat!" Billy Laporte shouted from the back of the room.

First came some howls and hoots from the guys in class. There is something about that bodily function that rouses kids, and Tommy's farts were no exception. But the laughs suddenly turned to panic when Tommy let loose with another one. This time, kids sitting around him scrambled from their seats to find safety. Tommy's fart blasts were no longer funny.

"Crap!" Frankie Malone yelled. "You trying to kill us or something, Tommy?"

Tommy, with a weird smile on his face, nodded his head. "Bombs away!" he yelled out. And he gave it to us again.

The class spun into chaos.

Miss Crouse tried to take back control, waving her arms frantically. I didn't know whether she was directing kids back to their seats or in some futile way trying to clear the air. In either case, our teacher didn't stand a chance.

Not to be outshined, Plotz in the back row contributed

his own fart, one that didn't let up for a full ten seconds. It struck me that this may have been his only effort in class participation for the entire year. Plotz's blast stunned all of us into momentary silence. That is, until a huge wave of his excretory stink climbed into our nostrils.

"Oh my god," Margie Gubitosi cried out. "I'm gonna puke, *now*." And then she did, letting loose a puddle of barf that spread across the front of the classroom, blocking the door.

Class 710 had concocted a smell so deadly that it likely could kill every human being if unleashed upon the Earth. Too bad we were the first victims, not that JHS 82 was going to mind.

I was about to join Margie, on the verge of a full-fledged heave. I barely held out, making my way to the large classroom windows, desperate for fresh air.

Sid Bladner was already there, hoisting a long wooden pole with a metallic hook on its end. The pole was used to pull open the top windows, but Sid was having a tough time attaching the hook to the window catch. Then the pole toppled from his hand into the window, cracking a pane.

"Let me try," I told Sid, who readily handed over the pole. I had no better luck though, shattering another windowpane. At least a cool breeze was making its way into our stink hole.

A bunch of kids scrambled over, frantically sucking in fresh air.

"I didn't think I was going to make it," Billy Laporte gasped.

I turned to check on Miss Crouse, who had collapsed into her chair, all color drained from her face. Just sitting there without a word, staring into space.

Sammy ran up to me, pointing at our comatose teacher. "Hey, Paul, I think Snow White is dead."

I didn't think Sammy was being funny. Miss Crouse deserved better than this.

All the while, Tommy sat calmly, enjoying himself,

scrunching up his face, hoping that he had another one inside of him. He seemed to be running out of steam, but I might have been wrong on that one. Tommy then let out a trio of colossal fart bursts, the finale to his symphony.

At the same time, a group of girls had banded together, trying to tip-toe around Margie's puke puddle, to make their escape out the door. It was just too bad that Principal Stern stormed through the door at that moment, sending them flying headlong into the slop.

"For God sakes, *what is going on here*?" our principal shouted furiously, catching sight of the three girls, sprawled on the floor, drenched in vomitus, bawling their eyes out.

And then he froze in his tracks, his nose beginning to twitch. Kind of reminded me of a dog sniffing out a particularly awful scent.

"What *is* that smell?"

I mean, it *was* confusing given the choice of aromas. And then a tidal wave of stink hit him. Hard. His face instantly beaded up with sweat, and then his hand went to his throat. I could see him trying to hold back the sour stuff rising from his stomach.

"No, no, *nooo!*" Miss Crouse pleaded, shooting out her hands like a cop stopping traffic. Our teacher had come back to life! So I guess that was a plus.

And then Principal Stern retched, loudly, getting our full attention. No doubt that the guy was done. But to his credit, our principal managed to cover his mouth in time, holding back from puking all over Miss Crouse. By the crooked, pained look on his face, I could tell Principal Stern had just re-eaten his lunch.

It took a while until order was restored, not easy with a stink fog hanging over the classroom. Principal Stern was still pissed off big time, and I suspected he was thinking about padlocking our room to make sure the inmates in class 710 didn't escape into the general student population.

After a few hushed words with Miss Crouse, he angrily pointed to Tommy and Plotz, and marched them out of the room. For good measure, Tommy gave one last belt of fart bullets on his way out. No one could say that the guy didn't outdo himself.

The class finally settled down. Margie and the girls were sent to the nurse's office to clean up and calm down. The janitor came to mop up the floor. I got to finish reciting my poem. But by then the class had lost total interest, and so had I. I was sure that I'd never think of Paul Revere again without feeling my stomach turn.

It didn't help that the stench lingered throughout the day, fouling the air along with my mood. Even John F. Kennedy's stirring inaugural speech later on couldn't revive my spirits.

It turned out that the morning disaster wasn't the end of it. Tommy Branigan was still on the prowl, and ready for more trouble. No surprise there. He had found purpose in his cold life. Just a sick guy with a violent stomach and an armful of ugly Nazi scars. It was just too bad that I was the next target of his angry stroll through life.

CHAPTER 15

Retribution

I heard Tommy's back today," Sammy griped, as we made our way to the school entrance. "You'd think he would've gotten more than a two weeks' suspension. I mean, what kind of punishment is that for attempted murder?"

"I guess Principal Stern couldn't keep him out of school forever," I said, resigned. "Tommy must have promised to stop farting in class."

"Don't think Tommy would go for the deal," Sammy added. "Probably thinks his farts are protected by the Constitution. Kind of a free speech sort of thing."

"Yeah, he can be a stubborn guy when it comes to his fart rights."

Even our stupid talk couldn't joke away the fact that Tommy's return to 82 was a drag. Then again, maybe the guy used his time away from school to reevaluate his shitty life? Maybe picked up a book making a buzz called *The Prophet* by this guy Kahlil Gibran with advice on becoming a better person? Yeah, I lived in my imaginary world.

Just thinking about Tommy Branigan was a bad mistake—and had I been paying more attention, I might have seen him stalking us at that very moment.

Suddenly, Tommy was there, hovering next to Sammy and me. "Hey, how's life?" he hissed, and tried to shoulder past us. Then he reached out his hand and smacked the clarinet case I was holding to the pavement.

"Damn, Tommy!" I cried out.

"Accident, shithead. You should be careful with that thing," he smirked, strolling by.

"Hey, man, cut that crap out!" Sammy hollered, taking him on.

Tommy turned back to Sammy, shoved his hand into his jean pocket, and took out a razor blade. He held it up to give us a good look. "How would you like me to cut you both a new asshole?" he snarled.

I could feel the blood drain from my face. "Hey, Tommy—not funny." I barely choked out the words.

Tommy gave me his cross-eyed murderous stare. I could see that he was thinking of his next move. I was positive that a group hug was not one of his options.

"See you later, faggot!" he warned, pointing a finger in my face.

I really hoped not.

"He's a real stupid bastard," Sammy fumed after Tommy was out of sight. "But what can you do, Paul?"

We both knew that there wasn't much of anything I could do. I wasn't a fighter, and besides Tommy was taller, stronger, older and, by far, meaner.

The clarinet case had suffered a dent. I guess I was lucky enough that the instrument survived intact. Of course Tommy wasn't after my clarinet. He just liked the idea of humiliating me, and he'd won out. Again. The situation was only getting worse, and dangerous. Threatening Sammy and me with a razor blade—I mean sick, and really scary. I suppose Tommy was looking to join his father at Attica, maybe share a cell and re-live fun times with his good old dad. I was only afraid that I'd be included in their fond memories of favorite homicides. Actually, nothing was funny about this at all.

I anxiously made my way to class finding it hard to shake off the morning scare. I took my back-row seat only to find Tommy sitting next to me in Psycho's Corner. I was hugely relieved to see that he was already into his morning snooze, his head rolled back and snoring away.

Things didn't get better over the next two weeks. I tried to avoid the guy, but he was keeping an eye out for me. Why? I had no idea. Maybe it was because I played the clarinet, or sometimes needed to wear my glasses, or recited Longfellow, or that Dee-Dee O'Hara talked to me but ignored him.

Whatever crazy thoughts crept into his head, Tommy had it in for me. I prayed that Halloween had been the last of his bully act, but who was I kidding? The "accidental" bumps in the school hallways, the taunts, had become a regular part of my school day. I don't think Tommy even knew my name. To him, I was just "shithead."

I couldn't find a way out of this, until I did that Saturday afternoon.

⌒⌒⌒

I'd been hanging around Mel's candy store, leafing through Superman comics, and sipping a chocolate malted, when Tommy strolled in. He lived around the corner, so I wasn't entirely surprised to see him there. I wasn't jumping for joy either.

He wore that contorted, snarly look of his, the one where his eyes became squinty and his mouth twisted. Kind of a Cagney impersonation though the actor had nothing on him. Tommy would've been a natural to play Al Capone if he ever took his act to Hollywood.

Too bad he was still living on the block—and at the moment giving me the stare-down.

Tommy didn't waste any time sauntering over. Before I knew it, he had pinned me against the comic book rack.

And then he lunged forward, his shoulder thumping into my chest, at the same time slapping the comic book from my hand.

"Oops, shithead," he sneered, his crazed eyes shooting hate. "You should really watch where you're going."

I should have been terrified. Really. Tommy was nastier, more poisonous than ever. Just a scary creature disguised as a human being. But another feeling hit me instead. Hot spikes of energy were suddenly shooting through my body. Taking over. I was in some crazed head that could not possibly have been my own. Except that it was.

I had flipped. And even if I wanted to, I couldn't have stopped myself.

So I took the extra-large chocolate malted I'd been drinking and pitched it right into Tommy's face.

My aim could not have been better. The thick liquid dripped from Tommy's face and body onto the floor forming a puddle around him. He rapidly blinked his eyes as if trying to excrete some foreign substance. For that second we both stood there, paralyzed in the moment. Stunned. It wasn't clear which one of us was more in shock.

And then things moved quickly.

Tommy, his face a mask of rage, shrieked: "I'm going to kill you!"

He meant it, but I wasn't listening, just reacting.

I took a step toward him.

And then it was on.

In that instant, I latched onto Tommy's head. Bruno Samartino, my favorite wrestler, destroyed his opponents with his famous headlock—no one ever escaped that vice-like grip. Neither would Tommy as I took hold. I could feel his bony face trapped under my armpit, wanting nothing more than to yank his head from the rest of his body.

Then the two of us crashed into Mel's counter knocking to the floor an empty malted glass that exploded into pieces.

"Shit!" I heard Mel holler out. But I had other things on my mind at that moment.

Tommy and I were now spinning wildly out of the store and onto the sidewalk, locked together in a violent four-legged dance, then spilling into the avenue with cars whizzing by.

I heard the screech of cars, braking, swerving to avoid ramming into us. Traffic on Tremont Avenue had come to a standstill.

I kept Tommy bolted in the headlock. I swung sharply to the right, then left, snapping his head with each motion. I thought it might be possible to unscrew his skull. So I kept trying.

Tommy was screaming, cursing, his arms flailing, but I wasn't about to let go. I was caught up in my own rage, my mind wrapped around every one of Tommy's "shitheads," every push, slap, curse. Every humiliation.

Only one purpose existed in the world—to hurt Tommy Branigan.

At the same time, I began to wonder who the hell this lunatic was fighting back against the bully. I turned to my heroes to take on the bad guys. They made things right in the world. And here I was in the middle of Tremont Avenue, with Tommy's head under my armpit, trying to do the same. Could this kid actually be me, *Paul Wolfenthal*? I thought it best to consider the question later. First I needed to whack Tommy in the nose.

Tommy wasn't through, though, clawing at the back of my neck. But a wallop to the top of his head put an end to that. I kept pounding, aiming for his face. A shot to the mouth shut him up for a moment. Another to the nose. Tommy's spout of curses had turned into a wail.

So strange, with the fight now seeming to move in slow motion. I could also feel my rage slipping away, turning into something else, something utterly satisfying.

Retribution.

And in that moment I heard the Voice.

I was no longer afraid.

And Tommy Branigan knew it.

And that changed everything.

Mel was now out of his store and into the street to break us up. I could see that he was taking his time, half-smiling, not being a fan of Tommy's either. I gave him a serious look, shaking my head, as he struggled to pry me off of Tommy. I refused to let go. I wasn't done. Not with this hateful guy.

Another whack to his face.

I could hear Tommy choking in my headlock, and see his face moving from bright red to purple. I wondered how long he could go without breathing.

"Nuff, Paul," Mel now called out sharply, the half-smile gone, wrestling to unlock my arm from around Tommy's neck. Then more quietly, "He's through."

I finally let go, shoving Tommy to the side.

Tommy stood there shaking and sniveling. I could see his face already starting to swell. Then he instinctively felt the top of his head for bumps, wincing at the touch. The guy's eyes were red and wet, with a flood of snot dripping into his mouth.

He used the back of his hand to wipe away the nasty stuff, but only wound up spreading it across his face. I had never seen a prettier sight in my life.

Tommy wasn't happy at all, but not a single taunt or curse. No more "shitheads." In fact, the only thing I heard from him was a snorting sound as he tried to suck in the mucous bubble around his nose.

At that moment he looked like just any kid in the neighborhood, nothing special or dangerous. An ordinary, stupid kid with a swollen face and a mouthful of snot.

We traded some hard glares, but that was the end of it. There was nothing to say, or do. Only that we knew our Bronx lives would never be the same again. And that was really okay with me.

I waited for Tommy to go his way, and then I went mine.

ততত

In the coming weeks, I'd run into Tommy in the schoolyard or around the neighborhood. He hardly came to class anymore. Whatever anxiety I felt about him was gone. In fact, I was feeling pretty good about myself. Something was different about him too. To my amazement, every once in a while he'd come over and say hi, even ask how I was doing. He seemed calmer now, and, to say the least, it was strange. Even called me by my name—I was Paul—how about that? So odd coming from his mouth. I thought at those times Tommy was trying to be my friend. And maybe hoping I would be his.

I had no intention bringing Tommy into my circle of friends. He would never be a buddy of mine for sure. But some part of me actually felt sorry for him. The guy had serious troubles, just angry at the world. He was already far down the road to a miserable life. It did not take a psychic to see his dismal future.

And then, about a month after our fight, Tommy didn't show up for an entire week of class, and then missed the following week. He was a notorious truant, and I doubted whether the school was anxious to find him. Certainly no one in 710, including Miss Crouse, missed him. More days went by. Tommy seemed to have simply disappeared.

He never did return to JHS 82. In fact, I never saw Tommy Branigan again. I assumed nothing good came of him, maybe that prison stint in Attica with his dad. I couldn't really explain it, but when he came to mind, and it wasn't often that he did, I hoped that he was okay. Maybe he'd even found a little peace in his life. It was a crazy, stupid thought after all of this, but there it was.

It was only some years later, when my Bronx boyhood was over, that I ran across the guy again. Actually, his picture printed in a newspaper article. There he was dressed in a military uniform.

At first I didn't recognize him. He appeared older in the photo, lines around his eyes, less angry, but still troubled.

He wore the weary look of someone struggling to sort

out the demons in his life. At least that's how I took it.

I couldn't help but stare at that picture of him, and then read down the news story to come to his name. Thomas James Branigan. It was one on a long list of American soldiers killed in a place called Vietnam.

CHAPTER 16

Watching Eichmann

That spring the world had finally caught up to Adolf Eichmann. At least the Israelis had, and now Hitler's sidekick was in a Jerusalem courtroom facing his accusers. They were the survivors, the lucky ones I suppose, though I doubted whether they felt that way. At the least, they had lived long enough to see this day. This retribution.

"They captured the bastard in Argentina," Dad said tightly. "He was on the run fifteen years, but Mossad finally got him."

I knew Dad was angry, using language never spoken in front of "the children."

Each evening at six-thirty p.m. Dad tuned into the half-hour TV coverage direct from a Jerusalem courtroom. We watched together, a father-son ritual of sorts. Three months, night after night. One long nightmare. Stories of the camps, deportations, and always the gruesome deaths—kids, their parents, men, women, young, old—an endless march to the gas chambers. This was impossible. Only that it wasn't.

The television camera panned from witnesses to Eichmann, seated in a glass booth, wearing headphones, calmly waiting for his German translation. Two Israeli guards sat in back of him, a third on his left side. The guy seemed to always be scribbling notes on a large pad. Maybe an "I'm sorry" letter to each of the Six Million, but I didn't think that was it.

I found it hard to make any sense of this bald guy with black horn-rimmed glasses studiously writing in a notepad. This Eichmann. He easily could be mistaken for any middle-aged nobody. More like the travelling oil salesman he was before joining the Nazi Party. Could this be the lunatic who got his kicks deporting millions of Jews to places like Auschwitz and Treblinka death camps? Dad told me that most Jews were taken right from the trains to the gas chamber.

So this is what a psychopath looks like, I thought. But no one word could explain Eichmann. Were there *any* words to describe this guy in the glass booth?

I thought I had a better handle on the other Adolf. (I didn't think that the name was going to make a comeback any time soon.) The Fuhrer was a "Looney Tunes" cartoon character, easy for us kids to poke fun of with his brush mustache, spitting speeches, and pumping fists. When a silly mood hit us, we'd tramp around with our index finger under our noses and right arm stiffened in a Nazi salute. It was meant to be stupid fun, only it wasn't to survivors living in the neighborhood. We should have known better. Nothing was funny about Hitler and his band of homicidal maniacs.

I knew who the survivors were on my block. Most still carried the accents from their homes in Europe. They were branded with a tattoo, their camp number. But their eyes told the saddest stories, a heavy, hooded look of despair and weariness.

I couldn't forget the story that Sammy told me about his cousin, Louie. He had been eleven when taken to Auschwitz, and when he arrived he had been given a choice by a Nazi commander. Execute your father or be shot himself. Kill or be killed. A gun was placed in Louie's hand. Then he shot his dad through the heart. Sammy's uncle.

"Louie survived the camps but might as well have died there," Sammy recounted to me one day. "Hanged himself two years ago. Twenty-six years old. But he was a dead man long before that."

coco

Hitler was also long gone. Dad told me that he had put a bullet in his brain after first killing his new bride, Eva Braun—the type of lovely relationship I'd expect from the guy. Eichmann wasn't about to get off so easy.

My father took grim satisfaction watching the trial on television. Eichmann's victims included his relatives and friends back in Poland. I could see that tonight's coverage was especially painful for him. Dad hadn't said a word, but I saw it in his eyes. He was gazing past the TV screen, focused on something far away.

A survivor was now giving testimony describing what had occurred in and around the city of Livov in Poland. Dad's city, his home, before he fled to the United States. Others in his family who stayed behind had been killed, along with most of the 150,000 Jews who lived there. Dad continued to watch, silently. I didn't think it right to barge in on his thoughts, so I sat quietly and watched and listened to the horror stories…

"You are the only survivor of your family?" the prosecutor asked.

"I am the only survivor, not only of the immediate family but of the whole family including all cousins, uncles, which counted all of seventy-six members."

"Your grandfather and your uncle Yaakov, when were they liquidated?"

"He was liquidated end of December together with my uncle Yaakov, his wife and their two children."

"What about your sisters?"

"My sisters were liquidated the Friday before Yom Kippur, all four sisters with my grandmother and two aunts and eight cousins were taken away at this time—marched barefoot from Stajanow to Radziechow. There they sat at the railway station for two days and two nights without any food—my youngest sister was seven years old at this time—and then they were packed into railway wagons and sent away to Belzec."

"When they were there, did they have any clothes on?"

"They were undressed when they were put into the wagons…"

I didn't feel particularly Jewish in my day-to-day life, but looking at Eichmann changed that. Had Dad stayed in Poland rather than come to America in the early '30s, he most certainly would have been swept up in the madness. Fred was born in 1944. I came around five years later. Dad's fate was our own, our existence the result of chance, plain luck. Much luckier than those other kids, the invisible ones that were never born, the ones that never had a chance of life because of this guy on TV. This Eichmann.

I couldn't take my eyes off the man in the glass booth, emotionless.

"He's such a plain, nothing guy," I said to Dad.

"That's the face of evil," he replied pensively.

"Why don't they hang him and get it over with?"

"That would be too easy," he said. "Eichmann needs to face his victims."

"Dad, what could he possibly say to *them*?"

"This trial is not for him. He's *geshtroft*. He's cursed. This trial is for them, these survivors. The world must hear their stories."

"You know, Dad, Hitler was a lunatic, but Eichmann seems, well…normal. How does he explain what he did?"

"He says he was just following orders. He was like any other good German soldier. So he wasn't responsible."

"That's how he explains the Holocaust? *That's it?*"

"That's it," Dad replied, and paused. "There's nothing more that he can say."

I shook my head. Here was another demon in the world. One that brought so much pain.

"Then he'll hang, and I'm glad," I told Dad, yet knowing that even this retribution was hardly enough.

CHAPTER 17

The Catcher in the Rye

enji Shapiro was back on *The Daily News* front page that morning. There he was, that old photo that I'd seen a hundred times before on posters and in the papers—the same tow-headed six-year-old with those bright eyes, crooked smile and missing front tooth. Today was his seventh birthday, so I guess the paper had a reason to "update" us. A headline and a nothing story. Just a reminder that five months had passed since Benji had gone missing. One hundred-and-fifty days. Thanks for nothing. Couldn't a better story be written? That Benji was alive and well and back in his mother's arms. So much better. Did we need to know *this*...this nothing?

The no news was the worst, a dagger in the heart. A reminder of a birthday lost. A boy gone. A reminder that there was a hole in the world. Where there was something, someone, there was nothing, no one. No life, no Benji. What kind of reminder was that?

The article was basically a recap, nothing new at all. That Benji had been waiting for the school bus after his first-grade school day was over. And then he was gone. Taken.

A second photo of the boy, joyful in his mom's arms,

even more heartbreaking knowing what we already knew. Nothing.

I didn't need to read the story to bring back that awful night outside my building. The pictures in my mind still haunted me. A memory loop I couldn't escape. I was back again at my bedroom window, looking down into the courtyard. Laura Shapiro, with cops and neighbors around her, crying out her child's name. Agony etched on her face. Then Rosie by her side, trying to comfort her. What could Mom be telling her? Did any words exist that could bring Benji back from the demon who had abducted him?

This newspaper story was also filled with words that wouldn't matter. Just a message that we were helpless. The article had avoided bringing up the unspoken and likely end to this horror. That a body was never found. Instead, the police were still "investigating." I figured that such information was left out to give readers some hope. This on Benji's birthday. More cruelty, I thought.

I wondered where Laura Shapiro was in the world, how she must be coping. A dumb thought. How do you "cope" when your kid is stolen away? But if this woman couldn't have Benji back, then she needed an end to her misery. This misery of not knowing. The Jews sat *shiva* when a loved one died, a time to mourn and be held and hugged by people who cared and loved them. What pain must Laura Shapiro be suffering.

And who was there for *her* living day to day in this black world?

⌘⌘⌘

Benji often came to mind during these months. He would appear in the strangest of ways. Maybe it was weird, but I found myself thinking of him while watching some television show or after reading a book. There was this one story assigned by Miss Crouse that especially took hold of me. It was about some teenager named Holden, an odd, mysterious guy caught up in a dream-like but dangerous world.

There was a passage I read again and again, telling of "a thousand little kids" playing in a large field of rye. Holden is there is protect them from getting too close to a cliff—but it is treacherous place this field, and these kids are running free, as kids do, and don't really understand the looming danger. They could go over the cliff if they are not mindful. It is Holden who is fearful, keeping a close eye. All day long he tries to guard these kids from any mistake that might take their life. His job—to catch them should they get too close to the cliff's edge. This "catcher in the rye."

There had been no such luck for poor Benji. He couldn't have known that he was in danger out there on his own, with no one to watch over him. To protect him. That the world had more than its share of demons, lurking in the shadows. And that he would be caught by one of them.

It was so very wrong. And I couldn't help but sadly wonder where Holden had been that cruel afternoon, when this innocent kid with the bright eyes and crooked smile came too close to the edge and fell off.

CHAPTER 18

Joe Bailey

It was strange enough seeing the new kid in class more than halfway through the school year. He seemed friendly, big smile and all, and taller than most everyone else. He was also black, a difference that did not go unnoticed by any of us.

"Hey, what's *this* guy doing in *our* class?" Plotz spouted conspiratorially out the side of his mouth. His question sounded more like an accusation and, in truth, was one that silently ran through the class.

This new guy, in fact, was the only black kid in a class of Jews, Irish, Italians, and a few other Caucasian mixes. For the most part we got along well enough inside of school, though we tended to break into our cliques outside on the streets. Neighborhoods were usually broken down by tribes, and sometimes stupidity broke out—Jewish kids for one had a rough enough time facing parochial school toughs avenging the death of their Savior. But, as it was, we were all part of the same club by virtue of our white skin. So, to state the obvious, this black kid stood out in 710, and not in a good way.

When it came to race, in fact, some kids weren't all that far from their parents' attitude, which was closer to the Ku

Klux Klan than Abe Lincoln. The subject wasn't a big deal since the only blacks coming into the neighborhood were usually those hired to clean apartments or other house work. This kid didn't look like a hired hand to me, just perfectly content being one of our classmates.

"Man, he's black as coal," Plotz snickered. "And the fat lips on that guy, damn. Monkey lips!"

"Jeez, Plotz, *keep it to yourself*," I whispered sharply, hoping that the new kid seated next to us in the back row did not get his first whiff of Alan Plotz, so to speak.

"What's the problem?" he retorted. "These jungle bunnies belong in their own neighborhood. And, hey, the Bronx Zoo's not that far away."

"Enough of the stupid talk!" I snapped, barely suppressing the urge to throw my marbled notebook at him. "You sound like a moron. You are a moron."

Plotz gave me his offended who-ya-callin'-a-moron? face.

No one would ever mistake Plotz for a future member of the United Nations, though I did see his potential as an emissary for the Aryan Nation should Hitler be alive and considering a comeback. I put up with him because I had to, but he never failed to get on my nerves. He was doing his best now. It wasn't just that Plotz was a loudmouth bigot. It was that the guy was so very proud of that fact.

"Joe, would you stand and introduce yourself?" Miss Crouse announced.

"What *is* this?" Plotz mumbled to himself. "Some freakin' Academy Awards."

Joe had settled into the chair in Psycho's Corner and was my new neighbor. (It was too bad that Sid Bladner beat me to Tommy's old seat behind Dee-Dee, but what could I do?) The kid bounced out of his seat and bobbed his head to his left and right to take in his new classmates.

"Hey. I'm Joe. Joe Bailey," he said excitedly. "Real cool meeting you."

I have to say, the kid wasn't shy. Just flush with high energy and a flashing smile. He gave off the feeling that he'd rather be in no other place in the world than Room 424. Not an easy thing to pull off with this group.

"I'm not gonna like this guy," Plotz snorted. If anything, he was predictable. Plotz didn't particularly like anyone who exuded much self-confidence, and a black kid with such a personality? Well, I didn't think that Joe was about to be invited to his next gorge-fest at the all-you-can-eat Chinese lunch special on Burnside Avenue. Not that Joe would mind.

Joe sat back down in his seat, oblivious to the class silent treatment. And Miss Crouse got back to her lessons, weirdly enough about where all this race-hate stuff started out.

Our reading assignment had been about some "compromise" concocted by those nutty Founding Fathers. Miss Crouse made sure that no one was about to miss the point. She picked up a piece of chalk and wrote on the blackboard in her large block letters, THE THREE-FIFTHS COMPROMISE.

I didn't have a math brain, but I got the deal. It was right out of Bizarro world. Miss Crouse explained that the "compromise" turned slaves into a fraction of a person—three-fifths of a human being to be exact. She told us that the number of representatives in Congress was based on each state's population. So the dirty trick was to include slaves in the head count but not really as a full human being.

As if it wasn't bad enough being a slave, did these folks have to be turned into imaginary "amputees"? I conjured up the image of thousands of blacks minus their arms and legs being tallied up. At the end of the day, they were still slaves and couldn't vote anyway.

Our Founders loved a sick joke.

Not an inspiring story, though I doubted whether anyone in class cared much. I also wondered what was going through Joe's mind. He must have cared.

Miss Crouse was still into her American history lesson and turned the talk to current events. Something called Civil

Rights. She told us that black Americans were still not free. They were now demanding the same rights that white Americans always had. You'd think we would've worked this out by now.

Our teacher went on to tell us the story of a black woman named Rosa Parks, who had refused to give up her seat on a public bus to a white passenger—and was arrested "The bus driver had ordered her and three other black passengers to stand and take seats in the rear of the bus," Miss Crouse told us. "Rosa didn't budge even as the driver threatened to call the police. And then he did—and Rosa was taken away to jail!"

"Now, class, can *you* imagine being treated this way?" Miss Crouse said, shaking her head. "And why—because of the color of her skin."

"Maybe she should've taken that bus one-way back to Africa," Plotz muttered too loudly.

Joe shot Plotz an angry glance before turning back to Miss Crouse.

"Plotz, shut your trap!" I whispered furiously.

Plotz hunkered down in his seat and gave me another nasty look, as if I had turned down his free membership offer to the local chapter of the Ku Klux Klan.

We didn't say another word to each other for the rest of the day, which suited me just fine.

CHAPTER 19

Harlem

As it turned out, Joe Bailey and I became the best of friends. An odd match for sure. Joe was built like an athlete, with broad shoulders that tapered down to a narrow waist. Then there was me. I prayed that one day a growth spurt would add a few inches and stretch out the round surfaces molded around my waist.

There was something about Joe that I took to immediately. He was full of energy, and a guy that radiated likability. We also shared a common passion called basketball. Once the bounce of the ball became our heartbeat there was no turning back. And something else. The game was color-blind, so if you could play, then that was that.

Loving the game didn't mean I was especially good at it. My shot was okay, and I had the knack of seeing the court and making the right pass. But this was a game of rhythm, and my feet and hands were still catching up with each other. That didn't stop me from playing anytime and anywhere I could find a court, even if it meant digging out the previous night's snowfall. My yellow Voit basketball had taken such a beating one winter afternoon, that the ball actually exploded in my hands during a shoot-around.

I never figured out that one. I assumed that the ball simply couldn't take anymore and gave up.

Joe, on the other hand, was a natural, able to sky to the rim, effortlessly making shots I could only dream about. In our schoolyard games, my strategy was simple enough. Pass Joe the ball and watch him go. None of the white kids stood a chance. Even double-teaming Joe made little difference. He was lightning quick, and opponents were stuck in mud guarding him, suffering from our shared white-boys' disease. An inability to challenge gravity. We couldn't jump.

After games, Joe slapped me five, put his arm around my shoulder in that easy manner of his, talked sports or music—he actually played jazz trombone, of all things—or anything else on his mind. We just connected. And then one afternoon he spoke about getting out of neighborhood.

"Hey, man, I know where we can find a good full court," he said excitedly.

Full-court basketball was altogether different than the half-court game that I was used to. "Full" was the "real" game" that called for hard, fast play on the move. I wasn't particularly fast or strong and my stamina needed work. So I wasn't really up for Joe's plan, though I didn't want to let on.

"So, where's the game?" I asked hesitantly.

"One Hundred Twenty-Fifth Street. Harlem."

"Oh," was all I could say. I was thinking, "You gotta be kidding!"

"Don't think so, Joe," I finally said. "Lots of homework tonight."

I didn't even pretend to tell him the truth. Harlem basketball was rough for anyone, much less a challenged white guy. Getting on that court—and surviving—was way out of my league. And out of the question.

Joe shrugged off my lack of enthusiasm. "You're only going to get better by playing with good players," he said in his typical easy way. "Let's check it out, man."

My answer was a definite "no," until it wasn't. Joe was not about to let me back down. He gave me some more of the pep talk, clapped me on the back, and nudged me in the direction of the Jerome Avenue IRT.

And, so, I went with Joe to Harlem.

တၵတၵ

I had never been to Harlem before, and it seemed that no one there was particularly glad to see me there now. I hadn't come across a single white face, but it was more than that. The buildings were worn down, the streets gray, with groups of men hanging around, giving Joe and me the once-over as we made our way down Amsterdam Avenue. It wasn't a welcome-to-the-neighborhood look. No, that wasn't the feeling at all.

"Let's get over to Lenox," Joe said. "The best games are there."

"Joe, my ankle is acting up. Too risky to test it."

Joe laughed, not giving me any room to cut out. "No worries, my man, you gotta another ankle."

"You're gonna feel real guilty if I get hurt," was my only comeback.

"No problem. You probably won't come through the games alive anyway."

I was so glad that Joe was enjoying himself. Yeah, real glad.

It was around 110th Street that we bumped into a few guys Joe knew from his street days here before moving to the Bronx. Their eyes narrowed checking me out, as if to ask, "What the hell was this white kid doing here?" Exactly the question I was asking myself. I managed to become invisible while Joe engaged the guys in some small talk before we took off. Though he never let on, I sensed that Joe was also second-guessing himself about bringing his white friend into his old neighborhood.

Joe had left Harlem after a bad situation. His father had been shot dead in some holdup, and his family was barely getting by. His mom still lived here, cleaning homes in Manhattan, while he stayed with his grandmother on Loring Place, not far from my apartment building. A rough time growing up, but Joe wouldn't show it.

We were a few blocks from Lenox Avenue when a kid barely four feet tall, wearing a baseball cap, came up to us. "Any money!" The boy was no older than ten. He was un-smiling and his inquiry into our finances was more a state-ment than a question.

I started to laugh at the sight of this little kid trying to shake us down.

"Just ignore him," said Joe, "and them." He pointed to two other ten-year-olds that were coming our way.

"They look like babies."

"Yeah, but those guys don't."

I followed Joe's finger and saw that he was pointing out a tough-looking gang of some six teenagers. They were trailing the kids.

"They're using the kids to bait us. Let's hustle out."

I didn't argue and we hastily crossed the street and found a passing bus to hop onto.

We finally got to the court with a game already running at full tilt. Joe checked with some guys standing on the side-lines. We were next to run. I sat along a chain-linked fence, studying the play like it was some sort of new phenome-non—nothing like the games in my neighborhood.

These guys were incredible, racing up and down the court, driving ferociously to the rim. Competition was tena-cious. This wasn't a game but a war with its own soundtrack of street language, which I found educational and, well, scary. I came from a household where "bad language" didn't exist. Not an issue here on the courts. I never real-ized, for instance, that the word "fuck" could be used as a noun, adjective, verb, and adverb, with colorful variations on the ever-popular "motherfucker." Interesting stuff.

The two squads played shirts and skins, and even on this cool day the players' bodies glistened with sweat. The team getting to sixteen points would stay on, and neither side was aiming to sit. The intensity of the game went up another notch with the score tied at 14-14. "Motherfucker" also was in competition with the noun "nigger," as in, "Nigger, you got no game!"

I found the name-calling weird and imagined trying to egg Sammy on in a game, barking at him, "Kike, you got no game!" Somehow, it just didn't work for me.

Shirts finally beat skins, 16-15 after a muscular guy nicknamed Sky Jam slammed the ball through the hoop, letting out a whoop of "Motherfucker!" to emphasize the finality of the moment. The high-rise emotions deflated as players from both sides slapped hands, and it was a relief to see that any game fury didn't carry over.

Then Joe got me up and going from my seat on the side-lines. It was our turn to play.

I was now having *very* serious doubts. "Hey, Joe, these guys are bigger and too much. They'll kill me out there."

"My man, just play your game," Joe said with that easy smile. "You'll be okay."

I liked Joe but didn't believe him for a second.

"And keep an eye out for me on the backdoor," he winked. "The Big O's got nothin' on you."

Yeah, I knew the play, but I also knew that I was no Oscar Robertson.

We were joined by three other guys also waiting for their chance to play. Unfortunately for me, we were skins. I had no choice but to grudgingly pull off my shirt. Most of the players on the court had trim, defined bodies. I didn't and was immediately self-conscious of the handlebars molded around my waist that jiggled when I ran. I mentally vowed to abstain from the Twinkies and Snowballs that I was hooked on. That pledge, of course, did me little good at the moment.

I was one of the shorter players on the court, not to mention the only white guy. Joe matched me against the opposing team's guard, a speedy guy who handled the ball like it was on an elastic string. I decided to play off and give him a jump shot rather than get too close and have him swoop by me for a layup.

The game was fast, way too fast, but I managed to keep up on the court. I wasn't worried about scoring since that likelihood was slim and none. My strategy was simple—get the ball to anyone open on my team. Each time the ball was in my hands I made the pass and usually it was a good one, once even hitting Joe on the backdoor play.

"Hey, Big O," he shouted to me as we ran back down the court.

Another nifty pass earned me a pat on the ass by one of my teammates.

My opponent hit two outside shots off the jumper, but our team held on and was within a basket of the shirts.

It was then that Sky Jam and one of our guys started mixing it up under the boards, and I thought a fight was about to break loose as the "motherfuckers" and "niggers" flew in full force. The venting didn't come to any violence, thank goodness, but let's say that this game would never be mistaken for afternoon tea with the Queen.

I was relieved that none of the language and rough play was directed toward me, a curious hands-off attitude. I wasn't sure what to make of it. Maybe the regulars felt sorry for the flabby white kid barely keeping up, or just understood that I'd never be in their world with all the street machismo that came with it. In short, I could never be black. Honestly, I was okay with any explanation, and had no problem accepting their pity. Nor did I have any inclination trading "motherfuckers" with Sky Jam to enhance my rep. Nope, not one bit.

We wound up winning the game with Joe knifing through three players to score on a reverse layup. The celebration came down to a few hugs (gross considering we were half naked and drenched in sweat). Some of my teammates ambled over to slap me five, which seemed like a better idea. I didn't exactly feel like a "brother" but that was okay. I tried to stay cool, barely holding back from shouting, "Check out that Jew boy from the Bronx making good in Harlem!" I held on to that thought for a few more games before Joe and I had enough and took off for home.

"Not bad for a white boy," Joe chuckled softly with that big smile, placing his sweaty arm around me as we left the court that afternoon. I took his embrace happily without cringing one bit. "Not bad at all," he repeated, in case I had missed his joy about my basketball coming of age.

CHAPTER 20

Jumpin' Jim Crow

Joe stayed the cool kid he had been since day one despite the brushoffs that came his way. He was a real pal, and the mean talk around him got to me. Some kids in class could be plain dumb, suspiciously questioning Joe with their eyes. I could hear them thinking—Was this guy one of those "Negro malcontents" that their parents warned them about? And this after barging into their classroom uninvited?

The stupidity at school was one thing, but the stuff on television was just plain scary. Crazies in white robes and pointed masks with burning crosses and bad intentions. I had heard one report about this twenty-four-year-old black man named Willie Edwards. A couple of hooded morons had savagely beaten the guy, put a gun to his head, and then made him jump off a bridge. A 125-foot plunge into the water. The news story reported that the guy's body had just been found.

The Klan nut jobs weren't the only ones, though maybe they could whip up a costume party with their other lunatic friends roaming around America. I mean, I'd be glad to bring over the popcorn, soda and cyanide. This other crazy, George Lincoln Rockwell, kept making headlines by declar-

ing himself leader of the American Nazi Party, whatever
that was. Rockwell was quite a character with his corn pipe,
brown shirt, and a love thing for the Fuhrer. I wondered
what his mother thought of her son after naming him for our
two great American presidents. She must have been at least
a teensy-weensy disappointed.

The guy was apparently on his Nazi tour, holding a rally
in Washington, D.C., and planning one now for New York
in the summer. I thought that "Heil Hitler" salutes were
long buried in the great shithole of history. But Rockwell
and his brown shirt buddies had popped up like rats and
were looking for trouble.

I suppose Joe and I had that in common in our family
histories—lunatics in hoods or armbands that hated us. Joe
had told me his own story, coming from generations of royal tribal stock in Nigeria. No mistaking his roots with his
broad face, full lips, and wide eyes. I thought of my own
ancestors, some ancient Sephardic tribe that roamed the de-
sert way back then. Plain to see during summer months
when my skin turned a deep brown. My family were *Coha-
nim*, direct descendants of Aaron, the brother of Moses. So,
Joe and I were both royalty of sorts.

You'd think that would have counted for something, unless it didn't.

ᘓᘔᘓ

I was liking Miss Crouse more with each passing month.
My elementary school teachers had been older than my parents. Miss Crouse was young and optimistic, and made us
feel that way too. She spoke about "the 60s" as if we had
just landed on some heavenly planet.

"Your lives will be unlike your parents," she bubbled on.
"You will see such bright colors—amazing possibilities—
that they could never imagine for themselves. You can start
now. Maybe there are colors you can bring to mind that will

help you see your life differently. Wouldn't that be wonderful?"

"Even your black-and-white TV sets are becoming color," she added, smiling. "Maybe that's a sign of what's to come?"

Miss Crouse could sound wacky at times, and I can't say I entirely followed her color mumbo-jumbo, but something about her talk stirred me up.

Our teacher wasn't through talking about color that day—skin color. The subject wasn't on the school's curriculum, but Miss Crouse had made it part of hers.

"Who in class has heard of the Jim Crow laws?" she asked during our current events lesson.

"I once had a parrot named Jim," Mark Desapio called out.

Miss Crouse sighed. "Does anyone else have an idea?"

No one did.

In her block-letter handwriting, she wrote the words on the blackboard.

"Actually, the name came from a song called 'Jump Jim Crow' back in the early 1800s," she explained. "And it was performed by whites in black face and usually with a type of dance."

"Yeah, Miss Crouse, I saw that in a movie once," Sarah Nolte called out. "The guy was dancing crazy-like."

"Yes, Sarah, that song and dance became part of what were called minstrel shows."

Frankie Wachtel chimed in. "Couldn't they have gotten real black guys in the movies to do the jumpin' Jim Crow thing?"

"That really was the point, Frankie," Miss Crouse said, nodding. "The show was meant to mock black people. Make fun of them. Not very nice was it?"

"I don't see the big deal," Frankie replied. "I just cracked up seeing those guys hoppin' around like they were on fire."

Miss Crouse started to get that nervous face, worried where this talk was going.

From the corner of my eye, I checked out Joe next to me. His face was tight, not happy at all with the race talk.

I raised my hand.

"Yes, Paul."

"But doesn't Jim Crow mean something else today? That white people can keep black people away from their restaurants and schools and neighborhoods?"

"That's right," she said, brightening. "The word is called 'segregation.' How would you feel if you were told you couldn't live in certain neighborhoods, or eat in particular restaurants, or just take a drink at a water fountain that is for 'whites only'?"

The class seemed to be getting more into it. It was now Eddy Robinson's turn. "Miss Crouse, did you hear about those black students down south last month that sat at a food counter in a Woolworth's and wouldn't leave unless they were served?"

Before Miss Crouse could respond, Plotz blurted out his own answer.

"If they don't like it here," he snarled, "why don't they go back to the jungle where they belong!"

Miss Crouse froze, coming to grips with the miserable kid in the back row. Plotz was at it again.

I could see Plotz surveying the classroom. Maybe he was looking for others to back him up.

Joe Bailey definitely wasn't one of them.

"What the fuck!"

I could hear the entire class take in a sharp breath. I was shocked myself. Not by Joe's "four-letter word" but the hot anger behind it. Joe wasn't one for throwing around "bad" language, but Plotz had a way of inspiring it. And he wasn't letting up.

"Hey, no offense, brother. But this is America, and we're white and proud of it. Besides, my mom once told me that she had this Aunt Jemima maid who stole some things from our apartment. You guys gotta cut that out."

Joe shot to his feet, eyes on fire, fists clenched. "You

ain't my brother, motherfucker." Then he made a move to get at Plotz sitting on my other side.

I instinctively got between both guys, reaching out to grab Joe as he cocked his fist. It wasn't that I was trying to protect Plotz—a good punch in the nose and kick in the balls would have been fine. I just didn't think that any good would come of it for Joe.

"Joe Bailey!" Miss Crouse cried out, and then more softly. "Joe, Joe, *please*. You need to sit down." And then pointing to Plotz, Miss Crouse, furious, told him: "You—are—an—asshole, Alan Plotz. Shut—your—stupid—mouth!"

Holy moly!

There's nothing like having your teacher blow up to get your attention. And, my, such language coming from sweet Miss Crouse. You could hear a pin drop in Room 424—a beautiful silence. All of us, staring bug-eyed at our teacher. Could this be the Miss Crouse that I knew with the milk and cookies personality? I was instantly in love with her. Finally, she had let Plotz have it. And so eloquently.

Miss Crouse's explosion had its intended effect. Joe, still simmering, gave Plotz a hard stare, and slowly settled back to his seat.

Plotz, wide-eyed, shifted to his innocent face. "Hey, what did I say?" he called out to anyone who would listen.

Miss Crouse, still shaking with emotion, wasn't herself yet. She went to her desk, picked up a pile of worksheets, tossed them out to the class, and sharply told us to get busy. Our lesson on American race relations was over for the day. I had the feeling that my teacher wasn't about to return to the subject anytime soon.

CHAPTER 21

Beelzebub

I s this my imagination?" Sammy grimaced, looking down at his lunch tray, "or is my meat loaf alive and moving?"

Sammy was always good for a laugh. But he wasn't kidding this time. I checked out the lump of meat planted on his plastic tray, and something did seem strange.

"I see the problem," I said, seriously contemplating his dish. "It's the crap on top that's jiggling."

"That's the gravy," Sammy nodded. Then he put his index finger into the Jell-O-like goo and put it to his lips. "Tastes like doo-doo. Actually this whole lunch is a bad idea."

"Maybe you should've gone with the tuna fish."

"Had that last time. If you think this meat loaf is bad, the tuna fish will kill you."

Both of us had made the mistake of leaving our lunch boxes at home and were forced to risk our lives in the school cafeteria. It wasn't that we were picky eaters by any stretch.

But we did want to know that the food we ate was made from substances found on Earth. As long as we stuck to a container of milk and peanut butter-jelly sandwich in the cafeteria, we felt we were okay. Better yet to just stick to the milk.

Sammy had gone a little crazy that afternoon and decided to order the "Entree of the Day" highlighted on our lunch board. Unfortunately, the "chef" never mentioned what day, or which year for that matter, that this meat lump had been prepared. I was certain that the gravy had once been a different substance in a previous lifetime. I guess the chef figured we'd be fooled if he used a fancy French word to describe this inedible "entree." Sammy should have known better, but his grumbling stomach had gotten the better of him.

The lunch bell rang letting us know that we should be getting back to our classroom. "Well, better hungry than dead," said Sammy, giving in and dumping the remnants of his meal into the garbage. "Hopefully, they'll bury this deep."

We left the cafeteria for 424.

❧❧❧

Miss Crouse had yet to return to class when we got back. It looked like she was running late from her meeting, leaving us some free time.

I glanced over at Plotz, who seemed pretty content.

"What's up?" he said, adding a loud belch. "Good lunch, eh?"

"Yeah, Plotz."

"You should try the meat loaf. Had a double helping."

"Good for you, Plotz."

"Goes right through you, though." Another belch, this one sending out a puff of meat-loaf stink. Plotz clearly was versatile from both ends of his body.

Relief. Miss Crouse walked into the classroom putting an end to Plotz's critique on our public school cuisine.

The next period was spent with our English lesson—we were reading a book called *Lord of the Flies*. A really brutal story with kids marooned on a coral island, going crazy. I mean really crazy.

"Did you know," stated Miss Crouse, "that the title of book is based on a religious figure called Beelzebub? Does anyone have an idea who that was?"

"The Devil."

Joe Bailey hadn't even bothered to raise his hand.

"That's right, Joe," Miss Crouse said. "Why do you think the author had that figure in mind?"

"All neighborhoods have their devils," Joe replied quietly. "So did his."

Miss Crouse nodded, for a moment lost in thought. Then she was back to us. "Did any of the characters seem real to any of you?"

Yeah, I didn't have to think too long about "Roger" the bully. But no need to remind anyone about Tommy Branigan, so I kept it to myself.

"I felt so bad for 'Piggy,'" Molly O'Malley called out. "They crushed him with a boulder!"

"That musta hurt," blurted Plotz, sparking a few snickers.

"But, Miss Crouse," I said. "Aren't we like those kids? We can be stupid like them too. Not knowing right from wrong. Not thinking for ourselves. Believing in terrible things."

"Like that pig's head, with all the disgusting flies swarming around," Dee-Dee quickly added. "Those kids actually worshipped that scary pig. Killed for that thing. How could they?"

"That's something to think about, Dee-Dee," said our teacher, who seemed like she was thinking about it herself. "Sometimes we don't know what makes us do the wrong thing. Or even understand that it is wrong."

That idea hung in the air, only stirring up more questions. I had my own.

"Miss Crouse, doesn't your conscience tell you? Don't you just feel when something is right or not?"

"I wish that was true, Paul," Miss Crouse replied. "But some people don't always listen to their conscience, do they?"

"But isn't 'the beast' inside all of us," asked Sammy. "And gives us *no* choice?"

Sammy wasn't the reading type, but I could see that he was thinking about this one.

Miss Crouse gazed at Sammy. I could tell she was having a hard time coming up with an answer.

ⅇ⌇ⅇ⌇

The intercom buzzed, startling us, and putting an end to our talk. I was sorry about that. I had been grappling with demons since I was a little kid, and something about this story got to me.

An announcement reminded teachers that orchestra rehearsal was about to start, and to excuse student musicians from class. That meant me. I felt great being part of the orchestra as the lead clarinetist, and couldn't wait to get to rehearsal. Mr. Pagliaro was amazing, getting us in shape to perform Dvorak's *New World Symphony*. A real masterpiece with a beautiful spiritual clarinet solo that sang out of my instrument. I went to sleep with that melody in my head.

Miss Crouse nodded in my direction, giving me the go-ahead to pick up my instrument that I had left in the classroom closet.

I slid open the wooden doors to the closet where we all packed coats, bags, and belongings each day. The clarinet was stored on the right side of the top shelf, where I always kept it. The instrument sat in a black case imprinted with my name in large letters.

The sweetest sounds flowed from that clarinet—it was called a "Buffet"—and it was the one thing in the world that I cherished most. This magical instrument.

And it was gone.

ℰↄℰↄ

"Are you sure, Paul? Are you sure you left it in the closet?"

Miss Crouse was leaning over me, her hand on my shoulder. I sat in shock at my desk, my head buried in my arms. I was terrified to raise my eyes for fear that the truth would come tumbling back into my brain—my treasured Buffet was gone. Stolen to be more exact.

"Why don't we look for the clarinet together," Miss Crouse gently advised, patting me on the back. "Maybe someone accidently moved the case and we'll find it somewhere else in the room. It will be okay."

But it wasn't okay, would never be okay. I could not understand who would stoop so low. Why even take a clarinet? My clarinet? Was it jealousy because I was the only kid at JHS 82 that could play a chromatic scale? Or that Leonard Bernstein might give me a call for a tryout?

It didn't make any sense.

Our search turned up exactly what I expected. Nothing, except for a number two pencil that had rolled under a desk.

I had taken music lessons since I was seven, and Dad wanted me to have the best instrument. My Buffet was just that with its silver-plated keys and African blackwood. I felt that any music was possible. Even took on the challenge of George Gershwin's incredible opening solo from *Rhapsody in Blue*, notes that glided out from this clarinet. Now what was I going to do, George? I could only hope that he'd make room for me now in his mausoleum out in Westchester.

I was called into Principal Stern's office, and he did his comforting thing too. Some more pats on the back. By this time, my parents had been notified, and the word had spread through the school. I was more surprised when a policeman came to the school and into the principal's office. He seemed to take some pity also, but I was thankful that at least he wasn't going to start patting my back. I checked out his nametag, PO Antoine Brown, as he pulled out a pad and pen and started asking questions.

"So, when did you last see the instrument?"

"Right before lunch. In the classroom closet."

"Then you went to lunch. Who was left in the classroom?"

"Usually Miss Crouse. But she was at a meeting."

I turned to Principal Stern who nodded.

"Was there anyone else in the room?"

"Maybe. I guess there might have been. But I don't know."

PO Brown gave me that sorry-about-that-kid look and closed his pad.

Then he told me that my parents would have to follow up at the station. He promised that he'd be on the lookout, whatever that meant. I couldn't imagine anyone whipping out the instrument on the street for a rendition of "The Saints Go Marching In" while Officer Brown was on his lookout.

My Buffet was gone forever. And I was destroyed.

I bumped into Sammy and Joe after school. More pats on the back. I made a mental vow to kill the next person who even tried to touch my back.

❧❧❧

As it turned out, Officer Brown was telling me the truth. He had, in fact, been on the lookout for the clarinet. A week later, he'd found it—after a search of a student's locker. What was that about? But there it was, my precious Buffet, sitting perfectly intact in its black case on Principal Stern's desk as I walked into his office. I felt that I had drowned and someone just punched the water out of my lungs. I was breathing again.

"What—what happened? Who—"

Principal Stern held up his hand. "It's a police matter now, Paul. We can't say anything more."

"But who was it? Who stole my clarinet?"

The principal exhaled slowly, his eyes softened. "I'm sorry, Paul," he said quietly. "You should go back to class now. I'm glad we got back your instrument."

With that, I picked up my Buffet and left his office, incredibly relieved. I took a few steps into the first-floor hall when I spotted Officer Brown down the corridor. He wasn't alone. He had his hand on someone's shoulder, though I couldn't make out the guy as they both disappeared around the hallway. The thief.

"Officer Brown!" I yelled out, but was too late. I took off, my clarinet case in hand, racing to catch up.

By the time I skidded around the hallway corner, they had left the school by the side door. I followed, bounding out the exit door. I found myself in the schoolyard, and there was Officer Brown standing next to his squad car. Alongside stood his prisoner, his hands cuffed behind his back.

Joe Bailey.

I was drowning again.

I almost stumbled to the ground as I rushed up to the squad car.

"*Joe! Joe!* What's going on?"

Joe stared at me blankly as if he had never seen me before. And not a word.

"Damn, Joe, *what is happening?*"

Officer Brown put on his official voice. "Young man, you'll have to back away."

I ignored him.

"Joe. You gotta say something!"

Joe stood there silently. Confusion in his eyes.

Officer Brown then placed a hand on top of Joe's head and eased him into the squad car. Then he turned back to me as I inched closer. "Son," he said, less harshly. "You need to step back. You shouldn't be here."

I took a half step back, keeping my eyes on Joe seated in the back of the police car. He was leaning forward, his cuffed hands preventing him from resting against the back seat. All I could see now was his profile, his head slightly raised. And then something else. Tears rolling down his face.

Through the back window partly rolled down, I implored my friend. "Joe, *talk to me!* What's going on?"

Officer Brown was now on the driver's side, getting into the car.

Joe sat frozen into the back seat. Finally, he spoke. A single word.

"Beelzebub."

"Joe, what the hell does that mean?"

He turned and finally met my eyes. I could see that he was scared. Very scared.

"He's alive," Joe whispered, his cheeks wet with tears.

And then he was taken away.

CHAPTER 22

Spofford

Y ou never know with some people," Sammy said, sprawled out on the rug in my bedroom.

We were hanging out that afternoon with the talk all about Joe. It had been a week since he was arrested. Nothing made sense to me. I couldn't believe that Joe had stolen my clarinet, and I was pissed off at Sammy for saying otherwise.

"What do you mean 'some people'?" I shot back.

"Hey, I'm just sayin'."

"I know what you're saying, and it's lousy."

"Hey, listen," Sammy went on. "Joe swiped your clarinet, it was found inside his locker. Do you want me to make excuses for him?"

"I don't believe it."

"Sure you do, but you're giving him a pass because he's your pal."

"You're my pal too, and I couldn't see you ripping me off."

"We're different, Paul. We're lifers, together from the same neighborhood."

"And what about Joe?"

Sammy shook his head. "He never really belonged here, Paul."

"C'mon, Sammy. They were saying that crap about your grandparents back in Germany."

"Not a great comparison. Those crazies sent them to a concentration camp. Then they killed them."

"Sammy, what's happening to Joe, now? He doesn't deserve this."

"Bro. The guy's a thief. Suckered you into being his friend. And then stabbed you in the back."

Just then the phone rang from the kitchen, stopping in mid-ring. I could hear some hush-hush talk between Mom and the caller before Rosie called out, "Paul, it's for you. It's Miss Crouse."

What? Miss Crouse had never called me at home before. In fact, I don't think I ever had a conversation with Miss Crouse outside of Room 424.

When I came into the kitchen there was no missing the serious look on Mom's face as she handed me the phone. The last time I saw that look was when my parakeet Skippy suddenly died, and she sat me down to give me the terrible news.

"Hello, Miss Crouse," I mumbled into the phone, already jittery about what she had to tell me.

"Paul, I know you and Joe were good friends, and I wanted to talk to you before rumors got around. It's about Joe. He was taken to a juvenile center after he was arrested. He's waiting for a hearing and will be kept there until then."

"Where is he, Miss Crouse?"

"The place is called the Spofford Juvenile Center. It's in Hunts Point."

Every kid had heard of Spofford. "That's a horrible place, Miss Crouse," I said. "All sorts of bad things go on there."

I waited for a response but only heard Miss Crouse breathing coming through the line. "Yes, I know," she said finally.

"How long is he going to stay there?" I asked, my nerves on edge.

"Until the court is ready to hear his case."

"When is that?"

Another bout of silence.

"I'm not sure. I'm afraid it could be a while," she replied gently.

"Miss Crouse. He never could've done this," I murmured with less conviction than I intended.

I could sense Miss Crouse searching for words. "Paul...you've been a very good friend."

Left unsaid was the thought that Joe apparently wasn't a very good friend. Miss Crouse couldn't bring herself to hurt me with that opinion.

There wasn't much else for me to say either, and that's where we left it as she hung up.

I suppose I should have felt betrayed by Joe, furious that he could do such a thing—and to me. But I felt nothing like that. I thought instead of Joe in handcuffs and in tears in the back of the squad car. He didn't look guilty then. Only miserable, defeated.

"Nice of your teacher to call," Mom said, coming over to me.

"Real nice," I quietly replied, and turned to go back to my bedroom.

I was lost in thought as I plopped down on my bed. Sammy was still on the rug, reading a comic book.

"What's up, Paul?" he asked, tossing the comic aside.

"He's at Spofford."

"Not Spofford. That place is crazy dangerous."

"I know, Sammy. I know."

❧❧❧

It was nearly two weeks later when Dad drove me over to Hunts Point in the East Bronx to see Joe. Both my parents weren't thrilled with the idea. I couldn't blame them, but I wanted to see my friend. We had to talk. I needed to know what happened. And that was that.

Dad had called the Center and left Joe a message that I would be coming to visit that Saturday.

I had no idea what to expect when I got to Spofford. Someone had come up with the pleasant sounding "juvenile center," a kind of YMCA sort of hangout. Spofford was anything but that. Nothing less than a prison. Even from the street, the place looked dangerous. Huge slabs of concrete made up two four-story buildings surrounded by barbed-wire fences. Iron bars hung on rows of windows in rooms that housed young teens and even kids. A modern-day concentration camp.

Since Joe's arrest I had read stories of kids beaten, slashed, and worse, much worse. I was terrified walking into the place, thinking of my friend. What it must be like behind these barred windows with no way out.

Dad and I went into a long room and approached an angry looking guard sitting at a small desk. We told him we were there to see Joe Bailey.

"Yeah, Bailey," he said, checking a list. "Not today."

"What do you mean?" Dad persisted. "We called earlier this week. It seemed all right to come today."

"He's not taking visitors," the guard said testily.

There wasn't going to be any room for discussion. The guard had no patience with us and didn't care if he showed it.

"Is he okay?" I asked, breaking the standoff.

The guard turned and softened, but only barely. "He doesn't say nothin' to nobody, stays by himself all the time," he said. "That's probably just as well."

"Why is that?"

The guard stared at me in stony silence, taking a long hard look at this stupid kid with his stupid question.

"Come on, Paul," my dad said, taking me by the hand. "We'll try again some other time."

But we hadn't taken more than a few steps when we were hit by a sudden blast of shouts, threats, and curses reverberating off the Center's stone walls. They were coming from past the guard, out of sight behind closed doors, inside dangerous, dark places. I shuddered knowing that Joe was trapped there.

I turned back to the guard, who didn't even flinch at the chaotic uproar behind him. I expect it was just another day on the job at Spofford. I was set to plead with him again—that I needed to see my friend. But another hard squint from the guy shut down that thought and sent me away.

Dad and I drove home in silence. There really wasn't much to say anyway. And after a while it became easier to forget that Joe was in that hellish place. Not that I felt proud of the fact. Not at all. But once my emotions settled, I'd come to accept that Sammy, and others, might have been right about Joe. Life can be lousy. That even a friend, a good friend, or so I thought, can sneak up and clobber you with a sucker punch.

Maybe not a great revelation. In fact, a shitty one. But there it was.

CHAPTER 23

Dark Corners

It had been an ordinary spring day before it became something else. I mean, this was something a kid didn't see every day. In fact, shouldn't have seen at all. Then it became that other thing, and...well, I needed to catch my breath, slow down. I will get to this story, but in the end it was all Mom's fault. Rosie was to blame. You see, none of this would have happened if Mom hadn't ordered me to go and pick up the laundry from our building cellar. What else was I to do?

I came home that night exhausted after hours of street ball. Daylight Savings Time had kicked in, and I'd held out returning until the last rays of light had faded.

Mom had a burger and fries waiting for me, and then a television episode of *Bonanza* before turning in. Little Joe and Hoss were about to hang for a crime they didn't commit.

It's a good thing that Ben and Adam were around to save the day. Some family those Cartwrights. Nice neighborhood, the Ponderosa. The *Bonanza* clippity-clop theme song kicked in at the end, and I sang along. "Dant-de-de-Dant-de-de-Dant- de-de-Dant-de-de-Daant-DAANT..."

Then Mom came into the living room and blindsided me.

"Sweetie," she began in that sunny voice of hers. "Now that the show is over, can you please go and get the clothes down in the laundry."

I thought I'd escaped any house chore that night, but Mom was an expert in tracking me down. "Mom, it's pitch dark down there this time of night," was the best I could do. "You know, it's really not safe."

"Well, be brave, Paul," Rosie said, and smiled, a familiar look that told me not to bother arguing. "You need under-wear and socks for tomorrow, and they're in the dryer."

I really had to find a better excuse if I had any chance of getting out of this job.

The truth was, I hated going down to our building's cellar, a gloomy, coffin-like area with a washer and dryer crammed into the space. It was the one dark corner of 50 West Tremont that got under my skin. The cellar connected to a dimly-lit passageway that led to an adjacent building. As a very young kid I was certain that some creature was lurking about in some corner and ready to pounce. I was older now but no less jumpy.

I shut my eyes tight, found a glimmer of courage, and made my way downstairs and across the courtyard. I creaked open a small wooden door, ducked my head, and climbed into the cellar. I could already feel goose bumps sprouting on my arms. A forty-watt yellow bulb hung on a chain from the stone ceiling giving off more shadow than light.

During the summer, I had nearly peed in my pants after seeing the movie *Psycho* about some cross-dressing maniac who runs a motel and winds up killing Janet Leigh.

At the end, they discover the psycho's dead mother, at least her skeleton, resting her tired bones in a basement cellar. Just gave me the creeps and nightmares for the next month.

For all I knew, my dark, deserted laundry cellar might very well have been the set for that scene.

And so I made my way over to the dryer keeping my

eyes and ears open. I did not rule out the possibility of finding some psycho in a dress.

Instead, I found Anita Bonita. Without a dress.

I squeezed over to one of two machines, stuffed with my dry clothes. I was in no mood to waste time, hurriedly balling the pile of underwear, socks and T-shirts into a laundry bag. But apparently I wasn't alone. Frightening noises were coming from past the laundry down the dark passageway. A girl's voice, crying out, in pain. Her moaning was becoming louder and longer. I was listening to someone being killed!

Then again, there might have been another explanation.

Crossing my mind at that moment was Miss Crouse's class diction lesson. Each of us would take turns enunciating the vowels of the alphabet. And so, we'd stand, take a deep breath and forcefully release our letters into the air: "AAAAAAAA, EEEEEEE, IIIIIIIII, OOOOOO, UUU-UUUUU." And wouldn't you know it, these very sounds were identical to the ones now reverberating through the cellar, though I doubted that Miss Crouse was in the back passageway giving an English lesson.

Within seconds, the girl's voice had rocketed to a higher pitch, more like a scream. Actually, it was a scream, and she had company. A male voice had joined the duet, sounding remarkably like a pig's grunt. More *"UH, UH, UH, UH"* than the crystal pronunciation we were going for in Miss Crouse's class. Really, C-minus work.

What the hell was going on? I had ruled out my original murder scenario, along with the diction lesson. In fact, I now had a pretty good idea what was happening. Yeah, I had yet to turn fourteen but not completely dumb. Naturally, I decided to check out my suspicions.

I edged into the shadowy passageway and saw the two lying there. I certainly didn't want to scare anyone, cause a heart attack or anything. So I did the only thing that I could do, and hid behind a nearby column and watched. The gloomy walkway connected my building to 40 West Tremont, but no one was about to use this spooky shortcut at night. Except for these two naked teenagers lying on a beat-up mattress in the corner. And they didn't seem to mind being there at all.

A dim light bulb hanging from a slender chain cast shadows on the pair. It was hard to tell where the girl's body ended and her boyfriend's began. Their bodies were twisted together in a mound of wet flesh. I couldn't see the guy's face, only his hairy ass that kept pumping up and down, a frightening sight that was spotlighted by the overhead bulb. His back was slick with sweat that shimmered as he grunted away. Apparently he was working very hard.

I was terrified though I have to admit not necessarily in a bad way. So this was the great adult "secret" that kids on the block babbled on about. My immediate fear was that my pounding heart would give me away.

I had a good idea who was on the bottom of that fleshy heap. Anita Bonita, her hair a tangled mess, had her legs straight up in the air before wrapping them around the guy's sweaty back, pulling him closer. Really, a very flexible girl. By now, the syllable duel had reached a peak with "AHHHS" and "UHS" going back and forth like a Ping-Pong match.

Anita then turned, and I could clearly see her full face. Her eyes were shut tight, her mouth wide open. And then I freaked—after all the noise between the two, Anita was dead still, frozen, even as her partner grunted on. Then her face suddenly came to life, twisted into a mask of agony—and she had stopped breathing. I used to play that game myself to see how long I could hold my breath. But this wasn't that game. Anita Goldman, also known as Anita Bonita, eighteen years old from 50 West Tremont Avenue was about to die here in this creepy cellar. This was the end of her.

I might have been wrong on that one.

First, Anita violently exhaled, followed instantly by a very short religious prayer. *"Oh—My—GOOOOOOOD!!"*

And then Anita screamed.

And screamed again.

And again.

I found it hard to believe that any human was capable of reaching such astronomical decibel levels and was convinced that Anita had made her way into the *Guinness Book of World Records.* I would think quite an accomplishment breaking this particular sound barrier.

The screams didn't seem to bother her boyfriend, who at the moment was preoccupied with his own concerns. His pogo-stick of an ass was picking up steam. Unlike Anita, he didn't bother to bring God into the situation. Just some four-letter words that he let loose in between his pig grunts. Suddenly, his head whipped around, veins bulging from his tattooed neck. He shouted out one last *"F-U-C-K!"* followed by a strangling noise coming from the back of his throat. The guy obviously had a career in radio should murder mysteries make a comeback. He was finally done, plopping his head onto Anita's breast, then murmuring a sweet nothing to his beloved.

"You are some hot fuckin' bitch, 'Nita!"

Real nice. But no flowers?

For her part, Anita seemed content to lie there, twiddling the guy's crotch. You would think she'd want to break for a commercial.

The ups-and-downs had seriously given me the shakes. My T-shirt was soaked through from being trapped in this stuffy corner space. But that might not have been the reason.

The happy pair were lying on their backs now, and I had a clear view of them. I'd never seen a naked woman before not counting the *Playboy* magazine that Sammy slipped me on the sly one afternoon. A film of sweat covered Anita's body, and under the dim light bulb she seemed to glow. My eyes traveled from her large-nippled breasts to the dark patch between her legs. I couldn't keep my eyes off her nakedness or stop my mind from racing to "bad thoughts." I mean, would playing doctor with Anita really be such a bad idea after all?

I kept staring, lost in the naked sight of Anita Bonita when suddenly it hit me that I was way past laundry time. Rosie was not going to be happy—I warned her about this cellar! Neither Anita nor her friend seemed in a hurry to leave, just waiting for round two and getting primed for another screaming match. I could see that Anita's exploration of her boyfriend's crotch was starting to pay off.

Whatever, the situation was a problem since I needed to get going. I didn't think a warm greeting was in the cards if I stepped out into the open and greeted my two newfound friends. I mean, how was I exactly going to break the ice? ("So, Anita, what *about* those Yankees?")

I needed to escape and stay alive.

The two had been distracted when I first slipped behind the column and out of view. It would be tougher now making a clean getaway. But I had no choice. I shut my eyes and willed myself to become invisible. Then I made my move, tiptoeing from my hideout before busting down the passageway to freedom. The laundry would have to wait. Better to deal with Mom than Anita and her boyfriend at this exact moment.

I barged through the wooden cellar door to escape, but before slamming it shut I heard one more scream splitting the night. It was nothing like the ones earlier. This sound was filled with venom. Anita Bonita was yelling at the top of her lungs.

"PAUL!

"PAUL WOLF-EN-THAAAL!"

CHAPTER 24

Back in the Cellar

I thought I was home-free when I didn't see Anita
around the building the next two days. I had slipped into
my apartment after school in case of an ambush, but
Anita had failed to pounce. By now, she must had shrugged
off my Peeping Tom act, maybe even had a good laugh
knowing that she had turned on this dumb kid. Just like the
time she played doctor with Fred. Okay, she was older now,
but it only seemed fair to give this other little guy a preview
of the world to come. Hope he enjoyed it, and God bless.

Only it didn't work out that way. Apparently no Wolfenthal child could ever look upon the body of Anita Bonita
without paying the price.

I learned *that* fact of life when a letter was left under my
apartment door.

Mom had picked it up before coming into my room to
hand it over. My name was printed in bold letters on the
sealed envelope.

"A love letter?" she joked, but curious.

I didn't recognize the handwriting but had a strong sus-
picion who it came from.

"Must be Sammy's party invitation I've been waiting
for," I lied, already dreading the bad news waiting for me.

"Any pretty girls going to be there?" Mom went on, happily prying.

I was about to tell Rosie that this naked girl with incredible round breasts was going to be my date—and, Mom, good news—she's Jewish! And, hey, remember, she's practically family already, once showing her vagina to little Freddy.

But I thought I'd keep the stupidity to myself.

Instead. "Aw, ma, can't you cut it out?" Better to put on the self-conscious, innocent kid act.

I went to my bedroom and sat down on the rug, holding the envelope with both hands. I could feel my heart racing. The envelope seemed to be pulsating with hot energy. Something dangerous was inside. But my X-ray vision wasn't working that night, so I had no choice. Nervously, I tore it open.

No good ever came from anonymous letters, and this one was no exception. Inside was a sheet of paper with a single handwritten sentence in block letters.

MEET ME IN THE LAUNDRY CELLAR TONIGHT. NINE P.M.

Well, I first thought how rude it was to write a letter without signing your name. Not to mention that I was terribly busy that night working on my cure for cancer and preparing for my debut at Carnegie Hall.

Crap. What did Anita Bonita have in store for me? I knew she wasn't inviting me down for a game of "Who can scream the loudest when naked?" Nope, that definitely wasn't it—this was no love letter. I was more concerned that she, along with her tattooed boyfriend, was planning to dismember me and dump my body parts into the Hudson River.

I looked at the letter again, and decided to do the only thing that I could do. I ignored it. No way was I going to meet Anita in the laundry cellar late that night. Or any other night. I just needed to stay clear away from her.

There was only one problem with my strategy. Apparently, Anita disagreed and was unwilling to take "No!" for an answer. The next night a second letter with my name arrived under the door. Mom handed it over, but more suspicious this time around. "Another party invitation?" she asked dryly. "You must be quite popular."

I could feel blood rushing to my face as I reached for the envelope. Mom was onto me, and my world was becoming more complicated. Back in my bedroom, I opened the envelope. Again, a single page with a handwritten sentence. This one read: *MEET ME IN THE LAUNDRY CELLAR TONIGHT. NINE P.M. OR ELSE!!*

I thought the note was a bit of overkill, first underlining the threatening part, and then including *two* exclamation marks. I got the message, no need to hit me over the head.

So that night I made a silent plea for help to the Big Guy, barely calmed my shakes, and went back down into the building cellar. Only this time the place was still. Not a peep. Or a person.

Where was Anita?

It was just then that someone clamped a paper bag over my head. This time I was the one screaming, scared out of my wits. I ripped the bag off my head, letting out a long shriek, only to see Anita smugly standing there.

"What the hell are you *doing*, Anita?" I howled.

"That'll teach you to be a snoop," Anita said, not mean, but not friendly.

"That was really lousy."

Anita wasn't in a sympathetic mood. "You're too young to be a pervert," she went on. "How old are you anyway, fourteen, fifteen?"

"Thirteen."

I was still on edge. Where was this going?

"You're big for your age."

"Not really."

"Well, I'm sure you'll grow up big and strong like your brother."

If she still was so hot for Fred, why wasn't she bothering

him? In any case, Anita kept chit-chatting away, which was fine with me. At least I wasn't about to be chopped into pieces and thrown into the river. A relief. Just two old friends schmoozing about nothing much.

It was then that Anita grabbed my hand and pulled me toward the dark passageway. On the floor was the battered, dirty old mattress, still recovering from Anita and her boyfriend's workout.

I stopped in my tracks.

"Anita!"

"Oh, Paul, you're just a kid. I only want to talk. Sit down. Relax."

Actually I felt a bit insulted by the "just a kid" remark. I mean, I was starting to discover hair on parts of my body where it had never grown before. Anita should keep that kid stuff to herself but thought it best to let it go. Anyway, I sat down on the mattress.

Anita then eased onto the mattress, and we sat cross-legged facing each other. Two Indians at a powwow. This was okay. Anita actually was a beautiful girl, even more so close up. Her face was caught in the dark shadows, giving her a mysterious glow, but that was as far as I was letting my imagination go.

"Paul, what you did the other night was a very bad thing," she began earnestly. "A very bad thing. This was a very private moment between two adults."

I was content to sit there quietly and be lectured to, but I was already having some problems with Anita's logic. Okay, I was wrong to watch. But what about an eighteen-year-old girl, doing very, very naughty things on a dirty mattress in the building cellar with some tattooed Hells Angel guy. I, for one, disapproved. But, hey, live and let live.

Anita was still talking, but I was already losing interest in our heart-to-heart talk. Best to be patient, give her a few more minutes, and be on my way.

"By the way, Paul," she went on. "Did you tell anyone, but anyone, what you saw here the other night?"

I was actually planning to tell Sammy. I mean, what kind of best friend would I be without filling him in on the details with every grunt and groan. But I had yet to catch up with the guy, so I told Anita what she wanted to hear. "Nope, your secret is completely safe with me."

"That's really what I wanted to talk to you about," she said calmly. "You can't tell anyone, ever. You must promise to keep this between you and me."

"Absolutely, Anita. You and me. Our secret." I gave Anita a reassuring smile, then told her: "I'm glad we had this talk, but I have to go now. My mom worries when I'm out too late."

"That's excellent, Paul, good to know you can be trusted," she said, nodding. "And because I believe you, I want to show you something before you leave."

And like that Anita pulled her peasant blouse straight over her head.

I slurped in a sharp breath of air. The cellar atmosphere had suddenly turned heavy, and scarier.

Even in the darkened space, Anita's body shimmered. I stared at the swelling of her upturned breasts with their red-tipped erect nipples.

You wouldn't think that such a sight could cause paralysis. But I was frozen in place unable to utter a word. Other parts of my body seemed to work fine though. First I felt the rush of blood to my head. And then I felt something else—a rising in my pants. This wasn't the first time, recalling that day in the courtyard when Anita came by and cast her spell. She now peeked down at my tented pants.

"My, my!" she smiled crookedly.

Then Anita suddenly took my right hand and placed in on her breast.

"How does that feel, Paul?"

The room was spinning. *What the hell was Anita Bonita doing?* Was this another one of her games playing "doctor"? (Yes, I can feel your heart beating, Miss Goldman.) I was trembling, her breast cupped in my hand. I could feel

the spongy soft flesh that molded to my fingers. I instinctively began to squeeze—what else was I supposed to do?
Anita then gripped my index finger and ran it back and forth
on her nipple. It responded, instantly puffing up.

"Jesus, Anita!" I cried out.

The evil smile again.

The shakes were going bad now when Anita took my left
hand to her other breast and did the nipple thing again. Here
I was, with my two hands squeezing away on Anita
Bonita's breasts, looking like I was testing melons in the
market. I can honestly say though that squeezing Anita's
breasts was an entirely other experience.

"Anita—*Anita*."

"Yes, Paul?"

And just then I felt some sort of electric jolt. A circular
wet spot had suddenly sprouted on my pants.

Shit!

Anita nodded, seeming satisfied. "Emission accomplished," she smirked,

Just a lousy joke. At least, I thought so.

And then, like that, my getting-to-know-you with Anita
was over. She removed my hands one by one from her
breasts and slipped back on her blouse.

And now she wasn't smiling. No jokes. Her girly voice
had become deadly serious. "Now, Paul, if you ever happen
to let on to anyone what you saw with my boyfriend, I will
be forced to tell him what you've done to me. And such a
terrible thing."

"B—But you made me—" I sputtered.

"And you should know that Tony is a gang member of
the Fordham Baldies, and should he find out that you tried
to rape me, he will cut off your balls."

"Oh," I said, my voice creaking. "But you—"

"No buts, Paul," Anita warned, looking more and more
like the female lead in *The Astounding She-Monster*. "Remember."

Then she did the snip-snip thing with her fingers.

Cute.

But effective.

I got the message and became a true believer vowing forever to keep the secret of Anita Goldman and her dirty deed. Nothing could ever pry that knowledge from my lips. At least that is more or less what I told her. And this time I meant it.

Anita seemed to enjoy doing pantomime. Again, a reminder. Snip-snip. Balls gone. Thank you very much.

I was tempted to congratulate Anita for such a realistic impression, but I didn't think *she* could take a joke. Actually, I was the stupid one for not taking Anita seriously. The girl obviously was a pro when it came to these twisted games, getting an early start with Fred when she was seven. This time it wouldn't be her mom barging into our apartment to defend her honor. I had no doubt that Anita's gangster boyfriend would pay me a visit. The Fordham Baldies were true crazies with a reputation for shaving the heads of people who rubbed them the wrong way. I wasn't scared of a haircut, only interested in keeping body parts that belonged to me.

"Now, be a good boy and go home," Anita said, seeming pleased that her virtue had been protected.

I wasn't about to argue. "Okay," was the best I could do.

Anita followed me to the cellar door. "Careful now," she warned.

As I opened the door to leave, she offered a final bit of advice.

"And Paul," she said, giving me a wink. *That* wink. "You might want to change your pants when you get upstairs."

CHAPTER 25

Hot Cross Buns

*T*he early teens are years of upheaval and turmoil. They are years of physical and glandular change. Let's watch some of these youngsters as they spend their Friday night...

"Shit," Sammy cried out. "I've seen this crapola before."

It was our last day of school before summer break, but JHS 82 was not quite ready to let us go. One more torture session in the school auditorium for a final assembly—some "educational" film called the *Age of Turmoil*. After my shaky run-in with Anita Bonita, I felt like I was living it. I saw no sense watching these creepy kids on screen, nice and clean, and so polite, and obviously from some other planet. Maybe Krypton before it blew up.

Sammy read my mind.

"Where the hell *is* this place—straight out of Archie comics?" Sammy whispered in my ear. "Hey, there's Betty and Veronica."

Sally and Kay are typical teenagers. Their actions may seem excessive, but that is normal for teenagers. For instance, that giggling. Yes, they may seem crude and child-

ish, but they are at the beginning of an experiment in sex adjustment...

"A sex adjustment?" Sammy shook his head, stupefied. "What is this guy talking about, Paul?"

"Sammy, you know," I deadpanned. "It's kind of like getting braces. You go to the doc, and he straightens out your sex."

It was enough to get us cracking up.

"I need a sex adjustment!" one kid shouted out from the back row. A wave of laughter swept across the auditorium. Teachers keeping guard were getting nowhere shushing us quiet as the grainy black-and-white film sputtered on....

Kay and Sally didn't get far with the boys, but they found a substitute, identifying themselves with a glamorous movie actress who was very popular with men, giving them a satisfaction that they couldn't get any other way.

Sammy was back to the movie but only getting more puzzled. "Huh, what the hell is this 'satisfaction'?"

I got the idea, but I kept it to myself. I'd explain it to Sammy later.

"At least this beats the PS 26 assembly," Sammy went on.

"Doesn't take much," I replied.

Sammy's face lit up at the thought, and laughed. "Who could forget that crappy recorder concert?"

"Yeah." I chuckled at the memory. "I'm still pulling needles out of my eyes after listening to those kids."

❧❧❧

PS 26 had its own assembly embarrassment called the Third-Grade Recorder Concert, a performance like no other on Earth. Really.

Armed with a plastic bag containing their magical instrument, some forty third-graders trudged up to the auditorium stage while the rest of us prepared for the worst. The
kids didn't let us down. Their instrument, a cheap wooden
hollow tube, gave off a sound remarkably identical to that
of squealing rats caught in a steel death trap. Our principal
told us that we should be proud of these "talented musicians" that, I guess, represented the hopes and dreams of PS
26 as future recorder virtuosos. Too bad for the New York
Philharmonic Orchestra that no kid ever wanted to keep up
with the recorder after the trauma of his third-grade performance.

So we sat in assembly dressed in our required white
shirts and blue ties listening to the recorder kids open with a
version of the hit song, "The Itsy Bitsy Teeny Weenie Yellow Polka-Dot Bikini." But I might have been wrong about
that one. The beauty of the ensemble was that each listener
could sit back and imagine just about any song coming from
the ruckus on stage, since no one was quite sure what was
being played. That included the recorder kids.

It wouldn't have been so bad if the group wasn't produc-
ing the same ear-splitting sounds that the Japanese used during World War II to torture prisoners of war. On second
thought, nothing the Japs devised could ever have matched
the agony we suffered through.

I did, however, consider rising from my seat during the
concert, holding my hands up to surrender, and beg to be
shot through the head.

At the very least, I hoped to be buried in a deep, dark
hole where this noise couldn't penetrate.

The only light at the end of the tunnel was in watching
Mrs. Serrantino, grinning ear to ear, as she settled into her
position in front of the group. She would then lift her baton
high over her head before forcefully bringing the stick
down—a dramatic downbeat that ignited the recorder kids,
and likely awakened the dead. With her back to the audi-
ence, her enormous rear end shook wildly as she passionate-

ly led the kids in a yelping rendition of "Hot Cross Buns."

It was a song so perfectly appropriate given our view of Mrs. Serrantino's ass.

◌◌◌

The movie ended, and not a moment too soon. I'm not sure we were any less confused as teenagers having now experienced the *Age of Turmoil*, but as least we didn't have to hang out with those kids on screen. And so we went back to our classroom for our goodbyes before heading out to summer.

Miss Crouse looked forlorn as we lumbered into 424. "Boys and girls, this is our last day," she declared solemnly as we took our seats. "You have been such a wonderful class!"

Plotz mockingly rubbed his eyes, sarcastic and stupid as usual. "I think I'm gonna cry," he called out.

I really wanted to smack him.

Miss Crouse moved on to the business at hand. "Now your report cards, and I am proud to say that you are all graduates of seventh grade."

Of course we still had two more years to go to get our diploma. But I wasn't about to make a big deal of it.

Our teacher announced our names alphabetically. Naturally, I was one of the last ones called. "Paul," she said, giving me her sweet smile.

I made my way to the front where she handed me my card. My grades didn't point to a career as a brain surgeon, but Miss Crouse wrote that I had made "a lovely effort in my studies." At least she didn't write that I played well with others. I could only imagine what she came up with for Plotz's report card. I had a few ideas myself: Brush up on bathing. Should make an effort to develop a human personality. I really could go on.

"Now is my time to say goodbye to you, my children,"

she said, as if bidding us off to some distant land. Always the fairy princess.

I was going to miss her all the same.

In truth, though, I was way past sitting still in Room 424. The 710 chain gang hadn't been such a bad group after all. Yeah, a few exceptions for sure. But it was time to get moving on with my life. My summer was waiting, and I was ready to call it a day at JHS 82.

Only I couldn't have known that this day was just beginning.

CHAPTER 26

School Daze

The dismissal bell set us free from JHS 82. In an instant, the streets around the school were jammed with hundreds of us joyfully embracing the thought of the next two months. Summer vacation. My sights were set on a place called Tall Timber near Peekskill in upstate New York. It was one big clan-fest, with my family and cousins, aunts and uncles. We called it "the country," though any place with trees and grass qualified. In truth, the rundown bungalow colony had seen better days. But Tall Timber was magical in its way, a Bronx kid's paradise with grass ball fields, a swimming pool, and all the freedom to roam day and night.

But whatever thoughts I had of summer escape were jolted when a police cruiser, lights flashing, came barreling down University Avenue, skidding to a stop at the main school entrance. Our schoolyard celebration suddenly was over. Something was wrong and serious for police to come barging into the yard.

Two cops quickly exited their car and hustled into the school. I immediately recognized one. Officer Antoine Brown. His appearance instantly ramped up my anxiety.

Keira Jones, a classmate, dashed up to me. "Hey, what's going on?" she asked.

"No idea," I replied tensely.

I hung back while a crowd of kids, buzzing with chatter, crammed around the school entrance. All waiting for an answer.

We didn't have to wait long.

Sammy came running up to me out of breath. "Hey, Paul, didya hear, didya hear?"

"Sammy, so what the hell is going on?"

Sammy was still gulping air, trying to get his words out.

I could instantly feel the atmosphere changing around the school. And it wasn't a good feeling at all.

About a half-dozen kids from my class started coming up, circling Sammy and me. The word was out, and they all had that same strange look. Bewilderment.

"Paul!" Sammy shouted. "The cops got him!"

"What are you talking—"

"The asshole who stole your clarinet!"

"Sammy, they already—"

And before I could say another word, Officer Brown brought out a kid in handcuffs.

Plotz.

That feeling again, something bad in the air.

How could this be happening?

Alan Plotz?

No!

I ran up to Officer Brown, who was looking real pissed off. It was the type of look that took over when you knew you screwed up.

He recognized me immediately. "Paul, you can't be here," Brown said sternly but unsteadily. "You gotta stay back!"

It hit me all at once, staring at this obnoxious, putrid kid cuffed to the cop. "Plotz! *You* did this?"

Plotz, head down, sniveling, with tears and snot masking his face, reminded me of another jerk I once knew.

"Why, Plotz? *Why*?"

Plotz didn't say a word, just snorted out grief as he shuffled by me.

Sammy came up and pulled me back as the second officer put his hand on top of Plotz's head and guided him into the squad car. The cruiser then sped away with roof lights still flashing.

I tried to make some sense. I could only think of Joe, locked up at Spofford, that horror of a place. Four months in. What about *him*? *Jesus.*

Sammy eased up to me, his hand on my shoulder. "I overheard the cops," he said. "Plotz took your clarinet, then snuck it into Joe's locker. It was a setup."

"What!"

"It was Dee-Dee, Dee-Dee O'Hara. She saw Plotz do it, but she'd been real scared, didn't want to get involved. I guess it finally was too much for her to keep quiet."

"But Joe's been at—"

"I know, Paul. Just shitty, bro."

My head was spinning, and I closed my eyes. Nothing had changed when I opened them.

Sammy looked at me, worried.

"This sucks, just sucks, Sammy. How could this happen?"

Sammy didn't have to say a word. We both knew.

A wave of guilt came crashing down, and my head spun faster. I felt responsible but didn't know exactly why. Only that I did know why—I should have believed more in my friend. Joe had been out there on his own, with no one to rely on, trying to stay cool. Maybe in some way he was counting on me to help keep the demons away. But I let him down, big time. He never stood a chance. Just a black kid in a white neighborhood, an easy target for crap thrown his way by the Plotzes of the world. I wasn't really any different from anyone else, actually worse, pretending to be a friend. And then forgetting about him at Spofford, leaving him to suffer, alone, in that hellhole.

I could have screamed right then and there outside of 82. But what difference would it have made?

I closed my eyes again and this time saw stars flashing in and out.

It didn't take more than a few minutes for the schoolyard to settle down. Kids were more interested in getting their summers under way, rushing from the school for home. Plotz in cuffs was already a memory. For them.

Sammy hung back, leaning against the school gate.

"Real sorry about Joe," he said quietly, and meant it. "He got shafted. Screwed royally."

"All of this is so wrong," I murmured. "I should've been a better friend."

Sammy was about to say something else but bagged the thought.

We just stood there for a minute, silence between us.

"I gotta go," Sammy said, hesitating. And then he eased off the school gate.

We both realized that this would be the last we'd see of each other for the next two months. I was off to "the country." Sammy would stay to swelter on these Bronx streets.

I called out as he turned to leave, not wanting to let go of him yet. "Hey, Sammy, stay out of trouble this summer." It was enough to break the gloom.

Turning back around, he pumped a clenched fist and shouted, "I was born to cause trouble!"

We both let out a small laugh, a moment's relief, and a much better way to part for the summer.

I found myself the last kid standing outside of 82, lost in thought. It was then that Dee-Dee quietly edged up to me. I hadn't caught sight of her before, but here she was—and looking at me with sad, guilty eyes. A look we had in common.

"Let's go, Paul," she gently whispered. Then she took my hand, something she'd never dared before, and we walked together that way for home.

CHAPTER 27

A Bad Day

I had a day to go in the neighborhood before my summer breakout to Tall Timber. I still couldn't shake the scene in the schoolyard. Plotz. A self-made loser. But even in his own stupid mind, how could he have been so evil. Setting up Joe this way, cause this hurt. So seriously wrong and impossible to forgive.

Too much guilt floated in my head. I heard Joe had gone back to his home in Harlem to be with his mom. I wondered if I'd ever see him again, though I seriously doubted whether he was in a mood for a reunion.

So I found myself on my Schwinn desperate to find an escape from the craziness. I decided to journey over to the greenest pasture in the Bronx. Yankee Stadium. This was not just the Babe's House, but home to every die-hard Yankee fan. I was one of them.

The afternoon was gray, with a big storm brewing and threatening to wash out the game. I gave it a shot anyway, speeding across the Concourse, down 161st Street and past the mom-and-pop stores selling Yankee souvenirs. A shower of sparks flew down from the overhead EL as a train rumbled into the station, its eardrum-piercing brakes filling the neighborhood.

For me, it was all part of the natural music of the streets.

I always felt the same chill coming to Yankee Stadium. The building seemed to rise up off the streets as if lording over the entire neighborhood. Going to a baseball game was as close to a religious experience as I'd ever known. At night, the explosive sound of more than 60,000 fans against the brilliant, blinding floodlights coming off the top deck of the stadium made any baseball fan believe that there was a God. And He wore pinstripes.

I chained my bike to a lamp-post, and paid a buck at a ticket counter for my bleacher seat. I made my way to the right-field stands, taking in the players in the outfield warming up. It wasn't hard to imagine old Yankee ghosts like DiMaggio and the Babe hovering about—though I managed to push out of my mind last year's World Series championship game. The painful memory of Bill Mazeroski's ninth-inning homer that killed my Bronx Bombers had broken my heart. I was having enough angst for the day.

On my fifteen-inch, black-and-white RCA television the Yanks were small, blurry gray figures lifeless of color. At the stadium, I felt like I had been transported to another planet altogether. The field was huge and dazzling green. The Yankees themselves looked almost too "real" in their pinstripes, far from their fuzzy TV images or posed pictures on my baseball cards. These guys were living, breathing beings, and almost close enough to touch.

My cheap seat, first-row bleachers, was directly on top of the right-field wall—the best seat in the house as far as I was concerned. Only some 300 feet from home plate. The short porch was home-run territory for the big boys, and I'd brought my glove should a ball come my way.

There was something else about the bleacher seats that I found mystifying. After a batter hit a ball into flight, it would take a short second before I actually heard the crack of his bat—it was if my ears couldn't keep up with my eyes. I was told this was physics at work. Light traveling faster than sound. Something like that. Anyway, even if the game was out of sync, I didn't really care. My real concern were the drunks in the section that always managed to spill beer on me.

Right field was Roger Maris territory, the guy now roaming the field getting loose and playing catch with Mickey in center. The M&M Boys. What a pair. The two were on a tear, clubbing homers at a record pace. Talk was that the Babe's record was in danger—sixty homers in a single season! Could that even be possible? No way, though it was fun watching the guys chase.

Roger ambled over to the dirt warning track in front of me, and I clearly saw his face as he glanced blankly into the crowd. We bleacher bums screamed his name, but the guy remained stone-faced, seeming not especially glad to see us there. I gave him a break. Roger was having a rough time with the press. The sports guys loved Mickey, declaring that if any home-run hitter deserved to be worshipped, it was Mantle. I understood, Mick had it all: looks, personality, and this natural gift for playing the game. But something about Roger got to me. The guy just looked unhappy most of the time, and I felt bad for him.

It was then that the first raindrops hit. The bleacher bums let out a loud "Shit!" in unison, and within a minute the stadium was being battered by heavy rain. A washout. Damn.

The storm immediately pushed everyone into motion. The Yanks warming up on the field sprinted to their dugout while the rest of us hustled into the stadium walkways for cover. Not a single pitch had been thrown, and I was bummed. Just a crapped out start to the summer.

So I came up with a Plan B.

I knew the routine. Players waited for the game to be officially called before leaving the stadium. The plan: wait at the players' gate with a baseball in hand with a single aim in mind—to get Yankee autographs. I mean, the phony signatures on baseball cards were one thing. But to get my guys to personally sign a ball for Paul Wolfenthal—well, kind of like Moses getting God to sign over the commandments.

I picked up a new baseball at a concession stand and traipsed back to get my bike. Then I went over to the players' gate. Another five or six kids were already there with the same idea. The storm had seriously kicked up, and I could barely see their faces through the sheets of rain bombarding us. But we all carried the same determination, and a few raindrops were not going to get in our way.

Still, it wouldn't have been a bad idea if our Yankees got moving more quickly from the clubhouse.

And so we waited.

Twenty minutes passed. The storm wasn't letting up, the dark sky flashing with lightning bolts. The pavement had turned into a lake, and I found myself standing sneaker deep in a big puddle. My Yankee chums, barely visible, had become spectral creatures rising out of a lagoon.

What a nothing day, rotten luck, and I was finally giving up.

I puffed out a breath, got on my bike, thinking how the hell I would make it home.

Just then the side stadium door opened. And out hustled a group of men bundled in raincoats, a few holding umbrellas.

I jumped off my bike, letting it crash to the ground.

For a moment all of us kids just stood there in awe. Our Yankees. And less than an arm's length away as they tried to hurry past us.

Then the explosion of pleas as we reached out to our heroes with our baseballs.

"Whitey, can you please sign..."

"Hey Mickey, Roger..."

"There's Yogi!"

"Moose, Moose."

There they were, our guys—Maris, Mantle, Richardson, Boyer, Kubek, Howard, Berra, McDougald, Skowron, Ford, Ditmar, Turley, hurrying to their cars.

I thought I had died and gone to Yankee heaven.

Not all was what I expected. I was stunned as Roger and

Clete Boyer came by with cigarettes in their mouths. My Yankees didn't smoke, as I mentally tried to make sense of the sight.

Tony Kubek, the shortstop, rushed by. "Sorry kid, not now." At least he had said a few words to me.

The players piled into their cars, moving past us. Through his windshield, Mickey gave me a short wave, Yogi a brief smile—but not a single autograph—and then they too were gone.

Soaked to the bone, I pocketed my baseball, untouched by a Yankee hand, climbed on my bike, and headed home in the monsoon.

Just a bad, bad day. The worst. No game, no autographs, and now I was stuck in a lousy thunderstorm pedaling my Schwinn, just trying to make it home. Maybe I was being punished for some previous sin, not that I didn't deserve it. But at the moment I really needed a break.

The rain was not letting up as I skidded through puddles along the Concourse. Impossible. I had taken off my glasses, thinking that would help. They were useless in the storm, but I wasn't faring much better without them. The blinding rain, with gusts of wind belting me, had nearly knocked me off my bike. I had no choice but to pull over and find a place to wait it out. And I was about to, but then the strangest thing.

I first heard the screech before I felt the smash, metal on metal. Confusing. Sound then hit. Sound then hit. What? That wasn't how physics was meant to work. First hit, *then* sound. Hit then sound. Hit then sound.

I had been hit, hard, metal on metal, and the sound kept coming, too loud, too loud. Another sound, a frantic car horn. Blaring.

It took a second before I could put it together. My bike was being crushed. A terrifying crunch of noise, and I just knew that my Schwinn was dead and gone.

My world was now moving slowly. I thought I was flying. And then I was. Superman. In the air, soaring upward.

So this is how it feels? But it wasn't right. Very wrong.

Arms and legs flapping in the air. Hardly a smooth flight. And then I was tumbling back down to earth. I wasn't scared really, just watching myself in slow motion, looking ridiculous, wondering when this was going to all end. How this would end.

I landed, hit something hard, too hard. Then silence. Not a car horn now. Not a single sound.

The sky getting darker.

Rain hitting my face.

It wouldn't stop raining. Goddamn. Goddamn.

Rain…rain…rain.

Go away, come back some other day.

Shit, what a lousy day.

Bummer.

Mom…Dad…Fred…Sammy…Joe…Benji.

Too much darkness.

And that was that.

PART III

1961-62

CHAPTER 28

Back from the Dead

I survived.

The driver of the souped-up hot rod that hit me walked away without a scratch. Good for him. Yeah, the bumper of his car had to be replaced, and my blood had to be cleaned off his windshield. A bit of a mess but not a problem for the car wash. As for the guy, he spent a week in jail for drunk driving. Tough luck, but what can you do?

The bastard.

I can say that I wasn't as lucky. For a while, I was paying a visit to a black world, floating around, unconsciously praying that this was not a one-way ride. Does the word "coma" sound too dramatic? The doctors told me when I finally got back to Earth that I had been out for five days. This was a bit too close to my Woodlawn Cemetery pals than I was comfortable with.

Actually, I had no idea what space I'd been inhabiting. For all I knew this dark void was where you wound up when you left your Earthly being. Kind of a way station before the Big Decision is made. In my case I thought I might be in deep trouble.

My decision to stay home from the previous Yom Kippur services alone might very well have pushed God from entering me into the "good" ledger. And we Jews all knew what happened then. I can say for sure that pissing off the Big Guy was not a good idea.

Still, after all I'd been through, it didn't seem right that I'd end up in that other place. I already had spent a year in hell sitting next to Alan Plotz in seventh grade. Also, I was sure that Plotz was on a fast track to land here. Could life be so cruel to sentence me to eternal damnation with the fat fuck? Excuse the language, but I wasn't in a great mood when Plotz came to mind. No bygones-be-bygones. To hell with him, so to speak. He'd just better keep to his side of the underworld when he came around.

As it was, I was glad to return to the living, vowing to sit through every minute of the next Yom Kippur service. The doc later told me I'd been lucky. The coma wasn't exactly like taking a nap, he explained, but more a brain thing that had shut down. The idea was to get out of that mental pot-hole and back to the real world. Still, who wanted to face this reality? I'd been hit with a fractured skull, along with a shattered leg and five broken ribs. It struck me that I couldn't even move, strait-jacketed into place in a body cast. My leg was also wrapped in plaster and elevated onto some contraption.

My brain, though, was working just fine, making sure that I was feeling every blast of hot, excruciating pain coming my way. I hadn't been conscious for more than a few minutes when I was set to belt out a rendition of "Oh, Jesus! I Can't Take This Any More!" Kind of a religious hymn with a serious edge.

Still, every misfortune had its upside, and quickly I was developing a super appreciation for drugs. I particularly liked the ones that put some wacky pictures into my head and a drowsy smile on my face. So there was that.

Even my eyeballs were hurting, but when I managed to open them later that day I felt nothing but relief. There were Mom, Dad, and Fred, all looking real happy-sad. I had to give them credit. They were putting on their best smiley imitation, pretending that their Paulie-Boy was rousing from a restful snooze instead of some creature that had crawled up to earth from deep underground.

"Hi, honey," Mom chirped unsteadily, finally breaking the ice.

My mind was still dopey from the drugs, and I wasn't sure if this woman was even my mother or just another out-of-body hallucination. In any case, I went along and gave Rosie a smile, then my first conscious words in a while.

"Where am I, Mom?" This seemed like an intelligent question to me given that I wasn't even sure if I was still on the planet.

"You're in the hospital. University Hospital. You've had an accident. On your bike. But the doctors say that you are going to be all right."

That was good news since I decided I really wanted to live. A flash of bad memory hit me: the death of my Schwinn. More a sound running through my head. An angry, painful screech of sound followed by the crushing noise of metal on metal.

I shook my head to wipe out the thought.

Dad was now at my side, and took my hand, studying me with his worried, sky-blue eyes.

"Hey, Dad, who's doing the booklets now?" I asked jokingly to change the mood. It was good to hear him laugh.

Dad was the leader of the Max Wolfenthal Orchestra, a group of seven musicians that played weddings and bar mitzvahs at social halls on the Lower East Side when he wasn't working long hours at the family supermart in the South Bronx. My job each week was to paste dozens of black-and-white photographs of the happy couple or bar mitzvah boy into booklets of prayers and songs. By the time I was finished, my head was spinning from the fumes of rubber cement glue. Actually, it wasn't all that different from what I was feeling from the stuff coming out of the hospital IV.

"Saving the booklets for you back home," Dad replied,

lightening up a bit. "But, Paul, how are you feeling?"

Dad was having a hard enough time seeing his broken boy. No need to smack him with the truth. The drugs were wearing off and the "Oh, Jesus!" moment was coming back with spikes of pain starting to hit. It was just as well that Fred came over before I lied to Dad.

"Hey, pork 'n' beans." Fred had given me that nickname long ago. I still had no idea what he meant, but I let him slide now. He slowly shook his head, as if to say, "What did you do now, little brother?"

But I could tell he was glad to have me back.

"Gotta get you back on the court," he said. "Can't have you just lying around here."

I thought that the accident might have set back my career on the Knicks, but it was good seeing Fred. His own story came to mind. He actually played with a broken right arm for his varsity school team one season., dribbling and shooting the ball with only his left. Amazing to see. I imagined my own one-legged game, hobbling up and down the court on crutches—more Jerry Lewis than Jerry West. I let the stupid thought go, afraid I'd crack up laughing. Way too much hurt for the payoff.

Anyway, the Wolfenthal family spent that afternoon together, happily enough considering the circumstances. It would be a long haul coming back, and I wasn't sure what I was coming back to. I was a mess and only hoped that I'd feel like a human being again instead of a collection of body parts, each one screaming for mercy. At least I had opened my eyes, so I guess that was a good start.

A few days later curiosity finally pushed me to check myself out. The nurse reluctantly handed me a mirror, and I took a long look. Monster scary. A scar already was forming down the left side of my face. Shades of black, blue, and brown blotched my face. Really not very fashionable with the browns and blues clashing. I wondered if this was another one of God's jokes, turning me into one of the horror film creatures that I loved. A Funny Guy but with a perverted sense of humor if you asked me.

I was grateful though. Death didn't appeal to me now that I had a new perspective of the deal. I was even having second thoughts about that graveyard obsession of mine. I vowed to make amends for all the bad I'd done to mankind, a list I'd put together later. For now, I needed to heal, get better, even with the world still spinning without me. Eighth grade at JHS 82 would be put on hold. I'd miss hanging out with my buddies and, well, there was Dee-Dee O'Hara. My brains had been scrambled, but I wasn't about to forget walking hand in hand with her that afternoon after Plotz's arrest. I wanted to hold that hand again.

And so I rested, settling into my new reality, and waited to get back to life.

CHAPTER 29

Killing Superman

I left University Hospital in a wheelchair two weeks later, finally going home. Fred wheeled me past the
checkout desk and toward the exit with Mom and Dad
on my side. A few hospital visitors jumped out of my way
as they checked out the scary, mummified kid with a band-
aged head and casted leg. It would take another month before the plaster cast was hacked off along with all the hearts
and flowers my friends had drawn. Other images were less
poetic. Sammy had sketched a woman's breast. At least I
think that's what it was. Giving it away was a note in black
marker beneath his drawing that said "You Boob!" That's
Sammy.

"Hey, Paul, you're not leaving without saying good-bye,
are you?"

Nurse Helen came up to my chair and put her hand on
my shoulder. She had taken really good care of me, putting
up with my moans and groans, and feeding me my chocolate pudding and applesauce. I loved her in that you-are-the-
most-wonderful-nurse-in-the-whole-wide-world way, and
would miss her.

"Thanks a lot," I said, choking up.

"You are going to be fine," she said firmly, nodding her head.

A few tears started up, and I turned my head to avoid the embarrassment. Nurse Helen bent down and kissed my cheek. I could feel the spot as Fred pushed me toward the hospital doors.

My body still felt like I had gone fifteen rounds with Sonny Liston, but it was great knowing I was on my way home. Fred wheeled me down the street to our apartment building, a short ride from the hospital. It was the middle of summer, but the weather that day was more like fall, and I closed my eyes letting the cool air wash over me. I breathed deeply, filling my lungs, and feeling alive.

"Hey, Paul, how about a game of knucks when we get upstairs?" Fred teased, as we rolled down Tremont Avenue. My brother was at it again. Knucks was a card game that involved taking the deck and smashing the knuckles of your opponent with the intent of making them bleed. Needless to say, I had bled enough.

"We better stick to gin rummy," I told him, and we both had a laugh.

Mom and Dad buzzed around my shoulder with all sorts of nice promises. Mom already had my menu planned with her BLT's and malteds and legendary meatballs and spaghetti. Sounded fantastic. Rosie was intent on fattening me up after weeks of hospital food. In fact, I had shrunk. The coma diet was one I wouldn't recommend, though I did go down two pant sizes. Also, I was a year older now having celebrated my birthday in a state of unconsciousness. It wasn't as if I had a blast of a good time there, but at least I lived to turn fourteen.

Fred carried me up the three flights of stairs to apartment 3A. Mom unlocked the door, and I was back home. The apartment sparkled and smelled great. Dad handed back my crutches, and I dragged myself from the kitchen to the living room to get the warm feel of the place again.

"Just as you remember?" Dad asked with a soft smile.

I had been in a coma, but I hadn't lost my mind or my memory.

I wasted no time and hobbled down our long foyer and over to my bedroom. Unlike most of my friends, I had my own room, and it never felt better being back. It must have taken Mom a week to clean, but the place was immaculate with clothes, balls, games, and comics neatly tucked away. Everything in order. That would certainly change once I got back to being a slob.

I plopped onto my bed and surveyed the room, checking out the stenciled pictures of horses that covered each wall the wire basket of balls next to my bed, a container of plastic toy soldiers that I had kept from my younger days.

I couldn't help but notice my large wall poster of Superman flying into space, his left arm pointing skyward, fists clenched, looking for "Truth, Justice and the American Way." At least that was the television version. I had to say, though, that George Reeves didn't quite cut it for me in that baggy costume.

Superman had forever been my hero, and his adventures played out in my treasured comic books that were jammed into a large dresser. The chest stood taller than me, and with its five large drawers had plenty of shelf space for hundreds of comics. I didn't have any real organizing principle at work. Whatever comics fit into the drawers stayed. Those that didn't found their way onto the rug. A real mess, but at least my comics were handy to read.

It didn't take me long to miss the superguy so I hopped over to the chest on my one good leg relishing spending the next hour with him. I balanced myself before pulling out the top drawer. Then the second drawer. The third. Fourth. Fifth...

And then I let loose a shriek that almost put me back in the hospital.

I expect my family thought I'd been run over by another hot-rod that somehow had made its way into my bedroom.

But my situation was worse than that. Far worse, as I stared into the empty drawers.

Every one of my comics was gone. Gone!

I picked up my crutches and staggered around in a panic, a chicken without a head *and* a broken leg. Then I collapsed onto the rug, frantically checking under the bed, crawling over to my closet. The results were all the same. Not a single comic could be found anywhere. The room was stone-cold empty.

Just then Mom hustled in. Taking a look at my face and then the open chest of drawers, she paused and instantly saw the problem. And then she nodded, as if to say, "Paul, you are absolutely not going to be happy with this news."

"My comics!" I pleaded, seeing the doubt in her eyes, praying that my treasured collection was only being held for ransom and that a deal could be worked out.

Mom then hit me with a sledgehammer. "I guess Selma threw them away a few days ago when she came over to straighten up," Mom said sheepishly. "We were in the hospital and she wanted to make sure you were coming home to a clean room." Then she added, hesitantly. "Wasn't that so nice of her?"

"Mom, not my comics!" I cried out.

This time Rosie just gave me the helpless look.

I would have screamed again, but my ribs were already shooting bolts of pain. Besides, who would listen?

The reality had seriously set in. Superman was gone, a victim of the most heinous act of comicide imaginable.

Could Rosie's sister, my beloved Aunt Selma, have been the cold-blooded culprit behind this catastrophe? How could she? And then it suddenly struck me. Her cleaning move hadn't been an act of kindness at all—but vengeance. Yes, revenge had been on her mind all along!

So that was it. Aunt Selma never did forget the accident back in the spring. Yes, I'd nearly killed her kid, my cousin Mitchell. But it had been an accident, and Mitch was okay, just fine. Only that it wasn't fine. Aunt Selma apparently had a long memory and had it in for me all along, lurking in the shadows, waiting for the right time to hit back at her nephew. And that time had come.

ത്തെ

Of course I never meant to hurt my ten-year-old cousin. I swear. It had been a typical Saturday afternoon, and I was over at Montgomery Avenue when Mitch and I decided to head over to Square Pizza. So in a bit of fun I dared Mitch to a race down Montgomery. I admit the race was not exactly a fair one since he was on his two legs and I was on my bike. But he fell for the bait, instantly breaking into a sprint down the sloping avenue. I gave him a healthy head start knowing that he didn't stand a chance as I pushed off.

I was quickly at max speed, closing in on my cuz now pumping his arms wildly, his short legs running at full tilt. I was having a blast, coming up fast on his right side, ready to breeze by. The little guy was dead meat.

"I'm coming through!" I shouted, giving him fair warning.

Mitch was obviously a poor listener. Either that or I was a moron for coming up too fast on the kid's tail. Whatever. I think both of us would agree that the race didn't end well. In that split-second, Mitch cut sharply in front of my bike leaving me with but one choice. I had no other place to go but over him. And so I did.

The collision slammed Mitch facedown to the pavement. It also sent my bike spinning into a cartwheel and catapulting me to the sidewalk. I was shaken up, but okay. I rushed over to Mitch lying on the sidewalk. He was bleeding from his mouth. The left side of his face had a nasty scrape, and his two front teeth were broken.

I gathered Mitch up. He barely whimpered, determined to be the brave soldier. Between the two of us, I was the real coward, and terrified leading the poor kid back to his apartment. You see, Mitch's father, my Uncle Sol, was a butcher and owned large carving knives and…how should I put it?…he could get a bit overexcited at times. The combination of a large, sharp weapon and a hot temper simply didn't appeal to me. Henry VIII came to mind, and at that moment I knew precisely how Ann Boleyn felt the second before her head was lopped off. And that was the optimistic picture going through my mind. At least Ann's execution was quick and neat. I imagined what slow torture Uncle Sol could devise with those long butcher knives upon seeing the state of his eldest child.

I felt terrible for Mitch, I really did, just loved the kid. My survival instinct said to run. But, in reality, I knew there was no way out, no place to hide. I saw with horrific clarity that Sol, Selma, and the Almighty Himself would be after me now.

I supposed I was lucky finding only my Aunt Selma at home when I knocked on 3C. I'd managed to escape from Uncle Sol but not my aunt's scream as she opened the door. She stared in horror at her darling mutilated son and then turned to me with accusing eyes that shouted *What Have You Done?* I stood there in the doorway regretting that Uncle Sol wasn't around to carve me up. So much better than seeing the horrified look on Aunt Selma's face.

Apologies were useless, even if I hadn't been suffering from paralysis of the throat. How could I explain the tire track running down Mitch's T-shirt, or that he looked like he'd been hit by a Mack truck?

Over Aunt Selma's cries of anguish, I slinked back home.

Rosie was waiting for me when I got there, eyes on fire. The word was out. *How could you!* I crept into my bedroom struck by waves of guilt. I thought that this would be the last I'd ever see of my cousin. I wouldn't have blamed Selma and Sol for keeping the family pariah as far away as possible from their kids. My aunt and uncle were very good people—it wasn't their fault that I was their nephew.

In the end, Mitch healed, his teeth were fixed, and life kicked back to normal.

As for me, all was forgiven. Aunt Selma still hugged me each time I came through her door. I sighed with relief. Montgomery Avenue was still welcoming. But the whole forgiveness thing had been an act. I saw that now.

All the while Aunt Selma had been hatching her foul plan. An avenging angel, waiting until her nephew was out of the apartment, then finding an excuse to "help out." And then strike where it hurts him the most.

S'long, Superman.

Superman's demise was nothing short of a death in the family. Okay, a slight exaggeration, but I also don't want to underestimate the trauma that I'd suffered.

❧❧❧

My friends had their own comic book heroes, but none could come close to the indomitable Superman. I fantasized about *being* the Man of Steel, battling it out with the evil genius, Lex Luther, and supervillains' Brainiac and Bizarro. My pillow substituted for any number of evildoers, and feathers flew in the air as I thrashed and punched and crushed my enemy.

By the time I was six, I was fully addicted, hooked on every Superman adventure. My "suppliers" lived in the neighborhood. Mel's candy store was always good for the latest issue filled with three eight-page stories, all for a dime. A new store on Tremont Avenue sold five used comics for a quarter, and was heaven for a comic book junky. Pile upon pile of old comics were stacked on long tables, and I couldn't wait to dive through the stacks. It would take a lot to satisfy my craving. I loaded up on each visit.

I dabbled with other superheroes. Batman, Flash, the Hulk. All second rate. It was Superman who had this mystical hold. The guy was God-like flying above the Earth, peering down from the sky. And what cool powers? Who wouldn't want to fly and have X-ray vision, shrug off bullets and bombs, or fight for the good of us all?

And there was one other thing that made Superman special to me—his secret, secret identity. No, not his alter ego, Clark Kent. Something else.

You see, Superman was a Jew.

A member of the tribe.

I'm not kidding.

Okay, so the Man of Steel was never circumcised—which would've been a tough deal given his impenetrable body type. Or bar mitzvahed. Didn't really think he had to prove he was "a man." Let's just say his resume spoke for itself. And so what if he didn't look Jewish with his perfect nose, blue eyes, and spit curl that hung on his forehead. Does every Jew have to look like my Uncle Hymie?

Nope, this was not some post-coma delusion. Only a fact for anyone who studied the guy's history. For one, it was obvious that Superman was born into a Jewish family on the planet Krypton—apparently, the Miami Beach of the cosmos. His birth name was Kal-El. In Hebrew, "El" stands for God. "Kal" means "voice." So, his dad, Jor-El, gave him the Hebrew name, "Voice of God." A bit much, but as names go this one had punch.

And then there was Kal-El's biblical story by way of DC Comics, describing the second coming of the Jewish prophet. I mean, how could anyone miss the point? In the story of Exodus, baby Moses is sent by his family in a basket down the Nile to save him from certain death, only to be rescued by non-Jews in a foreign culture. Then there is Kal-El, facing impending death, sent in a ship into the darkness of space by his parents as Krypton blows up. He is, of course, rescued by the Kents, a lovely gentile couple living in rural Smallville, Kansas.

And is it simply a coincidence that the Man of Steel sounds like a Talmudic scholar when he speaks about truth and justice? Or that his Earth identity ends in the partial

Jewish surname, "Man?" Better Superman, though, than *The Adventures of Klopman.*

Yes, Superman, the super-Jew from Krypton. No denying.

☙❧☙

Knowing Superman as well as I did, I'm pretty sure that he would've wanted me to forgive my Aunt Selma for dumping him in some garbage bin. After all, I loved her, and she adored me. And I was beginning to think that maybe it hadn't been vengeance at all, but that Aunt Selma had in fact acted out of kindness for her comatose nephew. My bedroom always looked as if a tornado had hit, and she had taken it upon herself to give Mom a hand and get the room ready for her wonderful nephew coming home from the hospital.

So what if she managed to wipe Superman out of my existence in some crazy flurry of housekeeping. So what if my champion was soaking in some rotting mess somewhere.

Okay, so I wasn't ready to forgive Aunt Selma.

It was just going to take me some time to get over the fact that the Man of Steel was gone. Rather than think about pardoning my aunt, I decided that I would feel sorry for myself and mope around my bedroom for the rest of the day, mourning my lost hero who had come to such a humiliating end. Could anyone have predicted such an awful farewell? And to think, it wasn't Kryptonite that finally knocked off my hero, the great Superman.

Who could have imagined it was my Aunt Selma?

CHAPTER 30

Middle Fingers and Snickers Bars

I didn't return to JHS 82 until the new year, 1962. I was itching to get back to my life. Bones had healed, and about the only leftover sign from the crash was a crooked scar running down my left cheek. Dramatic looking, but not enough to get me an audition for the next Lon Chaney movie. Sammy told me that the scar gave my face character, whatever that meant.

In any case, it felt great making my way to school, chatting away with my pal. Sammy had been a real friend these past months, filling me in on the gossip, helping me with some home schooling, getting me back to myself. We talked and talked. There was a new, nutty baseball team in Queens called the Mets. An idiotic dance craze, the Twist, with this guy who called himself Chubby Checker. Some British group, the Beatles, that was starting to make it big. These guys had bangs, wore tight suits, and had a drummer named Ringo!

"They won't last," I told Sammy, who agreed.

I even got to watch Roger Maris hit his sixty-first home run on TV. A blast into the right-field bleachers, my territory. Amazing! Sammy and I had stomped so hard on my living room floor that crotchety Mrs. Hochmeyer, my neighbor below, came storming upstairs with a broomstick in hand, threatening to call the police if "you lousy brats" didn't keep it down. Nothing though was about to stop our celebration, including Mrs. Hochmeyer and her excellent witch impersonation.

Eighth grade had been more of the same for Sammy. He was placed in Class 811, the last stop at JHS 82. He told me that his class was a training ground for future Arthur Avenue wise guys and Fordham Road Baldies gang bangers.

"One guy goes by the name of the Shamrock Killer," he said dolefully. "I told him I was Irish, so maybe he'd leave me alone. Actually I'm more afraid of the girls. At least I think they're girls. I mean they have Popeye's biceps *and* his mustache."

I shook my head, sympathizing. Sammy liked to pretend he was one step away from joining the mob, and I guess he had a better shot now in 811. But, honestly, Sammy was much more likely to end up as a dentist than running with the Genovese gang.

And so we yakked on as we made our way into the schoolyard. It was good being there with my buddy again.

Only then did we see Alan Plotz lumbering down the schoolyard steps. He had yet to see us and looked dazed and off into his own world.

"The fat man," Sammy said grimly. "The creep was sent back to seventh grade. He had a choice, being left back or enroll in the Bronx Zoo. But the Zoo didn't want him."

"What's Plotz doing here, Sammy?" I asked, dumbfounded. "Shouldn't he be in prison?"

"Maybe a pig farm," Sammy muttered, frowning. "Didn't even spend a day away from his home after being taken in by the cops. I heard they told him to be a good boy and then let him go."

"Jesus. The cops let him get off scot free, after all the trouble? After what he did to Joe?"

"Yeah, they said it was just a stupid kid's prank. That was it."

"And Joe?"

"Yeah, he was the criminal. So they locked him up at Spofford. Go figure it out."

It didn't take much to figure out, given Joe's skin color.

"Where is Joe now, Sammy?"

"The guy's gone, Paul. The word is that he went back to Harlem. Not a good situation there. Heard he was running with the wrong people."

All this grief because of Plotz.

I could see that he'd grown wider, a large mound of blubber slowly rolling down the steps toward us. He was still in La-La Land, mumbling to himself as he got closer. A breeze had picked up his scent and moved it in our direction. It brought me back to my vomitus days sitting next to him.

Plotz finally picked up his head catching sight of Sammy and me. He froze, his face morphing into that pig-like sneer of his. And if we had missed the point, Plotz underlined it. He flipped us the finger. The guy really wanted us to know what he thought of us. So he gave it to us again, this time with both hands. Two middle-fingers. Twirling them in small circles.

I felt instant heat, that old feeling, the one that exploded that day with Tommy. Sammy put his hand on my shoulder, enough to hold me in check.

"Hey, no way, bro," my friend said. "He's a sicko. And, besides, he'll just sit on you and crush you to death. You'd be better off getting hit by a car."

"Yeah, I did that already," I said, settling down. Sammy was right. I was in no mood for another coma and backed off.

Plotz had inflated more these past months and reminded me of the television wrestler Haystacks Calhoun. They called him "Haystacks" for a reason, weighing in over 600 pounds. He loved to finish off his match with the "Big Splash," leaping forward, landing stomach-first across an opponent lying prone on the mat. I wouldn't stand a chance with Plotz. If his weight didn't kill me, I would suffocate from the smell.

"Plotz, nice to see you again, too," Sammy smirked. Then his face lit up with an idea. Rummaging through his knapsack, Sammy took out two large Snickers candy bars. He peeled away the wrappers and then started to pump the chocolate fingers in the air giving Plotz a double dose of fuck-yous.

"Hey, big guy, you can eat these if you get hungry," Sammy called out. He was really enjoying himself now.

Plotz's triple chin started to quiver. He growled, angrily punching the air again with his middle fingers.

And so it went between Plotz and Sammy, middle fingers and Snickers bars flying back and forth, a fuck-you battle of epic proportions.

And so began my first day back at JHS 82.

CHAPTER 31

Falling in Lust

It was cool walking the hallways at school. I was no longer that seventh-grade twerp, but more a teenager, and feeling pretty good about myself. I also felt the eyes of a few girls as I made my way to class. Maybe my facial scar was going to help me out after all.

A gang of old classmates rushed up to ask me how I'd been. My accident had been the talk of the school, casting me as some sort of conquering hero—though I never quite figured out what was so heroic about getting smashed to pieces while riding my bike down the Concourse.

Well, maybe I was also overstating the hero bit given the mixed bag of sympathy coming my way. Molly O'Malley, for one, came up to me looking confused. "Hey, I thought you were dead," she said, then touched my arm to see if I was real. I had the distinct feeling that she was disappointed seeing me alive.

"Sorry, Molly," I said, thinking I needed to apologize.

"No problem," she replied, shrugging her shoulders.

❧❧❧

At least JHS 82 felt sorry for me. At least that's how I

took it anyway. I was no longer a prisoner of 710—much as I adored Miss Crouse and would miss her. I was out of lockup and could now attend subject classes with other "normal" kids. So, a step up.

My first class that day, Mr. Marianoff for social studies. The guy was the intellectual type, about forty years old, with short, curly hair, and round metal glasses perched on his nose. After settling us into our seats, he got right to business—an exercise on how to read the *New York Times* on a subway train. Why this lesson, I had no idea. I guess Mr. Marianoff assumed that one day we'd find ourselves on a crowded train, going to our Wall Street jobs, and boxed in from reading the newspaper. And he was about to tell how to avoid this disaster.

"Here is today's *Times*," he announced, pulling the newspaper from his briefcase. "Now watch." Then he folded the paper in half, and then in half again so that the *Times* was now one quarter its size. I wondered if Mr. Marianoff was going to keep folding the paper then shout "Poof" as it vanished before our eyes.

He wasn't going for the magic trick.

"Look," he said excitedly. "Now you can still read the paper, and even turn to other pages, without sticking out your elbows."

So that was it. I just hated those moments on the Jerome Avenue IRT when some guy clipped me with an elbow while reading the *Times.* Uncivilized if you ask me. What we needed was a teensy newspaper to avoid any ruckus. Actually, I was debating whether Mr. Marianoff was straight out of "Looney Tunes" or had taken a wrong turn on his way to Harvard and wound up at 82.

George Mullin in the third row raised his hand. "Mr. Teacher, excuse me, but I don't read the *New York Times*."

I remembered George from seventh grade, and he was a little slow. It might take him a while to even memorize Mr. Marianoff's name, but George had a point. I didn't read the *New York Times* either and knew no other kid—or parent—

that did. This was strictly a *New York Post* crowd.

"Well, George, one day you might," Mr. Marianoff said, encouragingly. "It is a very important newspaper."

Then Melvin Yablonsky waved his hand with his own complaint. "I throw up when I read anything on the subway."

Mr. Marianoff hesitated, seeing he had no response for Melvin. Instead, he gave him an I'm-sorry look, and scratched his head. I guess he was disappointed that his inspiring newspaper-folding idea was meeting such resistance.

I actually decided to try his experiment later that afternoon back home. Not a great success, with my newspaper ending up as a twisted pretzel. I decided to stay true to my *New York Post*, our revered family newspaper, which I never read on the train, and only the sports section in any case.

⋐⋑⋐⋑

Next class that day was English with Mr. Devlin. My brother Fred had graduated from the junior high five years earlier, but his memory of Mr. Devlin was crystal clear, and terrifying. "The guy is big, Irish and scary," Fred recalled. "No one messes with Mr. Devlin. You take your life in your hands if you do."

Mr. Devlin's reputation ran far and wide at the school. He was an ex-Marine who still wore a crew-cut and thought we were still fighting World War II. His enemies were students who dared to cross him, in which case the rules against torturing prisoners were out the window. Girls were exempt from such suffering, but I happened to be a boy and could have done without the special treatment.

I caught up on the talk about Mr. Devlin and his imaginative punishments. It didn't take long though before I saw him in action for myself. Here we were, barely settled into our seats, when Richie Smith began to act up. Nothing too bad, just some horsing around while we geared up for class. I had known Richie from seventh grade, a funny, stupid guy and a prime candidate for class clown. He would've been much better off in the circus at that moment and out of Mr. Devlin's sight.

"Smith!" bellowed Mr. Devlin, glaring at this miscreant who had dared to disrupt his class. "Take the chair!"

Richie froze in his seat, reality setting in. The world was no longer kind and understanding. Not with this red-faced, scowling Irishman coming toward him.

"But Mr. Devlin," he weakly replied. "I already have a chair."

"Not yours, idiot—*that* one!" Mr. Devlin thundered, pointing to a heavy wooden chair in the corner of the room.

"Pick it up, and lift it over your head," Mr. Devlin ordered.

Someone might have warned Richie that our English teacher was a psycho, but it was now too late.

"The chair—over my head?" Richie asked, confused, his voice quaking. "Uh, I mean, for how long?"

"For as long as I tell you, Smith. And don't even think of dropping that chair, or else."

The "or else" was two weeks in detention, a fate worse than facing a firing squad led by Mr. Devlin. Detention-torture meant spending two hours each day after school, sitting in the auditorium with nothing to do but pick your nose while your friends were outside in the schoolyard whooping it up.

I just hoped for his sake that Richie had strong arms.

I was certain that Mr. Devlin was violating the "cruel and unusual punishment" clause in the Constitution, but then I remembered those rules only applied to Americans. We were only junior high school scum to Mr. Devlin.

Our teacher went on with his lesson, but no one cared much as we eyed the kid behind us holding up a heavy chair. Any one of us boys could be going next.

Mr. Devlin was on to explaining noun-verb agreement. At least something in his class was agreeable.

Richie's grunts were already popping up from the back of the room. I turned around and the poor guy was jerking around, trying to keep the chair upright.

Mr. Devlin then asked us to write an example in our notebook.

I began to write: "The crazy teacher 'kill' or 'kills' innocent kids." I took some pride in my work until I realized that Mr. Devlin might call on me for my sentence.

"AHHHHH." Richie's grunts now had become one long syllable. He was finished. The chair was dipping to the floor with Richie headed to detention purgatory.

Finally, Mr. Devlin granted him a reprieve.

"Put the chair down, Smith," he ordered. "Now sit down and shut up."

Richie could not hold back from crashing the heavy chair to the floor, the collision snapping us back in our seats. Mr. Devlin's face turned a beet red, a green vein bulged from his nose, pumping wildly. He stared murderously at Richie as the kid collapsed into his seat.

I thought that if Mr. Devlin ever decided to give up teaching, he certainly had a career as a prison guard at Sing Sing. Better yet, an executioner in the Big House. The guy would be great pulling the switch, happily watching the condemned con twitching to his excruciating death. I had the feeling he was thinking along those lines with Richie, while sizing the rest of us up for his next torture experiment.

The bell rang for class dismissal, but not soon enough.

಄಄಄

Math class was my last that day, and I was ready to call it quits. After months being laid up, I wasn't used to all the moving about and hubbub. It didn't help that math was, by far, my very least favorite subject. I could not see how my life was any better off knowing how to convert decimals to percentages or finding some "unknown" in an equation. I was very willing to let unknowns stay unknown.

So I shuffled into Room 335, Miss Bonnet's math class, wanting nothing more than to go home, turn on the TV, and chug down one of Mom's chocolate malteds. How was I to know that my world was about to change—radically?

Nothing could prepare me for Miss Bonnet. Nothing. My teacher was out of a dream world. She reminded me of a young Marilyn Monroe but without the whispery voice and exaggerated way in which the actress threw her hips when she walked. Miss Bonnet didn't try to be sexy or gorgeous, she just was. She wore eyeglasses to signal that she expected to be taken seriously, and would have no problem with me. I was already taking her very seriously.

I found it impossible to stop from eyeballing her. It was sick to think of my teacher in any other way than the parent type. But Miss Bonnet did not look like any teacher, or parent for that matter, that I'd ever known. Not with those crystal blue eyes, and golden blonde hair that flowed down to her waist. My eyes were glued to her heart-shaped face before making their way down her body. Her red sweater and black skirt hugged the curves of her body. I sat spellbound in her classroom gaping at her breasts that jutted tightly against the sweater's fabric, at the same time afraid that she would catch my eye.

So maybe I was a little sick—okay, more than a little— and should've been ashamed. I mean, what was I thinking? The thing is, I knew exactly what I thinking. It just wasn't anything I was going to share with Rosie about my first day back at school. The truth was, I was madly, wildly, in lust.

It made no difference that Miss Bonnet was my teacher, or that she even taught math, a subject I hated. Only that I had suddenly taken a deep, abiding interest in the study of mathematics. In fact, I now considered the subject as a career move for myself—nothing could be more important than the teaching of math to the young people of the world.

Of course, it might be helpful if I first understood math, but I was counting on getting the hang of percentages and un-knowns with Miss Bonnet's personal guidance.

I was already suspicious of every other boy in class—I didn't want the competition—and needed to act quickly, moving into a front-row, dead-center seat. The spot was a favorite of nerds who incessantly waved their hands, squeaking like baby birds, "me, me, me, me," to let every-one know how smart they were. I wasn't that type at all, but I was ready to squeak "me" with anyone else if it meant get-ting Miss Bonnet's attention.

I was looking for more than just getting called on in class by Miss Bonnet, though I was very confused as to what that other thing could possibly be.

CHAPTER 32

Alien Invasion

I thought that Sammy's birthday might take my mind off of school—something had to, my jitters around Miss Bonnet were only getting worse. My best friend was turning fourteen on George Washington's Birthday, which seemed pretty cool. My birthday coincided with some Nazi general's, so I didn't have nearly the same feeling.

Anyway, Sammy invited a bunch of us over to his place to celebrate with a night of poker. Also known as gambling. We'd had our first taste of the money game two weeks earlier when Sammy's folks were out for the night. We played five-and-ten, a nickel ante to get into a hand, and dime bets on each dealt card. You'd be surprised how those dimes added up. I found out quickly enough that night, losing nearly fifteen dollars. How I was going to pay Fred back for his loan was another matter.

I was itching to play again, as I climbed Sammy's walk-up on Grand Avenue. He had promised another parent-free night, and even a bigger stakes game. Finagling some future allowance money from Rosie hadn't been easy, even promising to clean up my room. I'd deal with that later after I won a few big hands that night.

It was weird, though, making my way up to Sammy's

apartment. I could hear the garbled sound of some singer echoing down the stairwell. As I reached the top floor, the voice was unmistakable. Elvis "the King" was going at it in "Jailhouse Rock." And he was coming from inside 5C, Sammy's place. A bad sign. Card games never had music. We might sing "Happy Birthday" to Sammy at some point, but that was it for the musical portion of our night. Music only meant one thing. Girls were around.

Then it hit me as I rang the doorbell. This was not only Sammy's birthday, but Maude's, his twin sister's. And I don't think she was sticking around for a card game.

"Hey Paul," Sammy growled at the door.

"Maude's party too, right?" I said, glancing over to the living room.

Fluttering about were a group of girls that I knew from school.

"Yeah. My folks didn't want Maude left out—so this," Sammy groaned, sweeping his hand across the crowded room.

"I guess that means we're not play poker tonight."

"That's exactly what it means."

It was then that I noticed Dee-Dee O'Hara. She was next to a table loaded with party food, talking with the other girls. Her presence instantly raised my anxiety level. The girl was a world apart from those chatterboxes—with those hazel-green eyes that sparkled. I could feel a knot in my stomach begin to tighten.

"I guess we'll just have to change plans, Sammy. Too bad." I tried to stay cool, but heard the shake in my voice.

"Damn, Paul, can't you just shoot my sister?" Sammy angrily went on, getting more worked up. "She even turned the living room into a crappy dance floor. What is this, freakin' *American Bandstand* with that loser Dick Clark?"

Then I saw Maude. She was Sammy's twin, but they were nothing alike. Sammy was short and slim, and a wise guy.

Maude was a half-foot taller than her brother, and really

pushy. And I mean really. She was squarer than the last time I saw her, but her barking voice had stayed pretty much the same.

Maude looked determined that her party went as planned. She had gone a little nuts, in fact, hanging a revolving plastic globe that gave off "moonbeams" that swept across the dark dance space. The light made me dizzy, swirling across some girls dancing together to Fabian's "Turn Me Loose." Most guys hung back, and I joined them at the soda and pretzel table. Then Maude changed records, turned on Elvis, and whispered something to each of the girls. Her message set off a bout of giggles.

The conspiracy was revealed as the girls marched over to the boy's pretzel table, taking us by the hand, one by one, to the dance floor. A couple of guys cringed and begged off, a good idea I thought. That is, until Dee-Dee came over. She gave me that shy smile of hers.

"Hey," she said softly.

I didn't resist as she led me to the middle of the room.

Neither of us said a word when she placed both her arms around my shoulders and nestled her head against my chest. I had nowhere else to put my arms but around her waist, and so I did. We danced that way to a ballad about being young and in love, rocking slowly, our bodies pressed. And Elvis sang to us.

I could feel Dee-Dee's soft breath on my cheek and caught her sweet-scented fragrance. Moonbeams swept over us. I closed my eyes, and we slowly drifted across the floor. The dance was no more than an excuse to hold her. Dee-Dee felt warm in my arms, the heat from our bodies mingling. Neither of us saying a word, lost in the silence. Nothing could be as perfect.

This feeling was not the craziness that battered me being around Miss Bonnet. Something else—this was real, and softer.

And it was then, without a word, that Dee-Dee reached up to touch my face. Just like that. It was enough to make me pull her closer, wanting nothing more than to keep her in my arms.

And we stayed that way, curled together, floating in the moonbeams—when we were suddenly jolted back down to earth.

The King had finished his ode to young love.

Couples started to break apart, but Dee-Dee and I were in no hurry to separate, swaying to our own music. And even when we finally let go, our eyes stayed locked.

"That was lovely," she whispered, a soft lilt in her voice.

"You're welcome," I babbled, making a mental note to kick myself in the ass for being such a moron.

Dee-Dee chuckled and turned back to the girls' side of the room.

I stood frozen in place, watching her walk away. Finally, I came out of my trance and back to my pals at the pretzel table.

The party wore on, and I found myself with the shakes again, working up the nerve to ask Dee-Dee to dance. To feel her in my arms again. But then I thought, why the need to rush over and scare the girl? I mean, what if she wasn't interested? Turned me down? Thought I was just being a creep?

Okay, so I *really* was a lamo—here I was huddling in a corner, hiding behind a bowl of pretzels, nothing but a chicken-shit, scaredy-cat with no-balls.

Instead, I watched Dee-Dee slow dance with pimply Stevey Blankfeld to the Everly Brothers. Dee-Dee had her head on his shoulder, her eyes closed. So were his.

Shit and more shit.

Abruptly, Phil and Don Everly were roughly scratched off the record player.

"Time for cake!" Maude declared, shutting down the music.

Birthday cake? What kind of stupid ritual was that anyway? Yes, I was pathetic taking my gutlessness out on a birthday cake.

Anyway, I moped over to a folding table and came to a giant white-frosted cake topped with strawberries and cream and a bunch of plastic hearts.

Sammy edged up, also unhappy.

"Just love the hearts," I muttered. "Your choice?"

"Yeah. I'm the romantic type," he said sullenly.

Sammy was still not over losing his birthday poker game.

I wasn't over Dee-Dee.

We made some pair.

And so, we all sang "Happy Birthday," and ate some strawberry shortcake. Sammy and Maude opened presents—an embarrassing moment given that I had come empty-handed—a move that usually signaled it was time to call it a night. I should've known that Maude still had one more idea brewing.

"Look, guys, Spin the Bottle!" she bellowed.

It wasn't a question, but a command.

Now the odds of me playing Spin the Bottle were as great as getting Dad's permission to convert to Buddhism. But I caught Dee-Dee eyeing me—was that my imagination?—and then she flashed her smile.

Spin the Bottle seemed like a perfectly good idea.

A dozen of us sat cross-legged around a Coke bottle while Maude stated the rules. No one really needed a refresher, but we patiently listened to Maude spelling them out.

"Okay, so one turn each," she told us. "And no tongues in the mouth."

"Eeewww." A collective groan.

"Hey, sis, we can do without the details," Sammy complained. "Let's get on with it."

"Just wanted to be clear," Maude shot back. "But nothing's stopping anyone from showing his or her true feelings, if you know what I mean."

I couldn't help but sneak a glance at Dee-Dee. She caught my eyes and kept hers on mine.

"Sammy, this is your birthday," Stevey Blankfeld said excitedly. "You're up first."

Sammy, suddenly recharged, bounded into the circle. Then he gave the Coke bottle a hard spin before it came to a stop. And landed on me.

"Hey, bro, you're not my type, and, besides, you're dirt ugly." Sammy smirked, and picked up the bottle. "I'm goin' again."

I wasn't about to object. Another spin. This time the bottle landed in front of Becca Bendetson, a cute redhead with freckles. Sammy ambled over and the two smacked lips while the rest of us hooted and hollered. That was fun, I thought.

We agreed it was the birthday girl's turn. "Go for the kill, Maude," Sammy called out, egging his sister on. Not that she needed any more encouragement. Maude's eyes were already shining as if she was some crazed vampire getting ready for dinner. A scary look. Obviously, it was a mistake to think of Maude in human terms.

Maude then stepped into the middle of the circle and picked up the bottle. With her eyes half closed, she began to spout some mumbo-jumbo chant while rubbing the bottle.

"Waiting for a genie to pop out?" Eric Heimbinder shouted out.

"Shhh, Eric. I'm making my birthday wish," she intoned in her best spooky voice. "To find my secret lover. Yes. He's right here. In this circle!"

"Yeah, pity the poor guy," Sammy chuckled in my ear.

"Hey, Maude, aren't you supposed to keep your birthday wish a secret?" Becca asked.

"Not this special wish. We shall all soon know who my secret lover is, dearest friends. I feel his presence only growing stronger!"

"Maude, enough with the witchdoctor voodoo crap," Sammy grumbled. "Spin the damn bottle already!"

Maude gave her brother a dirty look, then put the Coke bottle back on the rug. Gripping the bottle, she closed her eyes for a second—I guess she was doubling up on her wish—then snapped her wrist.

The bottle spun in a blur,
slowing, a final turn,
then coming to a stop,
and pointing to a boy.
Maude's mystery lover,
was no longer a secret.
Everyone could see
the bottle had landed...
on me.
No!
Nooo!
Not Maude!

Someone must have spiked the punch—I was hallucinating, living in a never-ending loop of Spin the Bottle, each time with a damn Coke bottle accusingly pointing at me!

Only that Maude Spigelman was standing on the other side of the circle, very real, and licking her lips.

"See, wishes do come true," Maude proclaimed gleefully to the group. "Paul, my one and only." Then she let out a belly laugh.

God, please, anyone else but Maude.

Apparently, the Big Guy wasn't in the mood to give me a break.

"How about one more spin?" I begged. "I mean, I'm your brother's best friend. This is sort of like incest, right?"

"I don't think that's it," Sammy shouted out before cracking up.

I shot Sammy a serious I-will-murder-you glare.

Maude's eyes lit up like one of her dancing moonbeams, and I saw something there that scared the bejesus out of me. It must have been what the Boston Strangler's terrified victims saw in his eyes before he cut their throat.

I desperately turned to Sammy. "Hey, man. You gotta help me out here."

"Paul, sorry, blood is thicker than best friends," he said

fake-solemnly. "Besides, Maude's horny for you. Bro, you're in deep doo-doo." Then he burst out laughing again.

Nice to see that the birthday twins were enjoying themselves.

In a heartbeat, Maude stomped over to my side of the circle. I was set to make a run for it, but the big girl already hovered over me. No escape was possible. Maude kept licking her lips, preparing for the kill.

"Hey, Maude, how about we give Pin the Tail on the Donkey a try?" I babbled. "Great party game."

Maude wasn't listening. Or merciful.

She intently eyed the shaking puddle of Jell-O—me—sitting on the floor, still silently praying for God's intervention. I had the feeling He was now looking down at me and having a good yuk for Himself.

Maude's brown-cow eyes had that crazed glint again. She wasted no time lifting me up by my armpits, wrapping her beefy arms around me, bringing me nose-to-nose with her. Up close Maude's oval face seemed twice its size and filled with blotches of blackheads and zits. I couldn't take my eyes off the tiny mounds of red pimples tipped with pus.

"Bro, you guys look like you're in love," Sammy hollered.

"Time for kissy, kissy," Kenny Spinelli joined in.

Blood was in the water. Sharks circling.

I found myself drifting back to when I was five. A neighbor's pit bull had rushed up to me, snarling and baring his teeth, ready to snap my head off. I peed in my pants then. I felt the same pressure on my bladder now. Another pit bull was ready to strike.

I'd never given Maude Spigelman a thought before. She was Sammy's invisible twin sister. Now no person in the world loomed so large, literally. Or was nearly as nuts.

Then Maude pounced—by which I mean she grabbed my head and kissed me. No, that wasn't really it. Not at all. This was an all-out frontal attack. Think of the Japs at Pearl

Harbor. Only worse. Maude lips bulldozed into mine, crushing my teeth.

"Maude, you're *killing* me," I pleaded, gasping.

"Yeah, I know," that crazed look back in her eyes. "Tell me you love it."

I really wanted to tell Maude to screw off, but who the hell knew what she'd make out of *that* idea? What, a marriage proposal?

Then she came in for the second bombing run even more determined. She was on my mouth again, sucking my lower lip into her mouth! *What was that about?* My lip wasn't a party snack! Maude was now chewing on it, having an entire meal!

I could only garble a protest—this spinning bottle thing was definitely no longer fun and games.

The guys were fully roused. "Kiss-Him! Kiss-Him! Kiss-Him!"

Sammy was the loudest. I really couldn't wait to kill him.

"Don't hurt him," Cathy Quinn called out nervously.

God bless her. But I was doomed.

"Kiss-Him! Kiss-Him! Kiss-Him!"

The chant had turned into a call for my execution.

Maude now had both her hands around my head in a vice-like grip.

"Maude!" I barely managed to suck in some air. "Game over. Time for cake."

"Already ate cake," she said zombie-like.

Thoughts of snarling pit bulls were back in my head. I could feel piss starting to leak into my pants.

Maude's face now was lit up like some sort of zit-infested jack-o-lantern. She grinned crookedly. The likeness was uncanny.

Maude had me locked down and about let me have it again. Still no mercy in her heart. She was back on my lips, wedging my mouth open with her tongue. *Her tongue!* Then she slivered the slimy worm-like thing into my mouth—

some alien creature was invading my body! I gagged, and tried to break out of her grip, but this Spigelman was strong. I mean, Hulk-like strong.

I desperately pulled my face away, gasping, angrily shouting, "Maude, no freakin' tongue in the mouth!"

Whatever happened to the rules? What kind of world did we live in without rules?

Maude read my mind. "Changed the rules," was all she said, before her alien tongue was at it again, snaking its way *down my throat!* This time I retched and had a momentary vision of throwing up on Maude's face.

Maybe sensing a vomit bath, Maude moved back. Her tongue was gone, but I could still taste the globs of saliva left in my mouth. I was exhausted, likely haunted forever by wormy alien tongues.

At least I had survived, dazed, but finally free from this lunatic.

So why was Maude pinning both my arms to my sides?

And what was that needle-prick sting on my neck?

Then another?

Jeez-uzz! Ahhh...

I crunched my head to where the pain was coming from.

Maude was chomping on my neck!

"MAUDE—NOT A HICKEY! ARE YOU OUT OF YOUR STUPID, CRAZY MIND? THIS IS SPIN THE GODDAMN BOTTLE!"

"More new rules," she garbled with her mouth still latched on to my neck, sucking blood up into a huge purple ring. And marking her spot.

"*MAUDE!*"

Dracula's daughter was now working her fangs on a second hickey. I could only pray that I wouldn't wake up the next day as one of her possessed disciples.

My survival instincts finally kicked in, breaking free of Maude's grip, before flopping to the floor. I clutched the side of my neck and felt where Maude's teeth had punctured my skin. Shit! I'm finished, possessed, and wondered how I would explain to Mom my new set of fangs.

Maude, wearing a raccoon smile, looked quite pleased with herself.

"Hey, Paul, you know what this means—my sister is your steady now," Sammy called out. "I expect you to treat her with respect." Then he rolled over, hysterically laughing.

I vowed to kill Sammy twice.

The other party kids let out a raucous cheer—I assume for Maude, the victor. I glanced over at Dee-Dee, sitting quietly. No smile this time, just staring wide-eyed at the hickeys that tattooed my neck. I didn't think she was about to ask me to slow dance again anytime soon.

"Man of my dreams!" Maude proclaimed, standing over me, still wearing her crazed, crooked smile.

I wiped my wet face with the back of my hand, fighting back a wave of nausea, and bolted out of Sammy's apartment. I barely made it down in time before puking all over some guy's Chevy. Too bad I couldn't package the stuff for Maude's birthday present.

☙❧☙

I was still sick to my stomach the next morning lying in bed. All I wanted to do was hide under the covers, but Rosie rustled me from bed.

"Paul!" she cried out, pointing to the purple blotches on my neck.

"Mom, you don't want to know."

She didn't, shaking her head, and leaving me to get dressed.

I slogged over to school absolutely not looking forward to the day.

Of course I had to run into Maude on the way to my locker. She was hanging out in the hallway with a few of her friends from the party. One by one they sauntered past me, not even trying to hold back the giggles.

I'd been pulverized and would've been justified in filing a police report. Instead, I hoped that everyone would just forget about the Spigelman birthday party, and leave me alone. Then Maude hustled over, running her tongue along her lips, and looking like she had a very good memory.

"Paulie, wanna come over later?" she purred. Then she noticed my bruised neck and started to slurp the air. A reminder, in case I was in the mood for another one of her love bites.

I fled down the hallway trailed by the sound of Maude's cackling.

But I was still being hunted, this time by the other Spigelman. Sammy caught up with me at my locker.

"Great party last night, eh?" He grinned, that idiotic look of his. "Hey, nice neck. Real colorful."

"Sammy, don't start. That sicko sister of yours is seriously out of her mind. Have you ever thought of electric shock treatment for her?"

"Whatsa matter? Maude has the hots for you. Didn't you notice?"

"Sammy, you're starting."

I hadn't forgotten my personal vow to kill Sammy the next time I saw him. The idea was still tempting.

"Hey, if it was Dee-Dee, you wouldn't have minded."

Sammy had crossed over to dangerous ground, and I gave him a hard stare hoping to shut him up. The truth was, I wouldn't have minded at all if Dee-Dee had taken a spin of the bottle. And the bottle neck landing on me. With what came next.

Instead, Maude.

"Let's just drop it." I was already wiped out, and the day had yet to begin. "I need to get to math."

"Hey, Paul." Sammy was not letting up. "I heard you have Bonnet?"

"Yeah, so what about it?"

"Betcha you'd like to play Spin the Bottle with her, too," he smirked.

"Sammy, go back to your cage," I groaned, way past my limit with the Spigelmans.

"See you later, bro," Sammy said cheerfully, and then he took off down the hallway.

CHAPTER 33

The Porno King of 82

I suppose I *was* a very confused kid, a condition only getting worse each time I checked myself out. I had grown a half-foot almost overnight, slimming out and losing my handlebars along the way. Hair was sprouting, and I don't mean on top of my head. And my kid's voice had dropped a half-pitch with a crackly edge. My eyesight was also getting sharper, noticing more the eighth-grade girls that had become taller, curvier, and, to quote Sammy Spigelman, "stacked."

Safe to say, I wasn't about to have a heart-to-heart with Mom about my roaring hormones. I wouldn't be surprised if she was still traumatized after seeing my gross blue-greenish neck, gouged with bites, thanks to Countess Dracula. And no sense letting on about my plan to propose to Dee-Dee O'Hara. That also would have to wait. At least until I stopped bringing my math teacher to bed with me each night in my dreams.

To repeat, I was a very confused kid.

Yes, Miss Bonnet—she was complicating my loopy brain, even if she had no idea that she was such a problem. I found my mind wandering to subjects definitely not approved of by the New York City Board of Education. Not that I expected extra credit for thinking out of the box. Not at all. And, so, no surprise that this obsession with Miss Bonnet had to end in some sort of trouble.

cso<c/ø

That afternoon in art class began harmlessly enough. Miss Sheldon, my teacher, had instructed us to use the time to come up with an "amazing" creative project. "Let your imagination fly and take over your artistic self," she dramatically told us.

Who was I to argue?

So I took her assignment seriously and let my imagination fly. I mean, that clearly was my teacher's instructions, right? What choice did I have but to listen to my brain, though that might not have been the body part urging me on.

At least that was my thinking before everything went wrong.

And so I gathered up my supplies—glue, scissors, and some metallic-glossy paper in different colors. I searched out an empty corner art table and, well, started imagining. It didn't take me long to come up with an idea. First I took a gold-colored shiny piece of paper and cut away an outline of a woman's body. I kept snipping away, until I was satisfied with the dimensions. She now had long, tapered legs and curved hips. Just perfect. Then I cut out two spheres and pasted them onto the figure's chest. Out of red-paper I created nipples and glued them on. A small triangular piece of black paper was attached to a spot between the legs. A bright, yellow piece for the hair, ruby lips, turquoise eyes, pink nose and ears. Finally, I glued my metallic picture onto a large piece of black paper.

And just like that, my creation came alive, looking ready to jump off the black paper and into my arms. Of course I didn't rule out the possibility that I was absolutely nuts, but

I'd deal with that later. For now, here she was—my naked Miss Bonnet. And she belonged to me. If anyone missed that point, I wrote her name in silver marker below her picture. She was just how I pictured her to be as I drifted off to sleep. And into my sticky dreams.

Okay, maybe I was a bit obsessive, sick maybe? I would settle for obsessive.

It really was too bad though that I failed to notice a shadowy figure sneaking up from behind me. I had been real content, happily cradling my Miss Bonnet in my lap. That is, until alarm bells went off in my head, and I whipped around.

Miss Sheldon, her mouth ajar, eyes wide open, was staring bug-eyed at me.

And then she let out a loud gasp. "Paul, how *could* you?"

Now, I could have taken this statement to mean that Miss Sheldon was flabbergasted to come across someone so young, so talented, that could produce such a brilliant piece of art.

But I quickly reached another conclusion, and started praying.

Miss Sheldon was in no mood for forgiveness, snatching the picture from my hand. With two fingers she held up my naked Miss Bonnet for all to see, a prosecutor with damning evidence before the jury.

"This is *disgusting*, Paul," she announced.

Some twenty kids were suddenly on full alert and having a good look at the "evidence." Emmie Kaiser, wide-eyed, had her hand over her mouth. Other kids let loose a barrage of cackles and hoots. I had no doubt, though, that I would've been found guilty of being a first-degree pervert had Miss Sheldon not immediately dismissed the group.

With everyone else gone I sat face-to-face with Miss Sheldon around a small art table. To be accurate, Miss Sheldon was giving me her hard stare. I was checking the cracks in the floor and having trouble speaking, or breathing for that matter.

"I'm really sorry," I mumbled, which I expect is how all these types of conversations start out.

I mean, what else could I say?

To be honest, I wasn't really feeling sorry at all. I had pretty much satisfied my raging artistic impulses, along with some hormonally charged feelings—and wasn't that the creative process at work? I was simply getting in touch with my very deepest emotions. Isn't that what my teacher told us to do?

I didn't try to push that line with Miss Sheldon, so I kept my mouth shut.

"I'm very disappointed in you," she went on, shaking her head. "This is not the kind of behavior I expect from you."

There must be a psychology book somewhere that lists all the responsible words that parents and teachers should say to their children when they've misbehaved—words to make you feel guilty, even when you don't. I wasn't feeling guilt as much as frustration. I had been caught, and now sat empty-handed without my naked Miss Bonnet. I suspected that confiding in Miss Sheldon my lustful yearnings for my math teacher was probably not the right move. I just needed to wait for her to finish up so I could get on with my day.

Miss Sheldon's words bounced off me, and there were plenty of them. Shameful. Appalling. Shocking. Disrespectful. Blah, blah, blah. But something wasn't right. I felt the heat from her scolding, but I was getting another message. Some other thought was floating in her brain. And it was then that I caught the flicker of a smile. A smile!

And her eyes. They seemed to twinkle.

Twinkle!

My mind must have been playing tricks. But before I had the chance to sort it out, Miss Sheldon dropped the other shoe.

"You know I'll have to take *this* to Miss Bonnet," she stated, holding up my picture again. "And you'll need to come with me."

What? Whoa! *No way!*

I was suddenly paying serious attention, waving my hands frantically as if trying to ward off an attack of killer bees. So I started to beg for her divine forgiveness.

"Please, Miss Sheldon, *Miss Sheldon!"*

That eye twinkle again.

What the hell?

I stayed nailed to my chair, sputtering, pleading that we keep this nasty little secret between the two of us. Now I really meant it when I told her how sorry and ashamed I was, and how such a terrible thing would never happen again, and how I would be good, but please, don't show my naked Miss Bonnet to Miss Bonnet.

"Oh, Paul," Miss Sheldon sighed, shaking her head, as if she had more important things to do then deal with this dumb kid.

I went on pleading and would have absolutely volunteered to crawl over broken glass if that would have made any difference. But Miss Sheldon was intent on her mission. With that strange, satisfied look reappearing, she stood me up, guided me out the door, and to a stairwell. Then she led me on a death march to Room 335. Miss Bonnet's classroom.

"Stay here until I call you inside," she ordered, leaving me in the hallway to contemplate my bleak future.

Through the door's glass pane, I could see Miss Bonnet. Both teachers were sitting at a small table in the middle of the room. Miss Sheldon was talking, probably itching to get Miss Bonnet's support that I was a pervert. Then she handed over my picture to her. I felt the shakes coming on, thinking how furious Miss Bonnet must be at this warped kid out to humiliate her.

I paced the hallway like some death-row inmate waiting to get strapped down and zapped with 2,000 volts. I was sure that "Old Sparky" was still running at Sing Sing. That worked fine for me. Better an electric death than facing Miss Bonnet.

The door to Room 335 finally opened, and Miss Sheldon, pointing her thumb over her shoulder, directed me over to a seat. I shuffled in, with Miss Bonnet eyeing me as I sat down next to her. I found myself staring down at my naked Miss Bonnet laid out on the table. The picture now seemed dirty to me with Miss Bonnet sitting there. Kind of like checking out the *Playboy* centerfold with Mom on your shoulder. Just not the person you wanted to share the moment with.

And my troubles were only getting worse with Miss Bonnet sitting so close. I could feel her body heat and smell her perfumed scent, my head spinning between the naked and very real Miss Bonnet.

I slowly raised my head hoping to find understanding. Instead, I saw Miss Sheldon zeroing in on me.

"Paul, can you explain yourself to Miss Bonnet?" she said sternly.

What could I say? That I was an underage sex maniac obsessed with my math teacher? Well, it was true, but did they really expect me to confess to the crime? To tell them how I *feel* when I think of Miss Bonnet—and in front of them? In front of *her*? They could pull out my fingernails, but no way.

"You see, I, really, like, I'm so sorry…" I babbled on, hoping for some sympathy.

Just then some raspy, choking sound cut me off. Like someone trying to clear her throat. What was that? Miss Sheldon, her eyes closed, was covering her mouth as if to hold back a hacking fit. But that wasn't it. I could swear she was laughing—*at me!*

Was I completely whacked out?

Before I had time to think, Miss Bonnet picked up the interrogation. "Paul, what made you come up with such a rude picture?"

I could have told my teacher that I saw this picture each night when I closed my eyes for bed. Or in class, when she hovered by my front row seat, so close that I could smell her soft scent as she swept by. But I think she already knew all of this.

Miss Bonnet was kinder than I expected. In fact, she didn't seem angry at all. More words without heat. Actually, another emotion altogether. Miss Bonnet seemed…pleased.

I *was* crazy. A nutcase.

"Do you promise never to do this again?" she firmly asked.

I wasn't quite sure what answer she was looking for. So I nodded my head and promised to be good even if nothing was about to stop me from imagining Miss Bonnet those late nights in bed.

"Then think long and hard on this experience today," she said plainly.

Jeez, Miss Bonnet—my mind was still in the wrong place.

Miss Sheldon seemed to have calmed down, and I guess both teachers were satisfied. I was told to go back to class, and I bolted from the room. Something, though, told me that this wasn't the end of my story. I turned to peek back into the classroom through the door's glass panel. The two teachers were still sitting at the small table. Pointing to my artwork on the table, they were curled over, howling. Their screeches of hysterical laughter echoed into the hallway.

So, my final disgrace, being ridiculed by my teachers for being so young, stupid, and very much in lust.

Head down, I let out a long breath, and staggered away.

And, worse, I was leaving empty-handed, failing to rescue my naked Miss Bonnet held hostage in Room 335.

ᘯᘰ

Of course the word got out. After Miss Sheldon dismissed her students to reckon with me, the gossip spread like wildfire. The bet around the school was either I'd be suspended or brought up on criminal pornography charges.

As it turned out, I was still allowed to come to school and wasn't facing jail time. Actually it was worse than that.

"There he is," Karen Brown blurted out to her friends. A buzz of fast talk was followed by bursts of laughter. I felt like I had officially been crowned the "Porno King of JHS 82." I could only hope that my school diploma did not note such an achievement—"Passed All Courses with Honors in Pornography"—especially with my parents looking for wall space in our apartment to hang the thing.

Along came Sammy with perfect timing as usual. "So, Paul, how's it hanging?"

"What the hell is that supposed to mean?"

"My, we're a little sensitive. Just asking how're you doing."

"Yeah, right," I muttered. "Just terrific."

"Well, things could be worse than being a pervert."

"Okay, so you know. Go break my chops."

Sammy wasn't about to let up. "What did Bonnet say to you?"

"How do you know I saw Miss Bonnet?"

"Paul, you are definitely out of it. Everyone saw you go into Bonnet's classroom—bro, you're famous, the talk of this place."

"I really don't want to get into it."

"Hey, did you check out the third floor boys' bathroom?"

"What do you mean?"

"You're an inspiration, like some Michelangelo. Someone drew a picture of Miss Bonnet on the wall, and he signed your name. Not a very good picture if you ask me. The boobs were way too big, but then again it's tough doing your best work on a bathroom wall. That picture wasn't yours, was it?"

"You'd better start running, Sammy," I snapped.

Sammy bent over laughing, clapped my shoulder. "Take it easy. You're the man."

Yeah, some man, I thought. Right.

I pushed past Sammy and went into homeroom to pick up my jacket. I desperately needed to get out of the school for some fresh air. A good thing it was lunchtime, and I could split. But then I noticed a large brown envelope sticking out of my desk with my name in large letters. What was this? The FBI deciding to investigate criminal charges? A shakedown demanding more porno—or else? I sighed, and ripped open the envelope. Inside were glossy pages from a *Playboy* magazine. Actually two large pages to be exact. The centerfold picture of Miss September. Scrawled on the bottom of the page was the name "Miss Bonnet."

I actually thought that Miss Bonnet was prettier, though I had to give Miss September credit for her other attributes. (I *really* needed to start focusing on something else.) Things had gone way too far. Mutilating your father's *Playboy* was a serious offense. I wondered how this John Doe's dad was going to react when he snuggled up to his magazine and found Miss September missing. I couldn't imagine he would be very happy without his naked picture.

That would make the two of us.

CHAPTER 34

Hiding in Plain Sight

It's when you're not looking that the demons come and blindside you. I thought I was through with them, but I should have known better. The truth was, they were never gone. Certainly not that night. I could not have missed this one if I tried.

That evening in early spring had been like any other. I'd been hanging out on my fire escape, gazing up at the cloudless dark sky. I thought I'd spotted a star and was amazed at the appearance of this speck of light. I suspected, though, that the sighting was nothing more than my wishful imagination at work. No stars ever came out in my neighborhood. Nights skies were usually a ceiling of murky blackness.

And it was then that Tremont Avenue exploded into sound and fury as a swarm of police cars stormed down the avenue, sirens on fire, shattering the peace. Leaning out over the steel railing to watch the cars fly by, I wondered whether we were now at war.

I didn't have to wait long to find out.

Fred rushed over to me, breathing hard. "Around on Davidson," he gasped. "The place is a battle zone. Cops everywhere, guns out. Looks like something out of a movie!"

"So, what's—"

"Must be something real bad, the whole block is barricaded."

We had our problems in the neighborhood, typical larceny stuff, sometimes a fight, but this was something else. Something serious.

Fred and I tore out of the apartment, following the noise down Tremont Avenue and around the corner onto Davidson. We stopped in our tracks, coming face to face with a mob scene. Hundreds of people were jammed onto the block. The neighborhood was out in full force, all eyes looking skyward. The crowd was not on the lookout for stars, but a madman.

I shaded my eyes. Blinding police lights spotlighted an apartment house that seemed to be electrified against the night sky.

Police cars were cattycornered along the street, their color flashers spinning wildly. A small army of cops had surrounded the building with guns out and pointing at a fourth-floor apartment.

"I've seen this movie," I told Fred, as we stood at the edge of the crowd.

"How does it end?"

"Not good," I grimly replied.

Police barriers kept the crowd back, but we managed to squeeze ourselves into a spot close enough to the building.

"What gives?" Fred asked an older man next to his shoulder.

"Hostage situation," he said. "The guy is crazed. A maniac."

And then we heard him, the maniac, shouting out his window. Some gobbledygook about heaven, about being God's Messenger.

Cops were bustling about with guns in hand, but didn't look like they were about to open fire.

"Too dangerous," Fred said, sizing up the situation. "They could kill the guy he's holding."

A sergeant had a bullhorn to his mouth, electric words

that bombarded the air. "Release your hostage. Come down, with your hands up."

The cop might as well have been talking to himself.

The standoff went on for the next half-hour. The lunatic rants kept spilling out the fourth-floor apartment into the night, with the cops on the ground getting more edgy, anxious, like the rest of us. A ticking bomb ready to go off. Something had to give.

"Fred, what can the cops do?" I asked.

"Need to wait him out, I guess," he said. "He's not going anywhere."

My brother might have been wrong on that one. The guy sounded like he was about ready to join his Savior, and take his hostage with him.

The maniac opened his window and stepped onto the fire escape. And then he reached back into his apartment and yanked his victim out. A heavy bag covered the person's face, and his hands were tied in back of him.

The hostage was small, half the height of his captor. Even from the street I could see him shaking violently, barely able to stand.

I finally had a clear view of the loony. A really bad version of Santa Claus, with his long, stringy, dirt-white hair and pointy beard, wearing a ragged robe that hung down to his feet. His face glowed under the harsh bright police lights.

A scary ghost of a guy.

He had his rap going strong, shouting down to the crowd. "But if you do wrong, be afraid, for he does not bear the sword in vain. For he is the servant of God, an avenger who carries out God's wrath on the wrongdoer!"

A psycho quoting the scriptures. A lunatic who was super serious and really sick. A bad combination. And then, suddenly, he reached under his robe and pulled out a large knife.

"A machete," Fred called out.

I shut my eyes, wishing this horror away.

I could hear the crowd take in a sharp breath.

Then shouts. "No! No! No!" bombarded the air.

Cops, still pointing their guns, swiveled around to their superiors as if to ask what to do next.

"Depart from me, you cursed, into the eternal fire prepared for the devil and his angels!"

The sergeant at the bullhorn was on it again, way more urgency in his voice. "Let your hostage go *now*. Drop your weapon, and surrender!"

The maniac lashed out, grabbing the hostage by his neck, and pushing him down to his knees. An execution scene.

Fred and I just stood there, watching, disbelieving. This could not be happening. Only that it was.

The crowd had swelled, even more charged, crushing Fred and me against a police barrier.

A local TV reporter was doing in a live standup on the other side of the barricade. He was lit up by an overhead light. A cameraman took aim. "Police have identified the hostage taker as Ernest Strump, sixty-three, an escaped convict from Attica Prison, where he had been serving a life sentence for murder. Strump escaped two years ago from Bellevue Hospital. He was being held at the facility for psychiatric observation after stabbing to death another inmate…"

I was caught between the reporter's words, and the action on the fourth floor. The lunatic was now pointing his machete to the sky as if he was summoning God Himself.

"…There have been no reported sightings of Strump since. That is, until tonight…"

I could see the maniac reaching down, struggling to pull the bag off his prisoner's head.

"Strump is now reported to be the kidnapper of a local boy missing and presumed dead after being taken from a school bus stop two years ago—"

And I knew before he said another word.

"—Benjamin Shapiro."

And there, illuminated by the bright lights, was Benji, on

his knees, barely holding onto life on that fire escape,

A scream rang out into the night.

I hadn't seen her at first, but then she was in front of me, standing next to a cop. Benji's mom, Laura Shapiro. Tinier than I remembered, lost in an oversized coat she was wearing. And looking older, her face lined, no longer Natalie Wood beautiful. Another survivor in the neighborhood.

It had been two years since that terrible night at my building. A lifetime ago. How could I ever forget her. So helpless. And now this night. She was screaming out for Benji again, her arm outstretched, pleading. Her son was there, finally in sight, but still out of reach.

"BEN-JI! BEN-JI! MY DARLING!"

She could not lose Benji a second time. God could not be so cruel, I thought.

Her cries made their way to the fourth-floor fire escape. I could see Benji flinch, bending his head down, desperately trying to pick up the voice that belonged to his mom. The boy and his mother were together, finally. Separated by a madman with a machete who was getting set to kill.

"You believe that God is one, you do well. Even the demons believe—and shudder!"

The lunatic was working himself up.

"Fred," I said hoarsely. "This can't be happening."

I felt myself trembling.

My brother stayed silent.

And then it came back it me. A flash of a memory.

That Halloween. Apartment 4G, with the old lady. The dead son's picture on the wall. Then I was on the street carrying a wooden box of her seltzer bottles. A crazy, weird, dark night. I had bumped into a strange, creepy man. *This man*. And he wasn't happy, calling me a stupid kid. But it was his black eyes that scared the hell out of me. Glaring. Dangerous. A kid was with him. He wore a baseball cap that hung over his eyes, and was slouched over in the shadow of the street. Benji.

"Oh, my god!" I shouted, as the memory hit.

"What?" Fred said, confused.

"It's him!" And I told my brother the story of that night.

"This guy's been hiding in plain sight," Fred finally said, shaking his head in disbelief.

"All this time," I murmured more to myself. "Here, in the neighborhood."

The poor kid, caged with this maniac.

And now it was about to end.

The lunatic then raised his machete into the air again, screaming some insanity into the night sky. I had no doubt that he was reaching out to his own God.

And about to give sacrifice.

My nightmare. So many as a kid, with demons haunting my sleep. My crying out, before Rosie nudged me awake. But Mom hadn't saved me from the memory, or the fear taking over me again.

"Hey, Fred." I turned to my brother, suddenly confused. "Is this some sort of bad dream?"

Fred gave me a worried look, much like the one after I woke from the coma. "Paul, nothing is more real than that," he replied, pointing to the fire escape.

I looked up and saw little Benji waiting to die. A maniac brandishing a machete and ready to strike. A living nightmare.

I found myself silently praying. I wasn't the religious type at all but had the habit of counting on Him when a big favor was needed. This was the biggest ever. Please keep this boy alive. Let him live.

I turned back to Laura Shapiro. Her knees had buckled, her eyes on her son, her mouth moving. We were both reaching out.

Benji also was on his knees. Silent, head down. This kid, what he had endured. He seemed ready to accept whatever was to come. Just wanting this over. Finally.

The crowd had become eerily still, also waiting for the inevitable act that would bring an end to this mad night.

And it was at that moment that the air filled with noise.

The shattering of glass from the fourth-floor window.

Shouts, policemen storming onto the fire escape.

Screams from the madman.

A fight, surreal, with police spotlights illuminating the struggle.

Yelling, grappling.

The lunatic still waving the machete, his screeches piercing the night.

Being fought to the ground, the knife wrestled from his hand.

More noise. Deafening. This coming from the sidewalk. The crowd exploding.

An uproar that climbed into the starless sky.

Fred and I joining in.

In another setting, we might have been at a sold-out Yankee game, exultant as Mickey hits one over the fence. But this was different. We were shouting out for the life of this kid. Benji Shapiro. Missing. But found. Alive. And safe.

❧❧❧

A police officer gently carried Benji out of the building as if he was precious cargo. The boy had his arm around the cop's neck, his head resting on the man's shoulder. A picture that easily might be mistaken for a father and son. Benji was thinner than his photo, but still the same face, the same boy.

And then I caught the rush of a woman, knifing through the police and over to the kid. Laura Shapiro. And her scream this time was louder than all the others. Her son was back.

And for the first time in my life, I gave thanks to God. And believed in Him.

The cop eased Benji from his grip and down to the pavement. The kid took off, sprinting over to his mother, a collision that ended as Laura snapped her arms tightly around her boy.

I could hear the crowd chanting his name. "Ben-ji! Ben-ji! Benji!"

A woman next to me started to cry. And I found myself breaking down as well, unashamed and overwhelmed. Life doesn't usually give us a break, but this little boy and his mom deserved one.

"Unbelievable," Fred said softly.

And that's exactly what it was.

CHAPTER 35

Scarlett Mine

W ell, there's Scarlett," Sammy announced, motioning to Dee-Dee down the hallway standing next
to her locker.

We had yet to start our school day and Sammy was already whacked out.

"What are you talking—"

"Scarlett O'Hara, you know."

"Sammy, what drugs are you on now? That's *Dee-Dee*
O'Hara. Who the hell is Scarlett?"

"Tell me you don't know Scarlett O'Hara! Are you kidding? She happens to be this hot chick that falls for this stud
with a mustache. But she's really a bitch, so he kind of slaps
her down and dumps her."

"Oh, thanks for that. So, to repeat, how're the drugs
you're taking?"

"Bro, it's an old movie about the Civil War. My folks
took me to see it at Radio City. Some sort of revival."

"And what does this have to do with Dee-Dee?"

"I wouldn't be surprised if the two of them are related.
Amazing coincidence, that's all. Dee-Dee has the same col-
or eyes, same hair, same last name. She's also hot."

"Sammy. Tell me that you're kidding," I groaned. "You

do know that one O'Hara is real, the other is not."

"If she's so real, why aren't you going for her?" Sammy shot back.

So that was the deal. Sammy playing matchmaker.

"I must be the stud with the mustache then," I replied, going along with his game.

"Nah. Not with your face. And she'll probably dump you anyway. But, hey, you only live once."

"Thanks, Sammy. A real confidence booster."

"C'mon, you know you want to."

Sammy was right. I did want to. I couldn't stop thinking of Dee-Dee O'Hara. How could I forget that dance in the moonbeams with her at Maude's party? Too bad I also couldn't wipe out Maude's mugging from my memory. But a "date" with Dee-Dee? That was something else. I'd never been on one and wasn't sure what that meant other than I'd be alone with Dee-Dee O'Hara—and for a couple of hours, and I'd be alone with her. Yeah, I already said that.

"So, where's your balls?" Sammy wasn't about to let up.

"Did you cut out on the bio class when we went over that?"

"Yeah, good one, but let's get back to the subject. Why not?"

"Nah. She always busy with her stuff."

"What stuff?"

"Well, uh, homework…and stuff."

"Paul. Remember Maude's party. Man, she was all over you."

"I don't think that was it."

"You dope. You still haven't gotten over her."

"I also haven't gotten over your crazy sister. My neck is still on fire."

"Forget that. You've had a thing for Dee-Dee forever."

"Yeah, I mean, she's nice and all, but—"

"Look, there, she's about to go to class," Sammy said, thumbing down the hallway. "Be a stud, bro, there's your Scarlett."

But we both could see that I was already too late.

"Shit!" Sammy exclaimed. "The competition crashed in. Would you believe this guy?"

Hovering along Dee-Dee's locker stood Arthur Solomon, better known as Artie "the Schmuck" Solomon.

I knew that other guys had an eye out for Dee-Dee. One was this ninth-grade jerk who moved in the fast lane at JHS 82. Artie was well deserving of his nickname. I was convinced that under the word "schmuck" in the Yiddish dictionary was a picture of Artie Solomon. He was never without a white T-shirt and his heavy black leather jacket, seeing himself as Brando, the tough motorcycle guy in *The Wild One,* instead of the moron he was at Macombs Junior High.

Sammy and I watched as he took out a comb and raked it through his greased-back hair. Artie kept forgetting that the '50s cool look was very uncool in 1962.

He had swaggered over to Dee-Dee's locker and now was giving her his rap.

I started paying more attention.

The two were chatting away, and I could see Dee-Dee taking in something Artie was saying. Maybe his explanation of Einstein's "Theory of Relativity." More likely, the guy was inviting her to touch his leather jacket and run her fingers through his greasy hair.

And then Artie's hand found its way on to Dee-Dee's shoulder.

"He's making a move on her, and in the hallway!" Sammy said.

We both stood transfixed next to my locker. I couldn't take my eyes off Artie's hand resting on Dee-Dee, and now rubbing her shoulder. What was that?

Artie kept yakking, all the while giving Dee-Dee a shoulder massage. Finally, she angled sideways and his hand slipped off. The guy didn't seem to mind the snub, pushing on with his gab.

"Look, she can't stand him," Sammy said.

"How can you tell?" I asked.

"He's laughing his head off, and look at her."

Dee-Dee had that you're-really-such an-asshole look. At least that was my interpretation. I then saw Artie's shift gears, lean over, and whisper something in her ear. Dee-Dee turned red, grimaced, and emphatically shook her head. Artie paused, shrugged, and took off. I could hear him call out as he sauntered past her, "Later, sweetheart."

I was glad to see that he wasn't looking too happy.

"He's an asshole," Sammy said, so a unanimous vote between us.

Just then, Dee-Dee glanced over in my direction. I'd been standing in the middle of the hallway, gaping at her talking to Artie like I was mental. My first instinct was to run, but I could feel Sammy's hand steady me on my back.

Then she waved and smiled. It was a very different look than the one she gave Artie. Open, friendly.

"Hey, wave back," Sammy whispered, and jabbed me on my arm.

I waved back.

And then Dee-Dee started to walk down the hallway toward me.

"She's coming over!" Sammy said, and snapped his finger. "Be cool, boy, real cool."

Sammy had to cut out his *West Side Story* impersonations. I was feeling anything but cool at the moment.

"Hi, Paul," Dee-Dee said cheerfully, coming up to my locker. "What's going on? I miss seeing you."

What was that? She missed me? Was this the "missing you" like in, "Haven't seen you around in a while?" Or was this the "missing you" as in, "I've been waiting for you to call me, you dummy, and ask me out for a date, and you haven't, and I'm dying for you to call because you are the most wonderful boy in the whole wide world?"

I thought that last idea was a tad optimistic.

"Don't want to be late for class," Sammy said to me, a bit too gleefully. He gave me a sharp poke on my back, a

message that said, "Show her you have balls, Paul!" Sammy
loved his testicles metaphor. Then he took off.

Without bothering to look over his shoulder, he raised
his fist and called out, "Catch ya later, bro."

I was already in trouble. Dee-Dee was eyeing me, waiting for me to say something. And I had no clue what that
was supposed to be. "I saw you talking with Artie," I finally
blurted. I didn't see how this observation could possibly
have inspired a conversation, but the words spilled out.

"Artie can be such an idiot," Dee-Dee said wryly. She
then gave me another look, hesitated a second, and asked
me a peculiar question. "So, Paul, I heard there's a great
feature at the Park Plaza. You'd like to go?"

What was that?

Was Dee-Dee O'Hara asking me out?

Dee-Dee O'Hara was asking me out!

I didn't answer right away. The question was the very
last one I had expected to hear coming from her mouth. In
fact, this question wasn't even on the list of possible questions I'd ever imagine Dee-Dee asking me: Do you have
today's English homework? A possibility. Do you think it
will rain today? Not a bad question. Do you want to go out
with me—and to a dark movie theater where we would be
alone?

Are you kidding me?

But she wasn't.

I finally found my voice. "S—sure," I stammered, failing
miserably to be "real cool." Yeah, thanks. Sammy. I'd even
managed to stumble over my single word response to her.

"That's great," she cheerily went on, and then without
missing a beat. "Want to hit the seven o'clock Saturday
show?"

Another question. Saturday night with Dee-Dee O'Hara.

"Sure," I replied, my responses adding up to grand total
of two words, actually a single word repeated twice.

Another smile from Dee-Dee that dimpled her cheeks.
"Saturday then, meet you in front of the theater."

And then she hustled off to class, leaving me standing there, shaking at my knees.

CHAPTER 36

Love at the Park Plaza

I got to the Park Plaza movie theater early, pacing around for more than a half-hour before I saw Dee-Dee coming up from down the block. For a minute I didn't recognize her—and then I did as she got closer. Her bright, red hair was tied back in a ponytail giving me a full view of her face. She looked, well, so grownup, with lipstick and makeup. Actually, beautiful is the word, not just the cute girl I knew since elementary school. I was relieved that I had listened to Mom and worn a clean shirt and plastered down my cowlick.

Dee-Dee didn't seem to mind my staring and bounded up and gave me a hug, a friendly squeeze, but I still felt her soft body as it rubbed up against me. I was having enough anxiety without the physical contact, not that I was complaining. As we touched bodies, I couldn't help myself and started to sniff her hair. Dee-Dee smelled like flowers.

"'Shalimar,'" she said, smiling. "You like?"

"You smell nice," was the best I could come up with.

A moment of panic, silently cursing out myself for not thinking of using Fred's "Old Spice." It struck me that my nervousness was working its way into a smell. Not the flower kind either. At least I had the sense to stop from taking a sniff of my armpits to check myself out.

"You waiting here long?" Dee-Dee asked sunnily.

"No, just got here," I lied, but I could tell she knew that.

I was beginning to think that this date-thing was a bad idea. I'd already run out of things to say after telling her how nice she smelled. Okay, not a great ice-breaker, but I had nothing else. The only good news, I wouldn't have to talk to her in the theater. I suppose, though, that we would be sitting next to each other. And close.

Yeah, I was an idiot.

I paid the dollar for both tickets—Sammy had warned me not to be cheap—and we made our way into the movie theater. The film was called *To Kill a Mockingbird*. From what I read in the papers, it wasn't exactly my kind of movie. Dee-Dee had made the choice, and I thought it best not to push the latest horror flick, *The Kiss of the Vampire*. I didn't want her to get the wrong idea.

It was the Saturday night crowd, and almost every seat in the theater was taken. So we shuffled around in the dark before finding two seats in the next-to-the-last row. I settled into my seat but not before peeking over my shoulder at some older teens that had taken over the back row. It was pretty clear that the pair were more interested in each other than in watching any film. Even before the movie had begun, they were going at it, grappling in the dark.

Both of us pretended that nothing else was going on while we watched the movie previews that had kicked in. But the sound of "oohs" and "aahs" were already background noise to the coming attractions featuring outer-space creatures invading Earth. A girl directly in back of us began sighing, "Oh, Johnny!" as a Martian-type monster devoured some poor Earthling. I glanced over my shoulder and caught a glimpse of the girl who'd been moaning, much to the appreciation of her boyfriend next to her—he must have been Johnny. He had one hand cupped on her breast, the other rubbing her thigh. She didn't seem to mind at all.

"So what do you think of the preview?" Dee-Dee asked,

staring ahead at the screen. She then let loose a light laugh, and I did too, nervously. There was no getting around the preview playing in back of us.

If I wasn't self-conscious enough, the back-row lovers made me hyper-aware of my "date." Dee-Dee and I weren't just "friends" but now "a couple," a thought that only made me sweat more, and horrified that my armpit stink level was on the rise. I glanced sideways to check Dee-Dee out. At least her face wasn't scrunching up in disgust, so I guess that I was okay for now.

Finally, I relaxed enough to get lost in the story of Atticus Finch, Scout, and Jem and their tale of growing up in the South. I found myself taken in by Tom Robinson, a black man on trial, accused of rape. I couldn't help but think of Joe Bailey, another victim.

What an amazing story. Even the couple in back of us had slowed down to watch the movie. And then, just like that, Dee-Dee rested her head on my shoulder. A shock, but, really, it didn't feel strange at all. It felt right. And, so, I reached over, and put my arm around her. That felt right, also. And we sat like that, together, our bodies connected.

I was still looking at the screen, but no longer watching the movie. Only thinking of this girl cuddled with me. Leaning over, I brushed back a strand of her hair. Actually Dee-Dee's hair was doing fine, but I simply needed to touch her. And wouldn't you know it—she felt the same with me.

And just then Dee-Dee raised her head, her hazel-green eyes on mine, and kissed me. A single kiss, but it stayed with me. And I sat there, dumbstruck, drifting back to the screen, staring at Boo Radley saving Atticus's kids from harm. I was floating in some wondrous space, sensing only the thump of my heart. I only knew one thing for sure in the world. I was absolutely in love with Dee-Dee O'Hara.

The movie ended, but we stayed in our seats, still nestled together. A beautiful story. Both Atticus's and ours. The house lights went on, breaking the spell, and we finally got up to leave. Our hands still laced together, we slowly made

our way out of the theater and back to her building on Burnside Avenue. We had held hands once before. That had been
different, a miserable day. After the nastiness with Plotz.
This was something else.

I thought this could be a good time to announce that I
was madly in love with her. Get down on my knee, propose,
talk about our wedding plans—I mean, why waste time? To
which she'd breathlessly tell me that she would absolutely
die if I didn't kiss her again. And that we couldn't wait another day for a wedding, but needed to elope this very instant!

Then again, I reckoned that I might be pushing it a little
bit. Instead, I brought up Gregory Peck as Atticus, who we
agreed was the perfect father and man.

We arrived way too soon at her apartment building.

"Thanks, Paul, this was wonderful," she said quietly, as
we stood next to the building entrance. All I saw were those
hazel-green eyes glowing underneath a street lamp.

I wanted to tell her that *she* was wonderful.

I also wanted to kiss her again.

"Yes, what a great movie," I said, my courage failing.

She then tilted her head and gave me a perplexed look.
"Well, be seeing you at school."

"Yeah, I guess so. I really had a great time."

"Me too," she replied, still gazing at me.

"Dee-Dee…" I couldn't let her go.

She just stood there. Waiting.

We both knew it had to end this way.

And so I did something crazy. I took Dee-Dee's face in
both my hands and kissed her. I did. I couldn't stop myself,
and beautiful Dee-Dee didn't seem that she wanted me to.
This kiss was longer than our first in the movie theater and
more serious. And then there was no turning back. I
wrapped my arms around her. Our bodies welded together.
Then another kiss with even more heat. I could hear her
sigh, and felt her hand stroking my hair. Neither of us were
willing to let go.

That is, until a voice—a furious voice shouting Dee-Dee's name—came down from the heavens. It was as if God Himself was getting set to strike us both dead.

But it was much, much worse than that—the voice belonged to Dee-Dee's mother. Mrs. Gertrude O'Hara.

"*Dee-Dee O'Hara!*" she yelled out a second time from the second floor apartment window directly above where we were standing.

We untangled in a flash.

"Hi, Mom," Dee-Dee groaned, red-faced. "I'm coming upstairs."

"Yes, *you are,* this very instant!" Mrs. O'Hara angrily barked.

In a panic, I meekly waved to the woman after being caught ravaging her daughter. I got the distinct feeling that I hadn't made a very good first impression to my future mother-in-law.

Mrs. O'Hara didn't say a word to me, just glared with murder in her eyes.

Dee-Dee gave me the I'm-so-so-sorry look. I hoped she meant it as an apology for her mother and not our passionate kisses. Then she opened the entrance door, and shuffled upstairs to face the music. I waited another moment, then turned and headed to Tremont Avenue. I could smell her "Shalimar" on me.

I was already aching for the girl as I walked home, so I went back to planning our life together. We'd buy a house in Riverdale, the fancy section of the Bronx, and have three children—three seemed to be the right number. There was the sticky issue that we were fourteen and virgins, but no matter.

And then there was the matter of God—Dee-Dee O'Hara was Irish-Catholic and outside the tribe. I might have a hard time explaining to Mom and Dad, but I was sure they'd understand once the grandkids came along.

I had it all figured out.

ℰↀℰↀ

Dee-Dee and I became "a couple" over the next two months, though there wasn't any official paper that we signed confirming the fact. It just seemed that we were. On weekends, we'd go over to Krum's on the Concourse for some ice cream and then catch a movie at the Loew's Paradise across the street, or watch the horseback riders at the stables at Van Cortlandt Park. Dee-Dee also didn't seem to mind shooting hoops with me in the schoolyard—I mean, how cool was that? I couldn't wait to surprise the girl for her birthday coming up—a bottle of "Shalimar" *and* a trip to Freedomland in Baychester with dinner at Nathans. (She loved their crinkly French fries.)

And everywhere we went we held hands and kissed. A lot. Under streetlamps, on benches, on her bed, though always keeping ears open for Gertrude O'Hara coming back to the apartment.

Needless to say, I kept both hands in my pocket around Dee-Dee's mother. Mrs. O'Hara wasn't the warm fuzzy type, and I didn't think she was about to break out the champagne and welcome me as her future son-in-law. She did a great impersonation, though, of J. Edgar Hoover, checking out Dee-Dee for any fingerprints each time we came back from a date—and, naturally, we made sure to tuck in our clothes and wash-up before walking into the apartment. During those times, Mrs. O'Hara would give me that squinty-eyed warning look that said, "Don't even *think* of messing with my daughter!" It was a good thing for me that she wasn't a mind reader.

Having a girlfriend cut into my street time, but that was more than a fair tradeoff. While my friends were out playing ball on the weekends, I hung out with Dee-Dee. She even took me shopping one day, so I must have seriously fallen for her.

One afternoon we decided on the movies, our favorite

hideaway, and found two seats in the back row. I don't re-member anything about the film, not even its name. We spent that afternoon in the pitch-black, and in our own pri-vate space, lips on lips and touching. I really liked the touching part.

It was all going so well between us. I woke up and went to bed each night with Dee-Dee in my thoughts and dreams. We talked on the phone every night until I heard the drowsy in her voice. She was just so perfect, and we were perfect together. Her hazel-green eyes lit up my heart, her soft kiss-es made me melt. Our love was the stuff of those sappy Hallmark cards. I could have written a bunch of them my-self. It was the most wonderful feeling being in love with Dee-Dee O'Hara, and, without a doubt, I was positive that she felt the same about me.

That is, until the day she dumped me.

CHAPTER 37

Shtupping Dee-Dee O'Hara

I never thought that there would be a time when I'd yearn to be back in a coma. But I really felt like revisiting that dark place again. How wonderful it would be to return to those days with my body broken, my mind gone. A nice distraction from the pain I felt now. I wasn't one for nostalgia, but where were those good old unconscious days? Floating around, not a care. I decided never to feel sorry for comatose patients again. They were the lucky ones.

I certainly had a way with girls—too bad it was the very wrong way. Anita Bonita. Miss Bonnet. Dee-Dee O'Hara. Strike three. You're out! Game over. I would have considered the priesthood as a good career move had it not been for the obvious.

I didn't know when the breaking up started since Dee-Dee never told me. But *she* knew and kept the secret to herself. It began slowly with one excuse or another why she couldn't see me. A plan to meet for ice-cream at Krum's was called off, something about seeing a sick aunt. And then the flu bug she caught an hour before our usual Saturday night out at the Park Plaza. Apparently some bad microbes were going around her family. She was quick to recover, though, showing up for school Monday looking chipper to me.

It didn't take long to notice that our nightly talks were getting fewer, and shorter—and more polite. Polite is not a good thing in romance. Polite is asking the deli counterman to make sure to cut the pastrami lean. Polite is making sure that the toilet seat is down for your mother before she walks into the bathroom. Polite is not your girlfriend telling you how sorry she is that she has lots of homework, so forget the date that afternoon. Or that evening. Or for the rest of the week.

Worst of all, she seemed to be boycotting our favorite activities together. The Big Three: kissing, holding, touching. I had gotten so desperate that I would've settled for a pat on the back. She threw me the occasional dimpled smile at school, but it was the eyes that gave her away. They simply didn't light up anymore. They looked past me.

To be accurate, Dee-Dee never uttered the words I dreaded to hear, which were, "I am breaking up with you." As for me, I denied that these words even existed in the English dictionary. It was actually Sammy who clued me in to the fact that Dee-Dee and I had broken up, which seemed peculiar to me. How did Sammy know before I did? As it turned out, it seemed everyone, and that included my best friend, knew that Dee-Dee had dumped me. Except me.

I was given the death sentence one afternoon as Sammy and I hung out on my building stoop. Not much talk. A real strange quiet. Sammy had this sick look not all that different than the one we have after eating in the school cafeteria. I knew nothing good was about to come.

"I'm sorry, Paul," he said finally, and he meant it.

Sorry? "What's going on?" I replied, instantly on edge.

Sammy didn't mince words. First he let me have it between the eyes. And then he cut my head off. "It's Dee-Dee. You're out. She's with some another guy."

I had refused to face the fact that Dee-Dee and I were through, though my vomiting twice a day was telling me otherwise. So, okay, horrible, terrible news but not really the electric chair sort of shock. I'd seen the breakup coming for sure. But there was this other thing that Sammy had said. This stuff about "some another guy." I could feel sweat starting to bubble on my neck.

"How do you know?" I asked anxiously.

Sammy hesitated again. Trouble coming. This time he was about to rip out my heart.

"I saw both of them together on Burnside Avenue yesterday and, well…"

"Dee-Dee told me she was doing homework yesterday," I mumbled.

"She was," Sammy sighed. "It looked like she was working hard on an assignment for her sex-ed class."

"She's not taking sex-ed," I said, my mind deep in a fog.

"You jerk. From what I saw she was having a private lesson."

"Okay, okay, I got it," I muttered. But the $64,000 question. "So, who is he?"

Sammy paused, staring down at his feet. "Artie Solomon."

I felt my mouth open wide, but couldn't utter a single sound.

"Artie Solomon," Sammy repeated, to make sure I understood.

Hold on. Just hold on. Hallucinations were kicking in. Some garble coming out of Sammy's mouth. Something about Artie Solomon and Dee-Dee—Artie? Dee-Dee? ARTIE, DEE-DEE?

"NOT ARTIE SOLOMON!" I finally cried out.

"Yeah," Sammy nodded glumly. "That's the guy. The schmuck."

⁓⊙⁓

I spent weeks in mourning, crawling into bed after school with a pillow over my face. Rosie had caught on, believing that the chocolate doughnut she brought into my room might help. But bringing back my handlebars was not the answer.

"Sweetie, why don't you go outside and play some ball with the guys," she urged gently one Saturday afternoon.

"Mom, I just want to jump off the George Washington Bridge, and hope that I get devoured by a gang of man-eating piranha that will ravenously rip every inch of flesh from my body." Actually, I never did say this to Rosie—a bit too dramatic for Mom. But I also didn't think playing stoopball was the answer. So, instead, I told her: "I think I'll go over to the library and catch up on some homework."

Mom threw me a real worried look now. Saturday afternoon at the library? I guess she was hoping that what had been bothering me hadn't infected my brain.

Too bad it had.

I tried to avoid Dee-Dee at school, not that my invisibility mattered in any way. She had adjusted to my absence quite nicely. I still couldn't help myself from spying on her. One afternoon, I caught the girl leaning against the school locker with the schmuck all over her. She was giggling while Artie whispered some sweet nothing in her ear. Then he ran his hand down her back where it settled on her ass, giving her butt a massage. Apparently Artie wasn't interested in any sweet nothing but one particular something. And Dee-Dee didn't seem to mind at all.

I couldn't figure it out. One day, I'm planning my future family with Dee-Dee O'Hara. The next, I'm hiding in the school hallway watching in horror as Dee-Dee gets an ass rubdown from this miserable creep. How could this have happened?

Of course, Sammy didn't mind sharing his theory. "Paul, you just ain't one of the bad boys," he told me as we lazed around my room one afternoon.

"What the hell do—"

"I mean, look at you. You're like that nice kid on *Lassie*.

"The kid on television with the dog? I don't have a dog."

"You gotta face facts, bro. The girl goes for the leather jacket guys."

"Like the *schmuck*?"

"You got it."

"No way, I don't believe it."

"That's the problem."

We both stretched out on the rug, staring at the ceiling, looking up at a bunch of plastic "stars" that I had pasted there. The things glowed in the dark when I shut off the lights. Now they looked like some crap that somehow got stuck on top of my room.

"Sammy, what am I going to do?" I moaned.

Sammy exhaled and gave me his stop-feeling-sorry-for-yourself look.

"You ever think of getting a dog?" he replied.

℮↗つ℮↗つ

The school year could not have ended too soon. I was still deep in the dumps, a mental state that sank lower each time I passed Artie and Dee-Dee in the hallways. Actually the pair were more like a single entity, Artie-Dee-Dee, since I never saw one without the other. Bumping into them felt like a sharp knife slowly being plunged into my liver and large intestines before working its way up to my heart. Only that this was much more painful.

Hating Artie Solomon came naturally. The guy was nearly two years older than Dee-Dee and walked around with a smug confidence. Artie also wasn't shy bragging that he was *the* stud at 82, counting his "conquests" on his fingers. I guessed he would move on to his toes when he ran out of fingers. Some guys at school seemed impressed by Artie's macho attitude. My opinion ran in a slightly different direction: I thought the schmuck was a supreme asshole. Objectively speaking, of course.

Dee-Dee seemed quite agreeable being the object of Artie's desire. The two were literally joined at the hip, sauntering through the school, their arms locked around each other. They made it clear to anyone watching that Artie-Dee-Dee were the school's hottest couple, with an emphasis on the hot.

I couldn't help but notice that something in Dee-Dee's appearance had changed. Her cheeks were flush, and she had a glow that wasn't there when I was around. Either Dee-Dee had taken in more sun recently or something else was going on. It had been a cloudy week. So I didn't want to think any more about it.

Not that Sammy was going to let me off the hook.

ೞೞ

We met up outside of Square Pizza that Saturday afternoon. I was hungry, thinking about two slices and a Coke. Sammy was more excited about the latest Artie-Dee-Dee school gossip. I knew nothing good was going to come out of our lunch.

"You know you want to know," he said pointedly.

"I'm not interested," I shot back, and thought I meant it.

"Yes, you are." Sammy was not about to let go.

"Am I going to throw up after listening to you?"

"Yeah, probably."

A pause, then Sammy gave me the news. "They're doing it."

"Huh? Doing it?"

"Yeah, they're screwing."

"I know what it means, but I don't believe it."

"The word's out," Sammy went on. "Artie told his best friend Danny, who told his friend Mike, who told his girlfriend, Gigi, who, well, told the rest of the school."

"So all of 82 knows that Artie Solomon is *shtupping* Dee-Dee O'Hara?"

"What's with the Yiddish—you sound like my grandmother," Sammy said. "And, yeah, they're getting it on."

"It's all bullshit. Artie likes to talk, but he's full of it."

"From what I'm hearing, Dee-Dee is the one getting full of it."

"You're a pig, Sammy," I snapped. I was really pissed though not exactly sure who I was pissed at.

Sammy had to be dead wrong. I saw the way that Mrs. O'Hara glanced over at her kitchen knives each time I visited. And I only kissed her daughter. If Artie tried *anything* else, well, he might as well have said goodbye to his balls. And that's even if he was allowed to stay alive.

"You're jealous because you hit a single with Dee-Dee," Sammy went on. "Artie has rounded the bases. Probably going for the home-run record."

"Thanks, Sammy, for the special sports analogy."

"No problem, bro," he said.

I couldn't take anymore Artie-Dee-Dee crap. Just needed to find some quicksand and peacefully sink into the ooze.

Sammy was also tiring of the talk more intent now on satisfying his stomach.

"Hey, do you want pepperoni on your pizza?" he asked without missing a beat, as we made our way into Square Pizza.

I couldn't have eaten if I tried.

CHAPTER 38

War and the Commies

I walked through the school hallway trying to get my head screwed on right. It wasn't easy. Dee-Dee still haunted me. Mental pictures of the schmuck, his tongue in her mouth, his hand on her ass. Even worse pictures running through my mind. Did I have to see all that?

Well, at least I was finally over my infatuation with Miss Bonnet. My hormones had finally calmed down, and, besides, I wasn't looking for any more rejection. Miss Bonnet still was Marilyn Monroe beautiful, but I had no desire to create naked pictures of her anymore. I'd settle for her with her clothes on. I guess that was a step forward, or not.

To her credit, Miss Bonnet never brought up the subject of my porno portrait. I suspected, though, that my art teacher, Miss Sheldon, still considered my humiliation a happy memory and probably had my creation secretly hanging on her wall at home. The bitch.

As for the rest of school, I was getting by. Mr. Devlin was still a drill sergeant dressed up as an English teacher. I had been lucky enough to avoid being hit by one of his flying board erasers. Poor Richie—he just couldn't control himself and found himself the target of Mr. Devlin's throwing arm. (I tried to stay away from the kid since I didn't trust our teacher's accuracy.) But I imagine even Richie was feeling better. He had avoided being tossed out the first-floor classroom window, a special "emergency exit" for Mr. Devlin's favorite student-enemies.

It was Mr. Marianoff's class, though, that opened my eyes to the idea that the world was bigger than the Bronx. Even so, I thought at times I might've been better off keeping my head buried in the sand. My teacher's lessons boiled down to his one basic opinion—that the world was a mess. And we had only ourselves to blame.

Not exactly the lesson I wanted to hear.

Mr. Marianoff was one of those peacenik guys who accused John of sticking his nose in places that we didn't belong. One of these places was called the Bay of Pigs. I can't say I saw the problem—I mean how important could a bay filled with pigs be? Okay, I was kidding, but my teacher wasn't, and complained that John and the CIA had sided with some Cuban rebels looking to take out this commie guy, Fidel Castro—a fight that didn't work out too well. "Those men were slaughtered or thrown into prison," Mr. Marianoff explained during our talk on current events. "The entire episode was a debacle for the US."

"Further military interventions are bound to lead to disastrous results," he went on. Then he mentioned another fight we were starting up in some tiny country on the other side of the world. Vietnam.

Honestly, I had no idea even where the place was on the map, only that a lot of heat was coming from all the political talk. John had already sent thousands of military "advisors" over there. I wasn't sure what advice those guys were giving, or why so many of them were needed, but I wasn't about to second guess my president.

I raised my hand. "Mr. Marianoff, if we wanted to we could wipe out Vietnam in a minute. We're strong, so why should we even worry?"

"Yes, Paul," he said, "but don't ever underestimate the willpower of countries fighting against an invading power."

I thought of Korea. A long war that didn't seem to amount to anything. My Uncle Ruby had come home a hero, but he was one of the lucky ones. So many men died there. And for what? The enemy was still around staring back at us from the other side. I was confused.

"We are the good guys—aren't we fighting for freedom?"

"I wish that was always true. It's not clear why we are getting involved in Vietnam. Do you know why?"

I thought we were there to defeat the Commies, but to be honest I was baffled about communists in general. There were the Russian Communists and the Chinese Communists, but these guys seemed to hate each other. Then there were the Vietnamese Communists, who had nothing really to do with Russia or China. We even had communists in the United States and they weren't Russian, Chinese, or Vietnamese. We studied in class how *Americans* were bullied and even thrown in prison by government types like my favorite perspiring politician, Richard Nixon. Even if some our citizens had been communists, how were they hurting us? They *were* us.

Crazier still, every day on TV I was being told that we were in a "Cold War" with "the Reds." But weren't Russians and Americans on the same side during World War II, in it together to clobber the Nazis? Then, suddenly, we were at each other's throats, with Stalin then our latest enemy. I was all twisted around. I wasn't sure who we should hate, or even why?

"We can't be the world's policemen," Mr. Marianoff insisted. "There are times when other countries have to deal with their own problems. If we step in to each crisis, we're heading for big trouble."

I just didn't know what to believe. My teacher was Jewish himself, and if it hadn't been for America kicking Hitler's ass who knows where we would be now. Even Mr. Marianoff thought World War II was the "good war." "Defeating Germany and Japan was a matter of our own survival," he told us. "We were attacked, and then we had no choice. We had to go to war."

Our talks about that war always came down to the Holocaust. No way around it. More than a few kids in class had family killed by the Nazis, and such talk quickly became personal. Auschwitz. Bergen-Belsen. Dachau. Death camps that hissed out of their mouths. Some had parents who were survivors, and still branded with their number from the camps. Other kids told of horror stories about relatives that were gassed or shot.

Mr. Marianoff then filled us in on the latest news coming out of Israel. Adolf Eichmann had been executed. Right before midnight, hanged, cremated, his ashes thrown into the sea. Some kids let out a cheer.

The news brought to mind the nights Dad and I watched Eichmann's trial on television. This man in the glass booth. This nothing of a guy. I didn't feel like cheering his death. Too easy an out, I thought.

We never did resolve the question of "good" and "bad" wars in Mr. Marianoff's class. I guess it boiled down to the idea that we fought some wars because we had to and others because we wanted to. It still didn't make complete sense to me. The only thing really clear was that we always seemed to be fighting someone somewhere.

You'd think we would have gotten tired of it.

CHAPTER 39

Mr. P

My eighth grade was coming to an end, and not a moment too soon. It hadn't been easy living a fourteen-year-old life with all the angst. My one refuge was the school orchestra, where I now sat with 40 other kids, waiting for our teacher, Mr. Pagliaro, to take his spot at the podium. It was our final meeting, and one I'd been waiting for. Each year, Mr. Pagliaro presented medals to the very top musicians in the orchestra. A big deal, the biggest in fact—and to get this award from Mr. P, well, it meant everything to me. I could hardly wait to have my name called.

"Hey, Paul, you or me?" asked Jake Steiner, sitting next to me.

I looked over at my woodwind partner.

"You gotta be kidding, Jake. Face the fact that the squeals and squeaks coming out of your instrument could scare to death the neighborhood dogs. Better to take up the trombone or tuba next year—better yet, the finger cymbals—but leave the clarinet playing to me. Okay?"

That's what I could've said to Jake if I wanted to set him straight, but thought I'd play it humble.

So I shrugged, maybe giving Jake the idea that Mr. P's

decision was going to be a tough one. In truth, the guy didn't stand a chance. I mean, not a teensy chance. Mr. P might have switched us between First and Second Clarinet during rehearsals, and that was nice of him giving Jake a shot at the woodwind lead. But Jake was only slightly better than lousy, and apparently delusional if he thought he'd take my medal. Only one musician from each section would be chosen—so do I need to state the obvious?

If Jake was disappointed, sorry bud, but that was life.

I really didn't want anyone even thinking about messing with my medal.

We all were waiting, though, for Mr. Pagliaro, to show up. Mr. P was the man, and all of us admired him. We had a good laugh when he told us after a particularly good rehearsal, "Ah, even the great Ludwig Van Beethoven would be impressed." I didn't think he was joking.

The orchestra had gotten off to a shaky start back in September, but Mr. P brought us together. We were mostly squeaky woodwinds, screechy strings, and farty brass instruments. From all of this noise, Mr. P brought us along to magically produce music. The end-of-the-year concert had gone terrifically well, capped by a standing ovation from the school assembly.

Mr. P even singled me out on stage for my clarinet solos in Dvorak's *New World Symphony*. I wasn't one to brag, but I had been good—actually I was stupendous and had no doubt that even Ludwig Van would've been mightily impressed.

I steadied myself, ready to accept my teacher's praise again. If only he would get started with the awards.

"Hey, Paul." Jake again. "I gotta good feeling about this medal thing."

"What feeling is that, Jake?"

"I mean, don't take this the wrong way, but I think it's mine."

I shrugged again. "Jake, besides being a lousy clarinet player, you are a moron if you think you won."

Okay, what I really said, was, "Well, good luck, Jake. May the better musician win."

I was getting real pissed but stayed cool. Maybe I'd rub it in his face after I picked up the medal.

Jake pumped both his fists, getting an early start to his imaginary victory.

Mr. P finally left his office and made his way to the podium at the center of the orchestra room. In his hand were four plastic bags. Each contained a small bronze medal.

"I want to congratulate all of you for working so hard this year," he said. "Your talent and dedication has shined through, giving Macombs Junior High School 82 the gift of this amazing orchestra. I am so very proud of all of you."

We kids wore ear-to-ear smiles, taking in our teacher's praise. Mr. P was something else, always perfectly dressed in a blue suit, with his dark hair slicked back, a real professional. And he treated us that way, pushing us to "make our instruments sing." He felt such passion for the music each time he picked up his baton to conduct the orchestra. And that rubbed off on all of us. "The New York Philharmonic has nothing on you," he told us after our assembly performance. And, again, I thought he meant it.

"Let's get in on!" Jake called out, getting shushed by a few of the more respectful kids. I glanced over, and the guy was cracking his knuckles, ramping himself up for his big moment.

This time I didn't bother with him—just looking forward to seeing him crushed.

Mr. Pagliaro then cleared his throat, and in that deep voice of his began to call students to the podium to receive their "Outstanding Musician" medal.

"For the brass section…Justin Flynn."

Justin was a terrific trumpet player, and a popular kid, and got a rousing hand, as he waved and collected his pin.

"Strings…Rebecca Rose Amdur."

More loud applause as Rebecca, a talented violinist, stepped up to the podium, and shook hands with Mr. P.

"Percussion…Robby Nathan."

Robby, a crazy timpani player, bounced up to Mr. Pagliaro, smiled broadly and snatched his medal.

"Woodwinds…" Mr. Pagliaro hesitated a second, but then announced—

I rose even before my name was called.

"—Jake Steiner."

Huh?

Huh?

Jake Steiner?

Lousy Jake Steiner?

I was caught standing, frozen, in the middle of the orchestra, all eyes on me.

This couldn't be true. Impossible.

But there was Jake in his chipper way dashing up the podium for the medal, looking like he thought he'd earned it. He slapped me on the back as he rushed by.

Screw you, Jake! I might've given Jake this congratulatory message had I not been in shock.

What the hell was Mr. P doing giving my medal to Jake?

That medal was mine.

Only it wasn't.

And, *crap,* I was about to fall apart! It started with a single sob and then the dam broke with tears spilling down my face. I couldn't help myself. Standing in front of the orchestra kids, I was blubbering like some baby who had his bottle taken away.

Mr. Pagliaro turned my way and started to come over, which only made things worse.

I had to get away—and bolted from the room.

I slammed through the school's exit door, out onto the streets. I wasn't about to stick around and face my schoolmates. The word would've spread quickly that Paul Wolfenthal was nothing but a cry-baby. And who wanted to play stickball after school with a cry-baby. And a loser without a medal no less.

My head was in a fog. Mr. Pagliaro was such a great

teacher, who helped me discover a beautiful language. My music. And it was this teacher who thought that Jake Steiner was better than me.

I rushed from the school building, still raining tears, and headed for home. It had been a rough time, getting trashed by Dee-Dee O'Hara and now Mr. P. Enough "fuck-yous" for a lifetime.

I was relieved that Mom wasn't home, as I banged through the apartment door before heading into my bedroom. I buried myself in bed that afternoon with a blanket over my head, determined never to show my face again. I stayed there until my stomach growled signaling it was time for a chocolate snack. But even that didn't help.

Sammy had gotten wind and gave me a call later that night and tried to make it right. "Dee-Dee is still in your head, getting you down," he told me. "Forget about this other thing."

This medal.

But I couldn't let go of either.

∾∾∾

Eighth grade was over, finally. I had nothing more to do than collect my report card from Mrs. Froelich, my homeroom teacher. I did better than I thought, even got a B in math, Miss Bonnet had been generous; A-minus with Mr. Marianoff; and, a real shocker, an A from Mr. Devlin—the guy was a softy after all. Gym was B-plus instead of an A because I couldn't climb the damn rope that hung from the gym ceiling; a C in art—I guess Miss Sheldon held a grudge, she was still a bitch; and an A-plus in music, which only made me feel more miserable.

And it was then that Mrs. Froelich came up and told me that I needed to report to the orchestra rehearsal room. Mr. Pagliaro had sent for me.

I asked her why, but Mrs. Froelich said she had no idea.

I hesitated then slowly headed down to the music room, not knowing what to think, and really nervous about meeting up with my teacher. I had made a scene during the awards, but I couldn't see Mr. P holding that against me. At least I hoped he hadn't.

I came up to his office door next to our orchestra space, and he waved me in. He gave me a real serious look as I shuffled up to his desk. Usually that look was directed toward us in rehearsal when he explained the correct intonation and feeling for a musical passage. Now something else was on his mind.

"I'm sorry that you were upset yesterday, Paul," he said quietly. "I know you were disappointed."

As he spoke I could feel myself welling up again, the emotions still raw.

"I thought I was better than Jake," I murmured.

"You are," he said. "I thought you wouldn't mind if I gave the medal to Jake to encourage him more. That was my mistake. I'm very sorry."

I nodded my head, understanding, and relieved, ready to tell my teacher that it was okay. I was okay. It wasn't really the medal after all, but knowing that he thought I deserved it.

But then he went into his desk drawer and pulled out a box with a picture of the American bald eagle. He opened it to show me a large gold medal, bedecked in a red-white-blue ribbon, lying in a blue-velvet silk lining.

"This was given to me when I was a member of the US Marine band during the Korean War," he said pensively.

We both paused to take a look at the glistening medal, engraved with a lyre, and the words, *Esprit De Corps*. It was the most magnificent medal I'd ever seen.

"This is for you," Mr. Pagliaro said, smiling gently.

What? I stepped back, and shook my head. "No, no!" I couldn't accept this.

He nodded.

And like that, tears were back rolling down my cheek. I

was really turning into a cry-baby. This was my teacher's medal, his incredible award. This was just too much to take from him.

"I can't, Mr. P," I whispered.

"You deserve it, Paul," he said softly. "It's a special medal for a special musician."

"But Mr. P, this belongs to you," I said plaintively.

"And now it belongs to you."

Mr. Pagliaro then held out the box. I paused a moment before reaching to take it from him.

I carefully held the box in both hands, gazing at this beautiful medal nestled in the blue-velvet lining. Nothing in the world meant more to me.

I looked back at Mr. Pagliaro, his warm eyes watching me. I would've hugged him if I had the nerve. But I guess it wasn't necessary. He knew.

I finally turned to leave his office, holding the box against my chest, choked with emotion, letting tears flow freely, unable to utter even a thank-you to my dear teacher, Mr. P, for believing in me.

CHAPTER 40

Blood, Revenge, and Penance

Paul, you gotta come." Sammy raced up by me near the school exit, barely able to catch his breath. "Now!"

He pointed to the main schoolyard.

It was Saturday, vacation break already in full swing, and I expected a two-hand touch game was already under way. But it wasn't a game taking place. A fight. But it was even more than that.

I rushed from the building down the stairs to the main yard. A crowd of kids had already formed a circle around the combatants. I could not believe my eyes. Alan Plotz was being pummeled, taking a terrible beating. A barrage of punches had knocked him down to the hard cement. He was weeping, but the other guy still wasn't letting up.

Joe Bailey.

I didn't recognize Joe at first. His face was scarred, and his nose flattened. A fighter's face. He was also taller now, hovering over six feet, more a man than the teenager I'd known. My easy, cool friend was now someone else. Crazed, fury in his eyes.

He had taken off his T-shirt, his lean frame had hardened. Muscles rippled with each punch. The hard blows kept coming, creating a loud smack against Plotz's head and body.

"This is what they did to me in there," Joe yelled, pointing to his scarred face. "Now you know how it feels, fat boy."

"Jesus!" Sammy said. "Plotz's face is mashed potatoes. This is too much to take."

Blood poured from Plotz's smashed mouth and nose. His face was sliced, nose broken and his eyes swollen shut. On his knees, Plotz blindly swung his arm, pawing the air.

The crowd egged Joe on, not that he needed more incentive.

"Kick— His—Ass!"

"Kick—His— Ass!"

Joe reached back and then let loose, bashing Plotz hard on the side of his head.

The sound of the blow jolted me.

Without question, Plotz was the most unpopular student at 82. I imagined his graduation photo would read, "The Student Most Likely to Be Hated." He deserved the rep—he was a miserable guy. But he did not deserve this. No one did.

I couldn't just stand there. So I stepped into the fight circle.

"Paul, no!" Sammy shouted, grabbing my arm. He was afraid for me.

"Sammy, let go!" I broke from his grip. I thought I could calm Joe down, bring peace. We had been friends. He would listen.

Then I eased up to him, and put my hand gently on his shoulder. "Hey, Joe, he's had enough," I said softly.

Joe whipped around and for an instant didn't recognize me, until he did. In that moment he also looked like a stranger. He was older than I remembered, his marked face a contorted, angry mask. He cocked his fist, and I thought I was next in line to be pummeled. Instead, he swiped my hand off his shoulder and menacingly leaned against me.

"Get the fuck away from me," he hissed.

The crowd of kids was getting even more ramped up and getting louder. "Kick-His-Ass! Kick-His-Ass!" They wanted to see more.

I was terrified being there with Joe. We were way past our history. Nothing to hold on to. Insanity had taken over with these kids calling out for more blood.

Plotz was now lying on his back, hands over his eyes. He was sobbing, heaving, his big body shaking. A large wet stain traveled down the front of his pants.

"Joe, don't," I pleaded. "He's hurt. Real bad."

Without a word, Joe grabbed me by the front of my T-shirt—I could feel his body quaking with rage— and then threw me hard to the ground.

"I'm not through!" he sneered, pointing a warning finger at me.

And then went back at it, viciously swinging his leg into the Plotz's ribs. I heard a bone crack. Another kick to the ribs. And another. Each time, Plotz let out a scream. His cries pierced across the schoolyard.

And then it over. Joe, his face covered in sweat, was finally done.

Even the big-mouth watchers had seen enough, and quieted down.

"I should kill you, you racist motherfucker," Joe rasped. "You put me away in some cock-sucking prison, and now I've put you where you belong. On your shitty ass, crying like a baby. Boo-hoo, boo-hoo, you stupid fuck!" Joe then turned to me, still quivering with the violence that he'd unleashed. "And fuck you too, Paul!"

I thought he was about to come at me, but he just stood there.

I looked back at this stranger, sad and scared to death of him.

It was then that two police cruisers, sirens blaring, screeched up to the school. Joe saw them coming, casually put on his T-shirt, and calmly waited as four policemen sprinted into the schoolyard. They came up to us winded, glancing at the big kid writhing in pain on the ground. One cop bent down to tend to Plotz. The others didn't take more than a second to grab Joe by his neck, shake him around, and cuff him.

It was a year to the day since Joe had been arrested for stealing my clarinet. I couldn't forget that guy, just a kid himself, sitting in the back of a squad car in tears, scared, questioning with his eyes, pleading for understanding. None was given.

We were both so much younger then.

A heavyset sergeant patted him down, Joe smirking at his handler, his eyes narrowing. Now the tough guy, Joe settled in, looking like he didn't have a care in the world, waiting to be taken away, as if he was off to a picnic.

I silently watched the police bring him back to the squad car. Joe was still defiant while a cop lowered his head and shoved him into the back seat. Then the cruiser took off down University Avenue.

It was only a minute later that we heard the sound of a single siren shattering the air. An ambulance braked hard speeding up to the school. Two paramedics jogged into the yard, one holding a black medical case, the other a stretcher. They reached Plotz, who was crunched over in pain, and wailing. The adrenalin in his body, a natural painkiller, was slipping away.

Plotz's face had been pounded into a bloody mess. A broken nose, broken teeth, and, likely a few broken ribs. Too many cuts and gashes to count. I could hear a rattling sound coming from his mouth. The paramedics quickly put a plastic mask over his mouth and nose, plugging him into an oxygen tank.

The men were having a tough time hoisting him off the ground. Finally, they managed to get him up, the stretcher creaking from Plotz's dead weight.

The crowd of kids stayed around long enough to see Plotz lifted into the ambulance and taken away.

"Jesus, bro, can you believe it?" Sammy said, unsteadily. "That was Joe."

I did believe it. This blood revenge. What did we expect after sending Joe to Spofford, that hell? Did we somehow think that the cool kid with the big, easy smile would come out the same? After all this hate and stupidity? That kid was gone for good. This other person, scarred, unrecognizable, and filled with rage and vengeance, was in his place. And we had no one else to blame for him but ourselves.

എൻ

Plotz was released from the hospital three weeks later, but by then I was away at Tall Timber for the summer. I never did understand him, this kid trapped inside a small-minded world that he couldn't escape. He never did stand a chance when he found life pushing back at him that afternoon in the schoolyard—a punishment that was brutal, even unfair, but inevitable, leaving him with no choice but to accept it.

It was Sammy who rang me up at the bungalow colony, something he'd never bothered to do during my summers away. But he wanted me to know. And, somehow, even before he said a word, I already knew.

Plotz had been back from the hospital, wandering around the neighborhood, looking depressed and lost. "Didn't say anything to anyone," Sammy told me.

And then one afternoon Alan Plotz, young and so dumb, went to the top of his apartment building and jumped. He lived long enough to say that he was sorry.

PART IV

1962-64

CHAPTER 41

Kissing Your Ass Goodbye

It was a ninety-minute drive from Peekskill back home after a summer in "the country." I never wanted my Tall Timber days to end. What kid wanted to give up running free in the world? But this time was different. I couldn't shake the feeling as Dad drove us home that something had changed. I had changed. I felt much older now at fifteen, somehow crossing some line, the kid in me fading, I wasn't especially looking forward to growing up. But it seemed to be happening whether I wanted it to or not.

When I settled in back home, that strange feeling only persisted. Tremont Avenue seemed different, too. My building's courtyard seemed to have sunk in, as if it could no longer carry the weight of us kids running around, playing our games. The block also was tired looking, feeling its old age. I know, a crazy thought. Brick and cement aren't alive, can't feel a thing. But maybe they are and can sense time quickly ticking down.

Okay, it made no sense, unless it did.

The reality, Bronx life was changing, and no one was asking me if I minded. But I did. The Bronx I came home to was not some shining Munchkin land with cheery little people greeting me back to the neighborhood. Not that it ever was. Still, I expected to see everything in its place. But that wasn't the feeling at all. Not with shops closing down, neighbors moving out. I was more likely to bump into the Fordham Baldies or Diablos, street gangs that I would never mistake for the Jets and Sharks dancing and singing in the streets. And the Cypress Lords, a tough girls' gang. I was sure that these girls weren't what Betty Friedan had in mind in her splashy new book about feminism, whatever that was. Not that I knew much else about Betty Friedan.

As it was, I could only watch my neighborhood slowly coming apart, moving too fast, becoming something else.

I know, it made no sense. Only that it did.

෴

My Bronx neighborhood wasn't the only place starting to come apart. The planet had become one humongous loony bin. Hot political talk was boiling over, enough to make anyone paranoid. And if that failed, I could count on JHS 82 to make me feel that way.

Yeah, I was now a big shot ninth grader, not that 82 cared much. Instead, the school had another way of preparing me for my future. The humiliating "safety drill." The drill had not changed since kindergarten and still carried the exact same message: our eventual annihilation was at hand unless—and here's where it got really hilarious—we learned how to duck.

Clanging school bells told us that Principal Stern was about to come on the air. His raspy voice crackling over the wall speaker told us that we needed to "remain calm." In fact, I'd been quite calm before his announcement. It was only after he issued his "safety" instructions should we get hit with an atomic bomb that I began to have real worries.

The drill brought me back to my elementary school days. Then we joked about "kissing our ass goodbye" should a nuke fall on top of us while we crouched under our desks with our head between our knees. But we were young and stupid without a clue about the big, bad world. This time the exercise felt different, and not funny at all.

Warnings about death and destruction were in every headline and television news broadcast. So many enemies. If it wasn't some Vietnamese guy called Ho Chi Min, then we could count on cigar-chomping Castro, or the bald guy, Khrushchev, who liked to pound his shoe on a table to make his point. Whatever that was. I guess there were even more countries and people that hated us, but this list seemed quite enough for the time being.

Mr. Weston, my new social studies teacher, explained that the drill was good training should our enemy drop a bomb on us. That kind of woke us up, but, really, he had to be kidding, though he wasn't smiling at the time. Actually, my main worry was not *a* bomb, but "*The* Bomb." The Bomb was a popular topic these days. This "race" going on with the Russians was not the kind reported on the back sports pages of the *New York Post.* The idea was to see how many nukes each country could build—sort of a "mine is bigger than yours" mentality. I was confused why we need-ed more bombs when we had enough to blow up the world fifty times over. If you asked me, a wee bit of overkill, so to speak.

You would think we would've learned from our past cra-ziness. Dropping The Bomb on Japan got high marks from Mr. Weston. "That decision saved many, many American lives," he declared, not mentioning that 200,000 obliterated Japanese might have had a slightly different opinion. Also, I wasn't thrilled with the idea that some country might share Mr. Weston's philosophy—"Better to be safe than sorry"— and drop The Bomb on us.

A screaming siren then went off, scaring the hell out of me. The signal that it we needed to hide. I tried to scrunch under my desk but wound up halfway in the aisle. No jokes were being tossed around this time. After all, the Grim Reaper himself might be around the corner and coming to get us. No use poking a finger in his eye. So we held onto our butts and hoped for the best. Unspoken, this insanity.

Cowering under our desks in the event of a possible nuclear attack was so mind-bogglingly wacky that it made such a strike actually seem possible. And, as President Kennedy warned us two weeks earlier—it was.

❧❧❧

It had been two years since I'd seen John at the Concourse rally, so alive and chipper then. This was a different guy that October night on television. John grimly told us the latest news coming out of Cuba—super serious talk. U.S. spy planes had confirmed that the Russians were secretly building missile launch sites in Cuba. These missiles would be capable of destroying every major city in the United States.

Such an "explicit threat" to the nation, he warned, was "a clear and present danger" and "could not stand."

So, John told us all his plan—something about a naval blockade around Cuba. Russian ships carrying "offensive weapons" to the island would be turned back, he explained. He also wouldn't rule out a nuke fight with the Russians should they give us a hard time.

I remember thinking that all this talk was out of some movie. But John's face told me how real this fight was—and he wasn't kidding around. This type of war, he warned, would be "without a victor" leaving the world with "ashes in our mouths."

I still was waiting for the feel good moment.

But John went on about "the cost of freedom" and how Americans would never choose "the path of surrender."

And so on.

This call to nuclear arms.

❧❧❧

I recalled those photographs of Hiroshima and Nagasaki, so many tens of thousands dead, a humongous ash-heap and a history that my teacher seemed okay with. But now we had more than one big guy on the block with The Bomb, with each side ready to blow up the other. Enough tough talk to scare me shitless.

We all exhaled when the eyeball-to-eyeball standoff with the Russians finally calmed down. But for me there was nothing very cold about this Cold War. Way too much heat in the air. One pushed button. The end, sayonara, finito. And this "safety drill" that morning did nothing to stop me from thinking that I was simply another inmate trapped inside the asylum, hiding under my desk, just waiting to kiss my ass goodbye.

CHAPTER 42

Girl Gone Wrong

I should have been over Dee-Dee O'Hara by now, but truth be told, I still felt that bad ache. Those stomach pangs. Head in a fog. The dumps. The good news was that Artie "the Schmuck" Solomon was no longer around, taking his swagger and leather jacket over to DeWitt Clinton High School. The better news was that it looked like Dee-Dee and the guy were history. At least that was the blather through the school grapevine, along with other gossip. Loose talk about Dee-Dee that wasn't nice at all.

I didn't like it one bit.

"It's true," Sammy declared as we made our way home from school that day.

"Bullshit!" I said. "No way! No *freakin'* way!"

"Actually, there is a way, and it looks like she found it," Sammy said plainly.

The unspoken word was "pregnant," as in, "The stupid girl is—"

I didn't believe one word of it. Actually, that very word. Pregnant.

"Listen," I retorted, "the schmuck still lives, he's still in one piece over at DeWitt Clinton. So, proof that Dee-Dee's not pregnant. Not a chance."

My logic was infallible. I had no doubt whatsoever that if Mrs. O'Hara ever found out that her daughter was having Artie's baby, we all would have read about it in the *New York Post*. Not in the birth announcements—the obituaries. I'd bet my house, if I had one, that pieces of Artie Solomon would be found floating in the Hudson River—though his cock would never be recovered but preserved in formaldehyde in Mrs. O'Hara's kitchen cupboard as a warning to others.

"Talk about a double whammy," Sammy said, refusing to let up. "It's bad enough being knocked up at fifteen, but with Artie the Schmuck's kid? Jeez, I don't wish that on anyone."

"Man, you are warped."

"No doubt there, but you still have it bad for her, bro."

"Thanks for the psychoanalysis, Sigmund," I said, adding lamely. "You don't understand."

I was ticked off, especially since Sammy was right. When it came to Dee-Dee, I couldn't see straight, but I still wasn't in any mood for his opinion. Of course that didn't stop Sammy from giving it to me anyway.

"Don't understand? Hmm, let me see," Sammy said, stroking his chin, now Socrates in search of the Truth. "Dee-Dee dumps you. Without a word. She takes up with the schmuck. They practically rape each other every day in the hallways. Embarrassing, disgusting, but they don't seem to care. Then the dirty deed is done. Now Dee-Dee is going to have the guy's baby, giving the world Artie the Schmuck II. What about this picture don't I understand, Paul? Time to get over her, bro. If you play your cards right, Dee-Dee might be needing a babysitter pretty soon. So a job prospect there."

"Sammy, a personal question—how do you feel about being strangled?"

"We can talk about that later, bro. But, hey, why don't we just go and ask her?"

"A good one."

"I'm not kidding around. I mean it."

"Go ask Dee-Dee if she's pregnant, yeah, right."

"Actually, we should probably use the word 'knocked-up' to keep it friendlier, but pregnant works fine for me. Whaddaya say?"

"Sammy, you are so beyond sick, but we know that."

"Okay, I'll ask her myself."

"No you won't."

"Don't worry. I'll send your regards. Tell her your baby gift is in the mail. That sort of thing."

"Are you nuts? I forgot, you *are* freakin' nuts. Just forget about it."

"Paul, you want to know."

I didn't have a response to that. Okay, so Sammy was right, again. I wanted to know, but I didn't want Sammy to know that I wanted to know. My head was spinning. Dee-Dee O'Hara could not be pregnant. Unless she was.

"Just leave me out of this," was all I could say.

∽∾∽∾

It was at lunch when Sammy spotted her. Dee-Dee was standing on line behind a group of kids waiting to be served the usual school slop. We had a clear view of her from where we sat in the lunchroom. I was glad to see nothing out of the ordinary.

"See, look at her, Sammy, no 'bump,' just Dee-Dee, all normal like."

"Well, looks are deceiving."

"What? She's not pregnant. Simple."

"You say no, I say maybe," he said. "Don't worry. I'll ease into the conversation. Maybe tell her I'm doing an opinion poll about the Vietnam War, Civil Rights—and the Pill. Sneaky, yes?"

Before I could say a word, Sammy jumped out of his chair and jogged over to the lunch line.

I didn't bother to try to stop him. I needed to know.

And so I watched, intently.

Sammy had already broken into the lunch line and was standing directly behind Dee-Dee. I could see him tap her on the shoulder and begin his rap. I had the feeling he'd given up on his opinion poll idea. Dee-Dee's reaction was, well, interesting. First her jawed dropped, then her face turned blood-red. She was either really embarrassed or really pissed off. Now she was furiously wagging her finger in Sammy's face. I was betting on the pissed off.

Dee-Dee's voice suddenly ratcheted up, spilling out into the lunchroom. It wasn't her happy voice, not at all. Then she got even louder, and it was impossible to miss her message.

"Fuck you, Sammy Spigelman!" she screamed, instantly silencing us all at our lunch tables.

It was as if every kid was now suspended in motion, with all eyes on Dee-Dee and Sammy, and waiting to see what would happen next. And then something did. Dee-Dee flung her tray to the floor, her lunch exploding like a grenade going off. The kids on line bolted from their deep-freeze, ducking from the soda spray and flying macaroni and cheese.

Dee-Dee, sobbing, raced from the lunchroom followed by the buzz of cafeteria chatter. Before she even reached the exit, the gossip was flying fast and furious.

Sammy ambled back to our table.

"That went well," I said stone-faced.

"She was a little upset."

"I could hardly tell," I said, not bothering to hide the sarcasm. "I assume you took the gentle, sympathetic approach."

"Nah, just asked her if she had something cooking in her oven."

"Yeah, that's real good. Sensitive."

"Maybe a little too direct. You think?"

"Let's cut the crap, Sammy," I snapped, getting tired of the stupid talk. "What did she say?"

"I thought you didn't want to know?"

"Sammy!"

"Well, she didn't exactly say anything specific. I hate when people don't answer my questions. Kind of disrespectful, don't you think?"

"Yeah, yeah. Did she say *anything*?"

"Actually, it was more of a physical statement when she attacked me with her tray. Got Pepsi and mac and cheese all over my sneakers. Just rude, not to mention a waste of food."

"Maybe she was pissed off at you for being a jerk."

"True enough."

"Besides she looks…normal."

"True also, but—"

"So, then, what the hell are you saying?"

"Well. She was carrying a book by some guy, a Dr. Spock. It had to do with raising babies. Don't think it was beach reading."

I stared back at Sammy, without a word. There was nothing left to say.

CHAPTER 43

The Bumps of Life

I had almost worn out the record grooves of a new single that I had picked up. This Jewish guy was starting to make a name for himself, just not the one his parents gave him. Bob Dylan. A better choice than Robert Allen Zimmerman. His gravelly voice called out from my phonograph, some questions about being "a man."

This manhood thing wasn't coming easy for me either.

And it was just then that the doorbell rang. I could hear the front door open, and voices. Mom—and Dee-Dee O'Hara.

Jesus.

I hadn't seen Dee-Dee in over a month, not a trace of her since that craziness with Sammy in the lunchroom. She had disappeared from school, though the talk about her still ran hot and heavy around the hallways. As for me, I'd finally given up on Paul Anka love songs that left me with serious heartache, opting for Dylan and his troubles with humankind. Not nearly as painful.

The good news, I was absolutely, positively over my old girlfriend, and ready to move on. But then the doorbell rang, a visitor. Dee-Dee was back, and having a conversation with Mom.

So much for moving on.

I shut off Bob Dylan and shuffled over to the front door, my mind already in a muddle. There, the girl I carried in my dreams, that broke my heart. Now she was calling for me. And there was no mistaking the bump protruding from her stomach.

For the second time in three minutes, I called on Jesus, not that I expected much in the way of help.

Pregnant Dee-Dee O'Hara stood in the middle of my foyer with Rosie. Mom was throwing me a brutal look as I slouched over to the two of them. Then Fred, who'd been playing piano in his bedroom, happened to casually saunter in. He also gave me the eye after seeing Dee-Dee, as if to say: "My younger moronic brother! Are you out of your idiotic mind?"

The silence must have been deafening because Dad was next to come out of his office, sensing something in the wind. This was becoming one big family reunion. Dad stopped in his tracks, his mouth agape, staring at the very pregnant, red-haired Irish Catholic *shikseh* standing in the foyer. He might have been considering the prospects of becoming a grandfather, but first he had to kill his second-born son. I could swear he'd stopped breathing, and prayed that I wouldn't be forced to give him CPR. The evening was becoming complicated enough.

I guess it didn't help that I was staring bug-eyed at Dee-Dee's belly. This bump with a button in the middle seemed ridiculous sticking out of the girl. All skin and bones, and one big bump. A bump with a baby growing inside of it. For my parents and brother, Dee-Dee's appearance in our apartment pointed only in one direction. And their verdict was unanimous: I was guilty and about to be sentenced to a life of fatherhood. So, *mazel tov*, Paul, now pack your bags, and get lost. I made a mental note to set the family straight later on. The five of us stood in the middle of the foyer in some Mexican standoff waiting for someone to say a word. I decided to break the deadlock.

"Hey, Dee-Dee, nice seeing you, a surprise," I said evenly, going for the cool act now that my eyeballs were back in their sockets. "Hey, why don't you come into my room, we can talk."

I don't think my suggestion made anyone feel any better.

"Keep the door open, Paul," Mom blurted.

I might have cracked-up, if not for the mortified look on my mother's face. I mean, the damage was done. What did Rosie think was going to happen if the door was shut? Was I going for twins? (Yeah, I know, I know, it didn't work that way.) I would have liked to calm everyone down, letting them know about Artie, the actual soon-to-be-dad, and the once and always schmuck. But it was best just to get Dee-Dee away from this silent inquisition.

And so we headed for my bedroom. I kept the door open.

We had barely stepped into my room when Dee-Dee broke down in a heaving, I-want-to-die kind of wail. Her emotional carrying-on must have given Mom and Dad another push toward a nervous breakdown. Anyway, I didn't know what else to do but put my arm around her. She reacted instantly, latching hard onto my waist, plowing her head against my chest. This embrace was not the lovey-dovey kind—we weren't slow dancing among the moonbeams—though my heart was thumping hard all the same.

"Paul, what am I going to do?" she cried out.

I wasn't quite ready for the question, not to mention confused why she was asking *me*. I mean, I had my own question, like, what the hell was going through her mind when she dumped me for Artie the Schmuck?

But here I was with her on a one-way street with Dee-Dee asking the questions. Actually, one question in particular.

"What am I going to do?"

I didn't want to make light of her bump—the thing brewing about inside her stomach was serious business—but I had no idea what to say to make this feel better.

"I'm so scared," she sobbed. "Mom wants to kill me, send me away someplace."

I wanted to ask her where Artie was in the picture, but I already knew the guy was hiding out. After all, he's a schmuck—I think I've mentioned that before—so that explains him.

Dee-Dee was still in my arms as I peeked over her shoulder to the doorway. There was Rosie, partly hidden behind the open door, checking out the scene—her Cyclops eye staring me down. I imagined Dad and Fred were standing right behind her waiting for the lowdown.

I let go of Dee-Dee and went over to the door. My guess was right. The three of them were lined up like bowling pins. They jerked back as if I was a leper coming at them. I gave a shrug, as is to say, "We'll talk later." A message that did nothing to change the miserable looks on their faces.

I shut my bedroom door. Enough of the spy stuff.

I was back to Dee-Dee and, weirdly, happy being with her. She needed me, and it was good to feel some self-confidence coming back after being so long the loser.

"How did this happen?"

Dee-Dee whimpered, her hand over her eyes.

I was glad that Sammy wasn't around, cracking wise with his response—*"Weren't you around, Dee-Dee, when Artie stuck his dick in you?"*

My own feelings were in a jumble. I still had no idea what had happened—to us. Or, for that matter, why she was back with me now. In my arms. As if she never left.

I could not help but love Dee-Dee, even after all of this, but those mad-hot emotions were cooler now. I started to stroke her long, red hair, and mumbled some words that everything would work out okay. Not that I thought they would, but she needed to hear the lie.

We went over and sat on the edge of my bed still holding on to each other. Before long we were lying down, her head resting under my chin. The spot where she'd been that innocent, magical night at the Park Plaza with Atticus and his family.

We stayed that way for a while with hardly a word between us. I didn't know how much time passed, but Dee-Dee was calmer now, cuddly even, and feeling safe in my arms. I hoped so at least. And then softly she whispered, "What am I going to do now?"

Again, that question. I don't think she was asking me but thinking aloud. A broken record playing in her mind.

And then to me. "You know I'm a Catholic?" she blurted out as if a revelation.

"I know, Dee-Dee," I said quietly. "I know you're Catholic."

It was not so much a statement about her faith but her future.

"I am so screwed!" she stated. It took us both a second to catch on that she'd been right on both scores. Fucked and in deep trouble. We let loose, curling into laughter.

A sound stirred outside the bedroom. I wondered what Mom, Dad and Fred, with their ears to the door, must be thinking now?

At least the moment brought some small relief for Dee-Dee, though her future was, well, blowing in the wind. Her life was about to change drastically, and at fifteen, and there was no good answer to her question. Just the reality of what had happened, and what was to come.

CHAPTER 44

The Last Straw

I had no control over life. After fifteen years on Earth, I had come to this grand conclusion. Okay, so Plato I wasn't. But I had good ears, ease-dropping on my parents talk about the end of the Bronx. More exactly, the end of my relatives' lives in the Bronx.

I didn't like the talk one bit.

There had been lots of nervous chatter around the block—new families were moving into the neighborhood, with their own language and skin color, and others were moving out. A new term was going around, "white flight," and it looked like my aunts, uncles and cousins were about to fly.

"You should see over at my sisters," Rosie told Dad as they sat around the kitchen table. "The block is changing. I'm worried. They need to move."

"Where are they going to go?" Dad asked.

"They're talking about upstate, out of the city."

I could hear the disappointment in Dad's voice. "It might be time," he said quietly.

My mind was spinning. My cousins, and aunts and uncles, moving out of the neighborhood? And the unspoken question—were we next to take flight?

Needless to say, I didn't sleep easy that night.

∽∾∽

Jews were used to moving—though usually not under the best of circumstances—so maybe I shouldn't have been surprised at the talk. But I was still finding it tough to believe that my clan was about to break up.

I lived my second life on Montgomery Avenue. That's where Mom's sisters, Selma and Ethel, and my cousins lived, a floor apart. Our three families were joined at the hip, no coincidence there. Rosie, Ethel, and Selma were born the Cohen girls in the South Bronx. They had come from a rough childhood—their mom died at thirty-two, then they lost their dad to depression. Real tough times. Rosie, twelve, was the oldest of the three sisters and became the family caretaker. The three girls were inseparable since.

So when Selma and Sol married and moved into 1750 Montgomery Avenue, Selma had no choice—Ethel and her family had to move into the building. Bronx apartments were scarce, though, following the war with returning GI's needing places to raise families. My father managed to bribe the building super to get our Tremont apartment. Selma had a different idea.

Selma set her eye on 2C directly below her own apartment. There was this one sticky point—the couple living there had no intention at all of moving out. Selma decided otherwise. Mysteriously, my aunt's bathroom tub developed a serious drainage problem, flooding 2C on a regular basis. And when Selma aired out her rugs, somehow the dusty thing draped over the neighbor's window cutting off sunlight. Selma's three boys also were encouraged to do jumping-jacks that sent shock waves to the apartment below—after all, the boys needed a little exercise.

The downstairs neighbors never stood a chance and couldn't flee Montgomery Avenue fast enough.

⌀⌀⌀

Ethel and Ruby in fact were another Bronx story. They both grew up as teenagers in the same apartment building in the South Bronx, and yet hardly knew each other. Ruby then went off to war, a lieutenant and tank commander fighting the Nazis. Returning home on leave, Ruby, resplendent in his uniform, bumped into Ethel, a dark-haired beauty. And that was that. And then the Army called again. Ruby was back fighting another war, this one in Korea, writing Ethel every day from the battlefield. One wound up in a *New York Post* story—a birthday letter to Philip, his one-year-old son.

Although you don't know your daddy very well, I know you from your pictures, and you are just like I imagined you would be. But I miss so much seeing you grow up, taking your first step, hearing your laughter and listening to your crying. But we'll make up for all this when your daddy comes home again. Because of this war which keeps us apart, my being here is allowing you to grow up in a nice, happy land where thunder is heard, and children know it is raining and do not have to crawl into caves from the thunder of planes dropping bombs or of cannon crushing against their makeshift cradles. I should be there telling you happy birthday—and bringing you presents—but I am happy we are fighting here instead of where you are. I hope that you will be a good boy for the next few weeks until I get back so that Mommy will not have too hard a time doing my share besides all of hers. So until then, happy birthday and pleasant dreams to my little son.

My uncle Ruby never talked about his war years later on, much less his heroic deeds. That part of his life he kept to himself. I knew some of the story. His Silver Star for bravery. A citation for heroism, having saved an entire infantry company trapped by enemy forces.

I still hung on to the old newspaper clipping and picture now torn at the edges. There they were, Ruby, Ethel, and little Philip—a joyful postwar scene that, I imagine, played out in thousands of homes across the country. The story told how Philip, all of eighteen months old, had scampered over to Ruby upon arriving home from Korea, calling out "Daddy, daddy!"

Pretty remarkable considering the kid had no real living memory of his dad, only pictures that Ethel had shown him.

Thanks to Aunt Selma's harassment campaign, Ruby and Ethel finally moved to 1750 Montgomery Avenue. After years of challenges and heartache, the three Cohen sisters— Rosie, Selma, and Ethel—had families of their own, men they loved, and children they cherished, and life, regardless of struggles to come, was good to them in the Bronx.

But those days were about to come to an end.

I guess I couldn't blame my aunts and uncles for giving up on the Bronx, but one day Montgomery Avenue life became way too bizarre, and that was the last straw.

❧❧❧

The neighborhood "watchers" were a constant on the block. Each day, these women set up their aluminum folding chairs outside the building while their young kids played on the sidewalk. They also kept a lookout for unfamiliar visitors on the block.

But when a moving truck pulled up, no one thought twice when a trio of men busily went to work. Armed with dollies and packing gear, they made their way to an upstairs apartment.

"I wonder who's moving out," Emily Fletcher said. "It must be 5D, the Katzes."

"Yeah, I heard they were interested in Long Island,"

Minnie Stein chimed in. "Huntington, you know, near Leonard's of Great Neck."

"I went to the Shulmans' bar mitzvah there," Sadie Black added. "Some affair!"

The moving men were pros, working quickly to get the job done, earning the admiration of the women. "I should get their card," Enid Kornbluth said. "You never know when you need a good mover."

"Look," Sadie said, pointing to one piece of furniture being lifted into the truck. "The Katzes have your couch with that same floral pattern."

Enid had bought the very same couch a few months back, and she was now pissed. "It was that furniture sale at Macy's," she groaned. "And look—even their dining room table matches mine."

Enid mentally vowed never again to invite the Katzes—those decorating thieves—over for Yom Kippur break-fast. "Couldn't they have come up with their own plan?" she complained loudly.

The story had a mixed ending. The good news, the Katzes were innocent of all charges. The couple did not steal Enid's furniture ideas nor were they leaving the neighborhood for that matter. The bad news. No one had bothered to inform Enid that she, in fact, was the one moving out of the building. The "movers" had broken into her apartment taking every last piece of her furniture—tables, a couch, bed, chairs, lamps, the TV set, even the wheelchair that belonged to her ailing father. Nearly all of Enid's apartment stuff was now neatly packed into boxes and piled onto the truck.

Only when the building's super confronted the moving men did the scam fall apart, and the watchers woke up. By then it was too late. The super was thrown to the sidewalk to the cries of the women. The thieves then took off speeding past a lone woman standing in the middle of the street waving her fist in the air. Enid.

The watchers then accompanied her back to the apartment, empty except for a few wall hangings and a broken lamp. Days later Enid Kornbluth left Montgomery Avenue for good, heading out to Oyster Bay on Long Island.

"Well, at least the moving charges weren't so bad," one of the watchers cruelly joked later on.

⟨∾⟩

The daring break-in was the talk of the block for the next week. For Ethel and Ruby, Selma and Sol, the robbery struck way too close to home. The time had come to leave. My cousins weren't all that happy giving up their streets and everything else. I wasn't happy either, losing them along with my aunts and uncles.

Their new home was outside the city, across a long bridge called the Tappan Zee, in a place with green lawns, spiffy two-family houses, and all sorts of nice suburban things. It was called Spring Valley.

A name, and a place, that never would have stood a chance in the Bronx.

CHAPTER 45

Sammy

As it turned out, I was about to lose Sammy, too. His family was getting set to leave the Bronx for Bayside, a pretty, grassy neighborhood in Queens. He said something about moving into a garden apartment, whatever that was.

Sammy and I had been lifers. Real pals. Now that was going to end. Just wrong. And I couldn't deal with this new reality.

I met up with my friend that fall afternoon for our "last supper" at Square Pizza. We'd known each other since we were five, and now Sammy would be gone by the weekend. For the only time in our lives neither of us really knew what to say, as we silently chomped down the pizza cut into squares that we chased with a Coke.

"Did you hear the one about the kid who puked all over his pizza?" I said in a lousy attempt to break the ice.

"Paul, I'm eating," Sammy complained. "I can do without the picture in my head."

"Sammy, what are you going to do in Bayside? The place has grass and trees, and you have allergies."

"I don't have allergies. You made that up."

"Well, you're from the Bronx and you're not used to pollen, so there's a real good chance you can catch them."

"Thanks for the positive thinking," he said, resigned.

"Sammy, for God's sake. You're giving up the Yankees, and for what? The New York *Freakin'* Mets! The only person I know older than Mrs. Levine, and she must be 100, is Casey Stengel, and he's the Mets manager. The players are younger, but they play ball like Mrs. Levine."

"Hey, just because I'll be living in Queens doesn't mean I'm rooting for somebody named Choo Choo Coleman. I'm Yankees through and through. Pinstripes forever."

I nibbled on the pizza but had no appetite. Sammy also was in no mood to eat, so we sat around the table in silence for a while.

"Whose terrible idea was this anyway?" I finally asked.

"My folks. Except for the old people, neighbors are moving out every day. The block is changing, and it's time to go. At least that's what my parents are telling me."

"So, what are you going to do for stoopball? There aren't any stoops in Bayside."

"I guess I'll have to sacrifice."

"And do the kids there shoot hoops through a fire escape ladder? They don't even *have* fire escapes! And, Sammy, can you see your mother screaming for you from a garden apartment in Bayside to come home for dinner?"

Sammy slowly shook his head, and sighed. "Yeah, too bad about the fire escapes. As for my mom, I'm sure she won't stop screaming at me where ever I am."

"Sammy, you can't go."

"Yeah, I know, brother. I know."

CHAPTER 46

The World Turns

My hero was dead a month later.
I don't remember much in the weeks after John was murdered. I was sure other things had gone on in the world but I couldn't tell you what they were. But those four days in late November, well, they were unforgettable. Days that scar the mind.

I sat glued to a television set that weekend locked into gray images. Life and death played out on my TV set. Real and surreal. The craziness of the world crashing in on me.

I refused to shut off the screen. I felt like I owed John that. I know, real dumb, but we had been friends once, even if was years before when we met on the Grand Concourse for all of seven minutes. But still, we talked and shook hands. He had soft hands, a great smile. John and me. Pals. And then Mom came over, and both of them also hit it off. Just talking about family and life. That counted for something. And now he was gone. I was waiting to wake up to my old world, but when his murder finally sank in, I knew we somehow had crossed a dividing line.

The world had turned, with no going back, and I sadly wondered later on what might have been if this Bronx boy had lived.

ھۄ

Not much was happening in school that fall afternoon. A lazy Friday and we already had our eye on the short Thanksgiving week coming up. Mrs. Taylor didn't seem in a hurry to push ahead with her English lesson, casually jotting some blackboard notes.

It was then that Mr. Hardin came into our room and called her into the hallway. A few girls covered their mouths to stifle a bout of giggles. Rumor had it that Mr. Hardin, our science teacher, and Mrs. Taylor were "an item," awkward, considering that both were married to someone else.

Mr. Hardin looked grim as the two left the classroom for the hallway. This was no romantic encounter. Minutes passed, with some horsing around in class in their absence. When Mrs. Taylor returned, her face had lost color, and she was in tears. Tears like those shed at a funeral. All the silliness in class instantly stopped. Teachers don't cry. Bad news was ahead, and we saw it coming.

We sat silently while Mrs. Taylor tried to regain her composure. We waited for the other shoe to drop. And then Heidi Saskin sitting next to me started to sob. So very strange. We knew nothing yet something was terribly wrong.

Our teacher was finally back to herself, intently scanning our faces, and preparing us for what was to come. She first announced that we were about to be dismissed from school. And then she told us why.

"President Kennedy—President Kennedy has been shot."

We sat frozen in our seats. Silent. Confused.

John's been shot? What was that? The president. John. Shot. *What did these words mean?*

I didn't get it.

How were we supposed to make sense of the impossible?

Several heartbeats passed when Sophie Diamond cried out: *"No!"*

Then the walls came crashing down.

The class burst into "OH-MY-GODS!"

I still didn't want to believe my teacher. This could not be as serious as she made it seem.

But Mrs. Taylor's face told us that it was.

"Is he going to be okay?" Sophie anxiously called out.

Mrs. Taylor stood there, reaching for an answer. "We don't know much," she said, her voice cracking. "Only that there is trouble in Dallas."

I refused to give in to these words. John was all right, still in the world. No other possibility existed. I worshipped the guy ever since we became fast friends that day on the Concourse. I mean, we had something real in common. Our Bronx roots. We shook hands, bonded, pal to pal. My drawer was filled with his campaign buttons and posters; an old *Life Magazine* with John, Jackie, and baby Caroline on the cover; and other sorts of Kennedy things. My very favorite record album was "The First Family" by some guy named Vaughn Meader, and I laughed out loud at his goofy impersonations of John and his family.

All would be well. It had to be.

Mrs. Taylor got us up from our seats. "Please leave the school and go directly home now," she said.

We piled out of our seats to the front door.

"Why would anyone shoot the president?" Sophie asked me, as we barged out of the classroom.

Who could imagine *that* question before this day? And I didn't have an answer.

The hallway was in chaos. Teachers and students, jamming the space, heading for the school exit. We all needed to get home, to get the word. To see if this news was possibly true.

ᘒᘒᘒ

Fred was already home when I raced through the doorway, and he filled me in. There wasn't a lot. The president was in a motorcade when he was shot. Some place called Dealey Plaza in downtown Dallas. John was now in a hospital emergency room.

"He'll be okay," I said, determined to convince myself.

Fred's silence wasn't reassuring.

We flipped channels for more news. One station was airing "As the World Turns." It was hard to miss the irony given the day's events. Still, I was relieved to see that the show was on the air.

"It can't be all that bad," I said, instantly feeling more positive. "Look, they're showing a stupid soap opera and it's live TV. This wouldn't be on if something was serious with the president."

Fred nodded and almost seemed convinced.

And it was just then that a "Flash Bulletin" took over the screen. The soap opera was gone. Then the voice of Walter Cronkite, the CBS newsman.

"Here is a bulletin from CBS News. President Kennedy was shot as he drove from Dallas Airport to downtown Dallas. It is reported that three bullets rang out. A Secret Service man was heard to shout from the car, 'He's dead.' Whether he referred to President Kennedy or not is not yet known. The president, cradled in the arms of his wife, Mrs. Kennedy, was carried to an ambulance and the car rushed to Parkland Hospital outside Dallas…"

The audio bulletins had given way to live TV studio coverage. The news was only getting worse.

A Parkland Hospital doctor with bleak medical news about John's condition. A congregation at a prayer service. A report that a Father Hubert had administered last rites to John.

The nightmare news was finally sinking in. This could not be happening, but by then I knew it was.

Cronkite still was refusing to concede, and I was on his side. I watched as he paused, put on his eyeglasses to silently read a report that had come to his desk. He removed his glasses, and his face had changed. A look of defeat. The worst was coming.

"From Dallas, Texas, the flash, apparently official: President Kennedy died at one p.m. Central Standard Time, two o'clock Eastern Standard Time, some thirty-eight minutes ago."

Swallowing hard, he told viewers that the nation would move on with a new president, Lyndon Johnson.

John was dead. The Bronx boy was gone.

The world was turning too fast.

Fred and I stayed glued to the television with the horror story still unfolding. Cronkite spoke in hushed tones as the president's plane landed at Andrews Air Force Base. Robert Kennedy was on the tarmac, waiting for his brother's body to be taken off the plane to a waiting hearse. Jackie was by his side.

"What's that on Jackie's dress?" I asked Fred, a question answered by a television reporter. It was John's blood and brains. Jackie had refused to change her strawberry-colored outfit from that afternoon. She was another victim.

"How can she take this?" I mumbled to myself. "Just too awful to watch."

Lyndon Johnson, our new president, stood on the runway before television cameras. He spoke of "a loss that cannot be weighed."

"I ask for your help," he sadly stated, "and God's."

҂ѽҀ

I hardly left the TV the next day. Much of the coverage that Saturday was repetitious, but I watched in a daze, hour after hour. Only one story existed on any channel. A blur of images—old Kennedy family home movies with John and Bobby playing touch football, the Kennedy clan on a sailboat in the waters off Martha's Vineyard, John vowing to end the nuclear arms race with Russia.

A news flash suddenly broke into John's story. A twenty-four-year-old man had been arrested accused of killing a police officer. The report made it clear that the guy was also suspected in John's assassination. The network quickly cut to the Dallas County Jail. Bedlam with police and media jostling for space in a crowded hallway. A detective holding a rifle in the air for all to see. The weapon, police said, that killed John. In the middle of the scene, a man in handcuffs. Lee Harvey Oswald.

"The place looks like a hundred guys crushed inside a phone booth," Fred said.

The media mob turned toward Oswald.

"Did you kill the president?" one reporter shouted out.

The camera closed in on the guy.

"I didn't shoot anybody, sir," he replied. "I haven't been told what I am here for." A bruise above Oswald's right eyebrow was clearly visible. "A police officer hit me," he told reporters before being led to an interrogation room. And then a final protest to reporters. "I am just a patsy," he called out.

"Really strange seeing this guy being paraded around like this," I said to Fred. "You'd think they'd have him under lock and key."

"It *is* weird," Fred nodded.

"Kind of reminds me of those Westerns where the mob gets hold of some bad guy before they string him up."

"Well, I don't see anyone with a rope," Fred said. "The Dallas police must know what they're doing."

I shrugged. "If you ask me, it doesn't look that way."

❧❧❧

I couldn't take my eyes off Lee Harvey Oswald. Could *this* ordinary guy be an assassin? John's killer? I searched for anything that could identify him as a cold-blooded killer. He seemed sane, even intelligent, calm and cool. He was no John Wilkes Booth, the drama king, leaping to the stage at Ford's Theater declaring "Death to tyrants." Actually, if you believed him, then the police had the wrong guy.

I wasn't buying it, though. I had learned long ago not to be fooled by appearances. Demons came in all forms. Still, I brooded over how any person—this man—could do this. Kill John.

Rosie was on the phone in the kitchen sidetracking my attention from the television. Her voice penetrated into the living room, a sharp staccato response to some caller. "I don't believe it! I don't believe it!" The world was a mess, but yet another problem was brewing and setting off Mom. I couldn't imagine though anything being worse than these pictures on television.

Mom then walked slowly into the living room, her head shaking, apparently coming to grips with the telephone call. "That was your Uncle Harry on the phone," she said, seeming bewildered. "He gave me the strangest news."

"Yeah, lots of that going around," I replied.

I wasn't thinking about Uncle Harry and his news, just wanting to get back to Dallas.

But Mom went on, pointing to the TV screen. "That man, Oswald, was once Harry's neighbor back in the '50s."

Now I was the one puzzled.

"Mom, what the hell are you—?

"Over at his apartment building on 179th Street."

"I know where Uncle Harry lives, near the Bronx Zoo, but what does this have to do—"

"Oswald lived with this mother in his building about ten years ago. He was around thirteen, fourteen at the time. Acted out a lot, a bad kid, Harry said. Never went to school, got caught up in the juvenile courts. Harry wouldn't forget him."

"Uncle Harry told you this?"

I was incredulous. I'd been to my uncle's building at 825

East 179th Street a hundred times growing up. It wasn't any different than most other five-story walkups in the Bronx.

"Remember, you used to play around his building with the older kids?"

"Sure, tons of kids there—Jesus—Oswald must have been part of that crowd."

Rosie nodded.

I was stunned as the thought sunk in.

"And your uncle told me something else," Rosie went on, as we both kept an eye on the live news coverage coming from Dallas police headquarters.

"Harry remembered an incident back then. It involved Oswald. One day he had taken out a BB gun and started shooting up the building, breaking windows. Even taking aim at some old women who sat by the side of the building."

"He did *what*!" I exclaimed. "Mom, could that be true?"

"I guess it shouldn't be that hard to believe," she said.

And it was just then that Lee Harvey Oswald suddenly appeared on our television screen. Dallas detectives were leading him through an underground passage to a waiting armored car. He was being transferred to the nearby county lockup. A hundred bodies were suddenly in motion as a crowd of reporters and television cameramen surrounded the guy. Oswald, dressed in a dark sweater, seemed unfazed by the bedlam around him.

I studied the man, trying to dredge up any memory. Lee Harvey Oswald, a Bronx kid? Did I ever meet and pal around with him outside my uncle's building? Did we ever play ball together, talk about stuff? Could this older kid have been a big friend to me? It was all too possible. That's how things were on the streets.

And to think, this guy hadn't lived all that far away from the home that once belonged to another Bronx kid—the same kid that we were now told he murdered.

As I stared at the screen, yet another weird feeling came over me. Somehow, Oswald no longer felt like some stranger. Some abstraction on the tube. He seemed all too real, maybe someone I'd even known, if not by name, then in the ordinary passing of my street life. And here he was ten years later—no longer that kid from back then. Someone else. John's assassin.

I was jolted from the thought as the scene on television became more chaotic. Pandemonium, as a crowd of reporters and television cameramen surrounded the guy. Above the clamor I could hear a reporter shout out a question. "Do you have anything to say in your defense?"

A question that hung in the air for the briefest of moments.

Oswald might have considered the question. And maybe we would have gotten some answer from him. Maybe a confession. Did he pull the trigger and kill John? And why? We desperately needed to know.

But Oswald never stood a chance.

Another turn of the wheel.

It was just then that a man suddenly flashed across the screen. And, in that split-second, everything changed.

I jumped off the couch, and like everyone else on the planet watching I began yelling at the top of my lungs. "He's been shot! He's been shot!"

A reporter on screen was shouting out the same. "Lee Oswald has been shot!"

Dad and Fred came running into the living room. Mom and I pointed to the screen. The shooting of Oswald was being replayed.

We could clearly see now a burly man in a dark suit and hat, stepping in front of Oswald, cuffed and in the custody of two detectives.

A gun was in the man's right hand, and aimed directly at Oswald.

Then the sharp pop of gunfire.

Oswald is hit point blank, his face wrenched in pain, clutches his stomach and collapses.

And then we were back live with the shooter being wrestled into submission by police. Chaos spooled out on the screen with reporters and police frantic and scrambling. I looked for Oswald, but he was out of the camera frame. Then he was visible again, lifeless, hoisted onto a stretcher and into an ambulance.

A reporter described his condition. Ashen, unconscious. All shorthand to tell us that Lee Harvey Oswald was about to die.

We all just stood there, stunned. Another murder, this one in front of our eyes.

"This can't be happening," I mumbled, but no one in my family was listening, only watching the world unravel. I thought I wouldn't care that Oswald was dead. But I did care. I needed to know. *Why John?*

The answer would stay a mystery.

જ઼જ઼જ઼

Fred and I were back in front of the television that Sunday. I imagined that the entire country had stopped with everything else, all of us connected by our TV, and mourning our murdered president.

A horse-drawn caisson carried John's flag-covered casket along Pennsylvania Avenue to the Capitol Rotunda. His body would lie in state there. The procession was soundless except for the muffled drums and horse hooves clacking down the avenue.

One horse was led apart from the others. An agitated stallion named Black Jack, missing his rider.

Television images moved slowly, and quietly. John's casket now rested on a platform in the rotunda—a stand that once held the coffin of Abraham Lincoln.

Jackie, holding young Caroline's hand, arrived at the chamber, then knelt in prayer by her husband's casket, reaching out to touch it. So composed and heartbreakingly sad.

Afterward, an endless stream of people moved steadily past John's casket. They had waited as long as ten hours in the near-freezing temperatures to pay their respects.

I felt in some way that Jackie should have had this time alone with John, not with millions hovering over her shoulder. I was intruding as well. I had idolized her husband—and hoped she'd understand.

The next day, that Monday, was John's funeral. So sorrowful a family picture: Jackie Caroline and John-John outside of St. Matthew's church after the service.

It was John-John's third birthday, a day that his daddy would be put into the ground. The little boy then let go of his mother's hand, took a few steps forward and saluted his father's casket.

"He would never get to know his father," I said to Fred. "We lost our president, but this kid lost his dad. How can that ever be made right?"

Fred didn't have an answer, not that there was one.

Jackie, her face veiled in black, was joined by the brothers, Bobby and Teddy. The three of them led the procession on foot to Arlington National Cemetery, each looking straight ahead, stoic, impossibly so, as they followed John's casket to his gravesite.

One day I vowed to visit my friend there at Arlington. But for now, I could only watch.

"What kind of country do we live in?" Fred asked this time, shaking his head. Yet another hanging question during those days.

I thought back to my old fears, the ones that haunted my nights when I was a small kid. By this time, I thought I'd figured things out. Only I hadn't. Not at all. Confusing me even more was the gnawing feeling that somehow we weren't through with this insanity and violence, and that other troubles were lurking ahead. Demons biding their time, getting ready to make themselves known. That this horror was only the beginning of something more.

There was yet another heartache to those tragic days, though I can't say I totally made sense of it at the time. I worshipped my heroes. They showed me a life greater than my own. They could break out of chains and handcuffs, or fly and fight for truth and justice, or dare to shoot into outer space with the hope of one day reaching the moon—or shake the hand of some Bronx twerp on the Grand Concourse, capturing his heart and mind. I believed in them all. They made me feel safe, whatever my worries of growing up. And they made me think that anything was possible. Even the impossible.

Now John was dead. Heroes shouldn't die, not this way. Not with a bullet in the head, brains spattered. How could this be happening? John, just vulnerable like the rest of us.

This couldn't be, but it was. This turn of life, with no going back. And, so, I sat in front of my television that miserable, gray November day, my hero gone, deep in the ground. So lost in the confusion and sadness. All I could do was watch Jackie, shrouded in black, light the Eternal Flame next to John's grave, and say goodbye.

CHAPTER 41

The Someone in the Mailbox

I knew it was finally time to leave the Bronx when I saw
the drunk screaming into the mailbox.

"Get outta there," he was shouting furiously. "I know
you're in there. Get the hell out."

It had been late afternoon and I was making my way
back to Tremont when I caught sight of him. He was furious, kicking and cursing out the corner mailbox, demanding
that the person inside the box get out. And then he tried to
stick his arm down the mail slot.

"I'm getting you outta there, you bastard."

Why he thought someone was in the box was a mystery.
Maybe he mixed up the word "Mail" printed on the mailbox
for "Male," and believed that the box was inhabited by
some human refusing to budge. And certainly that was no
place for a person to be. People belonged on the streets, he
thought, like him, breathing fresh air.

Obviously, this matter of the mailbox was mystifying to
him—how could life have been turned inside out. Or, more
precisely, outside in. And he clearly was distressed that the
lunatic in the mailbox had the gall to violate the natural order of things.

If this was his sense of the world, I didn't bother to

straighten him out. I didn't even presume that he was crazy. In fact, between the two of us, he might have been the sane one. Perhaps he was seeing with the utmost clarity how his days were fast changing, how the order of things, even in his old neighborhood, was going to hell. Life was a mess, turning inside out. Or, as he angrily shouted to the imaginary guy into the mailbox, outside in. And, so, he was pissed, refusing to accept that he no longer had any control over these things—which was more than I could say about my own life.

I still knew where to find a good pickup basketball game. Or the latest double feature at the old Park Plaza. As usual, I was on a first-name basis with neighborhood shop owners, and the China Star was still the only Chinese restaurant in America to serve veal cutlet with gravy, my favorite meal.

Everything seemed to be right where they should be. Except for those things that weren't.

Neighbors, relatives, schoolmates and friends I had known my whole life had left. Storefronts had closed down (and most upsetting was losing my comic book store, now boarded up). Others had signs in Spanish. Replacing the neighborhood deli with a bodega was as close to a sacrilege as you could get. The Art movie theater at the corner of Tremont and Jerome avenues was now a church. Its marquee welcomed parishioners to Sunday services. And Mel was gone having sold his candy store. With him went one of the great egg cream makers in Bronx history.

But instead of getting angry at the tides of change, I was resigned, seeing no use in getting worked up over things I couldn't control. My drunken friend, though, had fought back. He was furious, unwilling to give in, demanding that the person in the mailbox get out. The neighborhood needed to be made right again.

It was just too bad that he didn't realize that the world, in fact, had turned. There was no going back. *He* was now the someone who didn't belong—the one on the outside looking in. And that's what made him nuts.

CHAPTER 48

Life Goes On

Time seems to speed up as you get older. And before you know it, you're in high school—mine was Music and Art—with both your attitude and basketball game rounding into shape. That's where I was at that spring of 1964. But I wasn't quite done with my past yet.

Dee-Dee O'Hara had come back. Again she surprised me, turning up at my apartment door. This time without the misery that had besieged her then. As it turned out, Dee-Dee had managed just fine. She was carrying her eight-month-old baby girl in her arms. With joy in her eyes.

Mom was at home when Dee-Dee came to the door. A flash of memory hit me. That look on Rosie's face the last time Dee-Dee, pregnant and panicked, came by. I was glad to see that this time the sight of the girl did not send Mom into cardiac arrest. Only gentle words from Rosie welcoming Dee-Dee and her new baby into our apartment. I had filled Mom in on Artie "the Schmuck" Solomon, who had hightailed it out of the Bronx, barely escaping the wrath of Mrs. O'Hara and the law. Something about statutory rape. Mom agreed that Artie's nickname perfectly suited the guy.

I came out of my room, and there they were, talking. Mother to mother.

"Her name is Fiona Rose O'Hara," Dee-Dee said, softly rubbing Fiona's nose.

"A nice Jewish name if I ever heard one," I teased.

Rosie, flustered having heard her own name, shot me that worried look.

I gave her a big smile to reassure her that she was not yet a grandma. It was a role she would've loved to play some-day, but I was certain that this wasn't the right time.

"Fiona Rose. It means 'beautiful flower'," Dee-Dee ex-plained, now stroking Fiona's chin.

And, indeed, the baby was that with her tuft of red hair and bright eyes. I was relieved to see that the kid had avoid-ed the schmuck's Neanderthal looks.

We all sat around the kitchen table chitchatting. Dee-Dee O'Hara, a mommy. I was still getting used to the idea. Our personal drama seemed far in the past. Dee-Dee was herself again, only more so, glowing and looking so…perfect. She told us that she and Fiona would be leaving the Bronx for Long Island, along with her mom. A nice place to raise a kid, she said. And I agreed, though I had no idea at all whether Dee-Dee was right. But I hoped so.

We went on like that for a while, talking about the fu-ture, what was in store for her and Fiona Rose. Dee-Dee was so happily optimistic, and I was so glad for her. Life inevitably goes on. Dee-Dee had found her way. And so had I. Still, I couldn't help but feel as I gazed across the table at this girl with these hazel-green eyes, rocking her beautiful baby girl in her arms, how much I still loved her.

CHAPTER 49

Bronx Boys

The Bronx had been the only home I'd ever known. It was here where all those days and months, some sixteen years, added up to a boy's life. And now I was about to leave.

Our new home was in Queens on the edge of the Long Island Sound. It turned out that I wasn't all that far from Sammy in Bayside, so maybe we had a future there. My new apartment building was weirdly 1960s, with each of the floors painted a different color. I heard that a new drug called LSD was making its way around the country, so that might explain the crazy color design. The complex also had some French name—Le Havre. Way too pretentious for my taste. Rosie had told me about the neighborhood's tree-lined streets, and swimming pools, tennis courts—and a basketball court. So I'd adjust.

Wouldn't you know it, I had my first visit to Queens—an unexpected one—only a few weeks before we were to make our move there. The University Heights Y had rented a school bus to take a group of us teens on a late-night "mystery ride."

The destination was all very secretive, but the word was out as we approached a parking lot and pulled into Flushing

Meadows Park. We had arrived at the New York World's
Fair.

Even before the bus had come to a stop, I could see the
Unisphere ahead, a fantastic metallic creation of Earth with
steel rings circling a huge globe bathed in a cascade of fountain water. An incredible sight. I hardly waited for the bus to
stop before leaping off and onto the fairgrounds lined with
the flags of countries from around the world.

Under the night lights, the World's Fair was a fantasy. A
kid's paradise. I floated through the park, coming to pavil-
ions that transported me to astonishing worlds. In one, I was
a time traveler moving through our country's history. Abe
Lincoln was there, or at least his robot look-alike, reciting
passages from a famous speech.

Then the Ford exhibit, where I wandered up to a futuris-
tic, muscle-bound car that looked like it was itching to
blastoff. The beauty was called the Ford Mustang. Definitely the car of my dreams, and I made a mental note to start
saving my allowance.

Next was a boat ride through the Disney Pavilion, filled
with animated singing, dancing dolls and animals—the
"world's children," I was told—and I found myself stupidly
singing along with its annoying tune, something about some
"small world" that we all cheerily lived in. I still couldn't
get that song out of my head weeks later.

And then onto "Futurama." I sat in a car as it travelled through incredible creations of polar caps, ocean beds, and jungles, before transporting me into outer space. My robotic guide welcomed me to "Tomorrow." And, just like that, I was on the moon, and visiting a fantastic future.

> "It is now tomorrow. Now we can find our way along the dark star-studded corridors of space, and make that long-dreamed voyage to our nearest neighbor in the great unknown, that silent satellite of Earth we call the moon."

John had predicted that we would land on the moon before the end of the '60s—now that would be something out of the fantastic! Well, we were on our way. I would never forget watching Alan Shepard on television that tense morning at Cape Canaveral. The guy had been scrunched in to a tiny capsule for over four hours with bad weather holding back the liftoff. And then he was blasting off on top of a fiery Mercury rocket—at 5,000 miles per hour! Our first American in space—what a fifteen-minute ride! And how cool was Shepard? "It's beautiful up here," he told us from space. The guy sounded as if he was simply taking a ride through the Catskills on his way to a weekend at the Grossinger's Hotel.

Only in my imagination did my heroes rise to the sky, and here was Shepard, in his shiny spacesuit, making it all real. I wondered though—would we ever go as far as the moon?

In "Futurama," we not only landed on the moon but were on our way to building communities that could be our homes. Amazing! That was one neighborhood I wouldn't mind hanging out in one day.

> "Never has the world held a brighter promise of things to come."

And by the time I left "Futurama," I also wanted to believe.

∽∾∽

I can't say I left Tremont Avenue kicking and screaming. It was time to move on, though I'd miss my neighborhood. I had grown up on these streets, finding my way. It hadn't been perfect, not at all, but good enough. More than good enough. Tremont Avenue had been a real home.

So I helped bundle up what was left of our apartment with the bittersweet pull of my old life. I once thought that the stream of time that added up to kid's life would never come to an end. Weeks and years move slowly when you're young, with each day its own adventure. I certainly had my share. But I suppose there was no escaping the inevitable, that we all grow up, packing those years into boxes of memories, and moving on. And that was that.

I took one final look around my old home before leaving. The place, once so alive, seemed sadly abandoned and defeated now. I could hardly look inside my bedroom with its beaten down rug and faded walls pockmarked from pictures that had been taken down.

The stuff that made the room alive was sealed in boxes—bats and balls and gloves, board games, stacks of LP records, containers with my hundreds of baseball cards, plaster busts of JFK and Beethoven, along with my new collection of Superman comics. (I'd managed to keep these away from my Aunt Selma this time.) Other boxes and furniture had already been shipped ahead to Queens. And soon I'd be on my way, too.

My reverie was shaken when the familiar thump of a stoopball game spilled into the apartment. I went over to my window and looked down into the courtyard. Two young kids were smacking a hard-rubber Spalding against the building steps, propelling the ball clear across the cement yard, barely missing old lady Goldberg's window. They were having the time of their lives, excited, laughing, chasing that ball around the yard. Shouts of glee echoed across the courtyard.

I envied those little guys, and had to smile feeling the pure joy of their play. How wonderful it was for them. So free in the world. And for that moment, their life was as it should be. Everything was good for those Bronx boys.

Epilogue

The Old House on the Road

The old house was nothing more than a shell, empty and long abandoned. It once had been a pristine twenty-room mansion with stone porticos and graceful, arched windows—a house filled with the rush and promise of life.

But that was then.

The man and his son strolled along the country path before settling next to the old house. It had been built long before the incursion of the tall, red-brick residential buildings that dotted this area of the Bronx along the Hudson River. Dense forestry still preserved some of the old country ambiance around the neighborhood.

Time had still taken its toll on the once stately home. Developers had tried to restore its luster after the last family had moved out years before. The house was gutted now, ringed by a plastic tarp laden with rainwater. Bringing it back to life would not be easy, if possible at all.

Still, the man wanted his son to see the place. It was where his long-ago hero played games in the grassy backyard, had gone to school nearby, where he lived a kid's life. That was before that family migrated to Boston. Before the boy grew to become president. Before that day in Dallas.

The man had walked these grounds before. He couldn't

quite explain it, but he felt drawn here. He once was pulled to such places, memorials that marked a person's life. This one was not too far from his own home where he lived with Amy, and the kids—Rebecca, Robby, and Matthew. When the mood struck, he strolled down the country lane to visit. This time he brought Matthew.

"If you look closely, you can imagine what once was," the man said softly to his ten-year-old son. "He wasn't any older than you."

Matthew went along with the imaginary game if only to please his father, squinting through the windows of the whitewashed building—but saw nothing except empty, broken rooms that looked under construction. Any ghostly remembrances had taken leave long ago and impossible to conjure.

Matthew shrugged. "Just looks run-down."

"Lots of rooms, big family," the man went on, this time more to himself. "Kind of amazing, he was a Bronx kid, like you."

"And you too, Dad," Matthew said. "But he didn't talk like he came from here. Are you sure he grew up in this house?"

The man chuckled. Yes, this was that kid's childhood home in the Bronx. Certainly, though, no one from these parts would ever admit to such a libel, city maps be damned. To them, the area was called Riverdale, a country enclave of the borough nestled along the wooded palisades that lined the Hudson River. Mark Twain once lived nearby. So did Fiorello LaGuardia, the New York mayor. Of course it would never be confused with the other side of the tracks. The other Bronx.

That was where the man was born and raised, in sight of the elevated train tracks with the relentless screech of steel wheels that penetrated the cement sidewalks and five-floor brick walk-ups that lined the streets.

His had been a neighborhood of gray, not this neighborhood with the pastoral-sounding name and magnificent homes resting under a canopy of long-branched trees.

Still, there was something about this house at 5040 Independence Avenue. When the man was much younger, he
had taken a bike ride from his old neighborhood to visit the
place and stood on this very spot, thinking of the kid that
once lived here. The two of them, Bronx boys.

They lived decades apart, but both men started their
life's journey here in the borough. The man had gone on to
find his way, traveling the world, writing books, teaching,
while raising three great kids, loving his wife. This other
Bronx boy also had made good.

"You know, he had a younger brother named Robert,
like you," said the man.

"Did they also call him Robby?" asked Matthew.

The man smiled. "No, he was Bobby."

Matthew thought of his own six-year-old annoying sib-
ling. "Don't even think of calling Robby that."

The man laughed. "Yes, I know better."

"Dad, in class we talked about him, and the day he was
shot," Matthew said. "Why would someone do that?"

It was the same question the man carried through his life.
Fifty years later he still hadn't come up with an answer. He
had visited the gravesite in Washington, DC many years
earlier, but decided not to go back. He had abandoned that
peculiar habit of his, visiting the dead. He was now interested in places more connected to life. That's what brought
him here. John's house.

The man looked at his son and basked in his good for-
tune. He loved this boy. Matthew was so much like himself
at that age, a connection that touched deeply. He had told
Matthew, and all his kids, the stories of his youth, but there
was always something lost in the telling. Children can't imagine their parents as kids and feeling their exuberance,
fears, and dreams that came with growing up. Perhaps it
was too much to expect that Matthew could see, and take to
heart, the abandoned house that once carried the dreams of
this other Bronx kid.

The man took delight in his sons' and daughter's own childhood days. The times, so complicated, more perilous, had not dampened their vibrant curiosity, their need to discover what more lies around the next corner of their lives. He only hoped that they could hold off the inevitable tide of adulthood to keep alive these imaginative days, so gleeful and liberating. A kid's life only comes around once, he thought, and then gone, irretrievable.

"Gotta go, Dad," said Matthew. "The guys are waiting for me."

The man's wistful turns could not compete with his son's basketball game. He took a final glance at the empty mansion on Independence Avenue. The sun, a glowing ball of orange light, was falling quickly over the palisades. He could hear the gentle chug of a passing locomotive as it wound its way to the northern hinterlands, a sound that barely interrupted the sounds of nature.

It was a perfect setting, the man thought, a moment to hold onto, as he took Matthew's hand in his, and turned to leave the old house resting on the country road.

A FINAL FEW WORDS AND ACKNOWLEDGMENTS

It's been said that all fiction is autobiography, and that is true of *Bronxland*. My own coming of age can certainly be found on many of these pages here. The fictional Paul's infatuation and encounter with his "Miss Bonnet" is cringingly accurate as I recall my actual eighth-grade math teacher (still beautiful in my mind's eye). "Dee-Dee O'Hara" is also a composite of my youthful struggles with the opposite sex and the heartaches that followed. "Tommy Branigan" was in my life as well, along with the fight that put an end to my torment. Mr. P, my wonderful music teacher is here as well. I will never forget his act of kindness that is relived in this story. And, yes, a classmate once did steal my beloved Buffet clarinet, but I'm glad to say that the real "Joe Bailey" was not part of that episode (though that guy was very much a terrific friend later on).

And, of course, my heroes are also an important part of this story—John F. Kennedy, Superman, Alan Shepard, Harry Houdini, Roger Maris—a group that I imagine many of my Bronx contemporaries also revered during those times.

I have tried to stay close to the history of the '60s, though I have drawn on one particular event that came later on. I have never forgotten the very real tragedy that was the abduction of Etan Patz, this adorable six-year-old-boy taken off the streets of New York back in the 1980s. Etan's tragic story still stirs the heart. Benji Shapiro was my Etan, and in some metaphysical sense I needed to find him and bring him home.

This book could only have come to life with the support of the team at Black Opal Books. A special thanks to Lauri Wellington for believing in *Bronxland*. My deep appreciation as well to my editors, Susan and Faith, for making sure I got the words right. And to Jennifer Gibson for her remarkable cover design. Black Opal Books has lived up to its promise, giving writers a gateway to tell their stories. I hope this book lives up to their expectations and yours, my readers.

Fiction has given me the freedom to invent but also the chance to honor people who have meant a great deal to me. As such, I have stuck close to their actual names. My parents Rose and Mac Thaler would have enjoyed the plight of Paul Wolfenthal (and likely recognize how similar he was to their own peculiar son growing up).

My brother Fred also plays a part in *Bronxland*, though he takes on a far greater role outside these pages. He is a lifelong best friend, who long ago showed me how to shoot the one-hand jump shot and still astounds with his musical brilliance.

Hopefully, my extended clan will excuse my placing them in the middle of Paul's adventures and mishaps, some fictional, others all too true (and that includes the cataclysmic end to my Superman comics). I lived so much of my early life with my loving relatives that I found it impossible to separate even the fictional Paul Wolfenthal from my aunts, Selma and Ethel, and uncles, Sol and Ruby.

The book is dedicated in part to Mel Wolfson. I am grateful for his editor's hand in *Bronxland* but more so for his singular presence in our family lives. I will miss listening to Mel's own story-telling, especially of his young Brooklyn days when he too ran free.

The book is also dedicated to my Bronx "guys"— Matthew, Robby, and Rebecca. I have been the most fortunate of fathers. These three are my inspiration, and each day they amaze me as they make their way in the world. Their exuberance and beautiful spirit have rekindled my own boyhood memories—recollections that have given rise to these stories embedded into *Bronxland*. In that sense, it is fair to say that they are the heart and soul of this book.

Their mom, and my wife, Amy Wolfson, has been my guiding light for so many years. She has also been with me throughout the long creation of *Bronxland*, joining me on this writing journey as she has in life. So, readers, Paul Wolfenthal finally does find the girl of his dreams.

And, yes, Amy and I, and the kids, do live a stone's throw from the old Kennedy estate in Riverdale. Every now and then I wander over to that place. And like my fictional counterpart, I still think fondly about the boy who once lived there.

Photographs Credits/Info
(Please note: all photographs are either public domain or are used with permission of the copyright holder)

Isidor and Ida Straus, undated

JFK school photo, 1927, Riverdale Country Day School

Mickey Mantle, Bowman rookie card, 1951

Kennedy-Nixon First Presidential Debate, September 26, 1960

Houdini gravesite, photo by Ron Chicken, Houdini Museum

John F. Kennedy on the Grand Concourse, Nov. 5, 1960, Bronx County Historical Society

Adolf Eichmann at trial in Jerusalem, April 18, 1961, Israeli government

"Fat Man" atomic bomb, US Department of Defense

Murder of Lee Harvey Oswald, Nov. 24, 1963, photo by Ira Jefferson "Jack" Beers Jr. for the Dallas Morning News

John Kennedy's family leaving Capitol after his funeral, Nov. 25, 1963, Abbie Rowe White House Photographs

New York World's Fair, 1964, photo by Ron White

The Kennedy House, photo by Paul Thaler

Also by Paul Thaler

The Watchful Eye:
American Justice in the Age of the Television Trial

The Spectacle:
Media and the Making of the OJ Simpson Story

About the Author

Paul Thaler is a former journalist and a media commentator for many national publications and network programs. He is author of the critically acclaimed *The Spectacle: Media and the Making of the OJ Simpson Story*, and *The Watchful Eye: American Justice in the Age of the Television Trial*. *Bronxland* is his first novel. Thaler lives in the Riverdale section of the Bronx with his wife, Amy, and their three children, Matthew, Robby, and Rebecca.

CPSIA information can be obtained
at www.ICGtesting.com
Printed in the USA
BVHW04s0234101018
529709BV00012BA/520/P

9 781626 947474